THE CAMELOT CODE

The Once and Future Geek

THE CAMELOT CODE

Book 1

The Once and Future Geek

MARI MANCUSI

DISNEP • HYPERION
Los Angeles   New York

First Edition, November 2018
10 9 8 7 6 5 4 3 2 1
FAC-020093-18278
Printed in the United States of America

Text is set in Adobe Caslon Pro, Brandon Grotesque, Billy, Penumbra Flare, Penumbra Sans, Eco Coding/Fontspring

Designed by Whitney Manger-Fine

Library of Congress Cataloging-in-Publication Data
Names: Mancusi, Mari, author.
Title: The once and future geek / Marianne Mancusi.
Description: First Edition. • Los Angeles ; New York : Disney-Hyperion, 2018. •
Series: The Camelot Code ; book #1 • Summary: When thirteen-year-old Arthur of Gal, the future King Arthur, accidentally time-travels to the twenty-first century, Sophie Sawyer, twelve, must convince him to return and correct the time line.
Identifiers: LCCN 2017034204 (print) • LCCN 2017045073 (ebook) •
ISBN 9781368023221 (ebook) • ISBN 9781368010849 (hardcover)
Subjects: • CYAC: Time travel—Fiction. • Arthur, King—Fiction. • Middle schools—Fiction. • Schools—Fiction. • Friendship—Fiction. • Humorous stories.
Classification: LCC PZ7.M312178 (ebook) •
LCC PZ7.M312178 Onc 2018 (print) • DDC [Fic]—dc23
LC record available at https://lccn.loc.gov/2017034204

Reinforced binding

Visit www.DisneyBooks.com

To my daughter, Avalon.
You make every day a magical adventure.

CHAPTER 1

The stench of death hung heavy in the air as the group made their way through the ruined castle. Dark shadows danced menacingly across battle-scarred walls while the windows rattled a warning. A nightmare scene to frighten off even the bravest of heroes, and Lady Bella knew she and her companions were far from that.

But they'd come too far to turn back now.

And so they pressed on, through cobweb-draped halls, down crumbling stone steps. Ducking low-hanging archways, crossing rotted-out floors. Until the corridor dead-ended at a matching set of ironbound doors, looming tall and wide before them. The entrance to the sorceress's chamber.

Lord Vanquish raised his glowing red blade while Sir Melvin mumbled protection spells under his breath. Bella's staff crackled with magical energy and a chill tripped down her spine.

This was it. This was really it.

"We have fought long and hard, my friends," Sir Melvin proclaimed, his deep voice booming through the chamber. "At last, we stand at the doorway of our destiny."

A small grin crossed Lady Bella's face. She couldn't help it. They'd waited so long for this day. And now it was finally here. Her heart pounded in a mixture of excitement and fear.

"I'm ready," she declared.

"I have one final question," Melvin continued. "Before we enter Morgana's chamber." He turned to her, his wizened eyes piercing her with a sharp intensity. "One very important question."

"Y-yes?" she whispered, drawing in a shaky breath.

Melvin gazed at her solemnly. "Why haven't you done the dishes yet?"

Wait . . . *what?*

"Sophie! I'm not going to ask you again!"

Lady Bella, aka twelve-year-old Sophie Sawyer, groaned as she yanked off her headphones and threw them down on her computer desk. Seriously? *Seriously?* Shaking her head, she banged out a message to her friends.

>>LadyBella: Hang on, guys. I'm getting major dad
aggro here.

Pushing away her mouse, she rose from her chair and walked around her unmade bed. She had to admit, her father had a gift. A really, really annoying gift.

She pulled open her door. "Sophie? Did you hear me?" her father was still barking from downstairs.

Oh, she'd heard him all right. All ten times in the past ten minutes. Problem was, she couldn't exactly explain to him that though it might appear to the un-geeked eye that she was just sitting in her room messing around with her computer, she was actually in the middle of something pretty epic.

And the dishes would have to wait.

She stuck her head into the hallway. "I'll be right down," she yelled, hoping to score five more minutes of peace. Enough time to get through this last fight. The three of them had been building up to this battle for over a year now, leveling up and gaining the skills it took to bring down the numero uno boss of *Camelot's Honor*, the evil sorceress Morgana. She couldn't log out now.

Returning to her computer, she jammed the headphones back over her ears.

>>LadyBella: I'm back. Let's do this. Quick.

Grabbing the mouse, Sophie placed her character into position alongside her teammates, Lord Vanquish (her best friend, Stuart Mallory) and SirMelvin01 (a surfer playing from somewhere out in California). Pressing a few hot keys, she prepped her shields, readying herself for the fight. As a shape-shifting druid, Lady Bella had the most important role in this battle. Also, the most difficult. She needed to morph herself into bird form, then fly above the sorceress, disarming her force field before Morgana could cast her annihilation spell. If Sophie failed to do it in time, it was game over for sure.

She gritted her teeth. But she'd practiced this. She would not fail.

>>LordVanquish: Go, go, GO!

They stepped through the doors, into the sorceress's inner sanctum: a windowless chamber with black walls and high ceilings disappearing into the darkness. For a moment, the chamber appeared empty. Then Morgana drifted out from the shadows, the music swelling in her wake.

"Foolish mortals," she purred. "Do you really think you can defeat me?"

"Go!" Melvin cried. "NOW!"

Lord Vanquish charged the sorceress, shield up and sword ready.

When he reached her, he slashed down hard, a bite that should have cut her to the bone. Instead, the blade bounced harmlessly off her skin—her magical force field protecting her from any harm.

Morgana cackled, raising her hands above her head, a cloud of black smoke swirling as she drew energy from the elements to aid her cast. A firebolt shot from her fingers, striking Lord Vanquish square in the chest. Only Melvin's lightning-fast heal kept him upright.

Melvin turned to Bella. "It's all up to you."

Bella nodded grimly, using her magic to transform herself into an eagle. Then, beating her wings, she took flight, soaring high above the rafters. Once in position, she locked on to the small tear at the top of Morgana's force field. The one weakness—sure to bring the sorceress down. She began her descent, heart slamming against her rib cage, ready to—

"You better not be playing that video game!" Dad cried, bursting into the room. Startled, Sophie knocked the mouse with her hand and the game spun, completely distorting her perspective. By the time she regained control, Lady Bella was on the ground. Dead. Along with Lord Vanquish and Sir Melvin. Utterly annihilated.

"No!" Sophie cried, staring at the screen in dismay. "You killed me."

Her father rolled his eyes. "Funny. You still look pretty alive to me. Which makes me wonder why you haven't done the chores I assigned you this morning." He wagged a finger in her direction. "Get to it, young lady. I'm not going to ask again."

Sophie slumped. "Fine," she said. "Can I at least say goodbye to Stu first?"

Her father frowned, looking as if he wanted to argue. Then he sighed. "Five minutes. Then I want you off the computer for the rest of the day. Go get some sunshine or something."

And with that, he stormed out of the room, slamming the door behind him. Sophie could hear his loud footsteps clomping down the stairs.

Awesome.

Leaning back in her chair, she scrubbed her face with her hands. Lady Bella now stood resurrected in the graveyard next to Lord Vanquish and Sir Melvin. Alive again, but all for nothing. They'd been defeated and the online game wouldn't give them another chance at slaying the sorceress for the next five days.

Her phone started ringing.

"I know, I know," she said as she answered.

"What happened? You totally had it!" Stu cried on the other end of the line. She could hear the disappointment in his voice. Stupid Dad. He had no idea how his interruption of Sophie's virtual world affected other people's real lives.

"What can I say? My father has an epic finishing move." She stared glumly at the screen, where Melvin was saying good-bye as he prepared to sign out of the game. She quickly private-messaged him an apology. After all, the guy was a good player and had become an online friend, though neither she nor Stu had ever met him in real life. She didn't want him to get annoyed at them and decide to leave their guild.

"You can say you're getting a lock on your door for a start."

Sophie snorted. "Yeah, right. Like my dad's going to go for *that*." She pressed a hot key, bringing up Lady Bella's Pegasus mount, then started her flight back to the main city of Camelot. "Don't worry, I'll think of something before Friday."

There was silence on the other end of the line and for a moment she thought they'd been disconnected. Then, "Friday?" Stu asked.

"Yeah, you know, we have to wait until the dungeon resets before we can try again," she said, surprised at having to explain. Stu was the ultimate expert on everything *Camelot* related. In fact, he often spent more time on the game's wiki boards learning the fights than doing his homework.

"I know, but . . . couldn't we do it Saturday instead?"

"Actually no. They're doing that patching, remember?" she said. "The servers are going to be offline all weekend."

"Oh. Right."

"What do you have against Friday?"

"Uh . . . nothing. I was just . . . thinking of going to that pizza-night thing with the team after the game."

Sophie frowned. "The team?" she repeated before she could stop herself. Then realization hit her. "Oh. Right. Soccer." She made a face.

It had been three weeks already, but it was still hard for her to believe that her best friend—for some unfathomable reason—had made the crazy decision to join the school's soccer team. An unexpected move that reeked of his stepbrother Lucas's influence. Lucas was the resident jock in the family. A star player on their school's football team. Stu, on the other hand, had always been more *math*lete than athlete. A geek of the highest order.

Until now, that was.

"Just tell them you're busy doing something actually important," she said. "Like downing Morgana with your best friend. I'm *sure* they'll understand."

She said it as a joke. She expected him to laugh. Instead, there was dead silence on the other end of the line, causing an uncomfortable feeling to worm its way to her stomach. What was going on here? Did he actually want to hang out with the team—off the field? Instead of playing video games with her? They always gamed on Friday nights. It was tradition! And he was going to break that now? Now that they were up against the most important fight of their gaming lives?

Stu cleared his throat. "Look, I'm sorry, Soph. Can't we just do it Monday instead?" He paused, then added, "I mean it's just a video game, right? It's not like Morgana is going anywhere."

She stared at the phone. "Just a video game?" she repeated. *"Just a video game?"* She drew in a breath. "Okay, who are you and what did you do to my best friend?"

She could hear the anger and confusion rising in her voice and was a little embarrassed that she was getting this upset. But still, who could blame her? For the past year she and Stu had lived and breathed *Camelot's Honor.* Slaving away on menial quests, gaining experience, and rising in levels. All to get to this point.

And now he was bailing. To hang out with the cool kids. Leaving her behind.

"Whatever," she said sharply. "Maybe I'll just find a pickup group and slay Morgana with them instead."

"What?" Stu cried, suddenly sounding concerned. About time. "You'd kill her without me?"

Okay, fine. Maybe that was going a bit too far. He'd only asked for one day. But still! She scowled. This *had* to be Lucas's influence. After all, Stu didn't even like sports. He didn't even play the video-game kind.

Also? He was terrible at them. In fact, that was how they'd first become best friends back in second grade. No one had picked him for the dodgeball game and she had found him, sitting on the swings all alone looking like he'd lost his pet puppy. She'd asked him if he wanted to play *Minecraft* on her iPad and he'd eagerly agreed. And the rest was history. Best friends forever. Happily ever after. Till death do we part.

Or soccer tryouts, evidently.

"Never mind," she muttered. "We'll do it Monday, or whatever. Just let me know when you can spare some precious time."

"Wait, are you mad at me?" Stu asked, sounding bewildered.

"Of course not!" she snapped, realizing she didn't sound very convincing. "Anyway, I've got to go. Dishes, remember?"

"But you're signing on later, right?"

"I don't know. The cheerleaders might want to go get manicures."

"Cheerleaders? What—?"

She sighed. "Never mind."

CHAPTER 2

The battlefield stretched out before him, drenched in the blood of the fallen. Though 'twould be easy to retreat to the safety of the forest, our hero forced himself to press on. The black knight still rode and there could be no rest until his enemy had been cast down. Evil vanquished once and for all.

A horse's neigh snapped him to attention. His eyes fell upon a tall figure astride a well-armored horse. He gasped as he recognized the twisted mark on the other man's shield.

The black knight. His sworn enemy.

The young soldier gripped his shield tightly while scrambling to unsheathe his sword. The black knight watched with apparent amusement.

"Say your last words," the black knight declared. "And may the gods have mercy on you, for I shall not."

The villain charged at our hero, their swords meeting with a clang, sparks flying between them. The horses passed, their blades slid apart and the boy readied himself for another round. As he urged his mare around, the black knight came at him again, and he prayed for some opening. Some small mistake that would give him advantage.

Instead, the black knight's blade came crashing down hard, knocking him from his horse. As he fell to the ground, his sword slipped from his hand, leaving him unprotected and exposed. He scrambled to his feet, and the black knight laughed again.

And went in for the final kill.

"You're dead! I win again!"

Thirteen-year-old Arthur of Gal groaned as he dropped his sword and shield to the ground and held up his hands in surrender as the evil knight in question, also known as Princess Guinevere, tapped his tunic with the point of her practice blade.

"A lucky break," he insisted, knocking the dull weapon away with his hand and scrambling to pick up his own sword and shield.

"Please," scoffed Guinevere. "Evil knight is three for three now." She danced a little victory dance, her golden curls bouncing off her shoulders. "Methinks our mighty hero might need a bit more practice."

"Well, *methinks* he'd get some if he wasn't always stuck in the kitchen, washing the evil knight's dishes all the time," Arthur retorted playfully. He grabbed his sword and swung.

Guinevere rolled her eyes, parrying his blade with an easy stroke of her own. "Trust me, this evil knight would rather be doing *anything* other than dirtying dishes at one of those boring banquets of your foster father's." She charged at Arthur. He raised his shield to block her blow. "You should have seen all the nobles my father tried to introduce me to. You'd think I was to be married off tomorrow instead of three years from now, the desperate way he's acting."

Arthur laughed, circling her with wary steps, pinning her sky-blue eyes with his own, daring her to make a move. "Maybe you should just marry me," he teased. "You'd never have to go to another banquet again."

Their old joke brought a blush to her face—enough to fluster her and give him a momentary advantage. Arthur charged forward, slamming his sword against hers, knocking it from her grasp. Then he threw his own weapons to the side and leaped onto her, pushing her to the ground.

"I win!" he crowed. "At last our mighty hero has felled the black knight."

But as he raised his hands in a victory salute, Guinevere managed to flip him over, pinning him by the shoulders. She looked down with a sly smile.

"A bit early for a victory celebration?"

He groaned. "The fight was already declared."

"Not by me."

"Guinevere!" A male voice suddenly rang through the forest. "Where did you go?"

"O wind and earth, save us!" Guinevere groaned, sitting up and pulling the dead leaves from her hair. "It's Sir Agravaine again. The man's determined to make me his betrothed if it kills him." She scrambled to her feet, giving Arthur a hand up. "Which it very well might," she added wickedly. "Come. Let's leave this place before he finds us."

She didn't have to tell Arthur twice. After hiding their swords and shields in the hollow of an old tree, the two of them ran out of the apple orchard, skirting the castle of his foster father, Sir Ector, and heading down toward the small village below.

"I've been meaning to check on Sara and her children anyway," Guinevere informed him. "And bring them leftovers from last night's banquet." She held up a burlap sack, stuffed to the gills. "You want to come with me?"

An angel of mercy, dressed as a warrior princess. That was his Guin. "Absolutely," Arthur replied. "After all, I promised Thom I'd give him another sword-fighting lesson," he added. Thom was Sara's adorable six-year-old son.

"Oh, excellent! Someone you might actually have a chance to beat!"

Arthur shoved her playfully and the two of them headed down the hill, toward Sara's thatch-roofed hut. Smoke curled from the chimney and it looked peaceful and cozy. Inside was anything but. Sara's husband had been jailed for not being able to pay his taxes and she had just given birth to her fourth child.

They reached the hut and Guinevere banged on the door. From inside they could hear a shuffling, a baby's cry, followed by a woman's voice. "Please go away," she begged. "We haven't anything left."

"Sara! It's me, Princess Guinevere!" the princess called through the door. "I've brought food!"

The door burst open and Sara popped her head out, a big smile on her face. "Well, why didn't you say so, Princess?" she demanded cheerfully. "Come inside at once!"

The dirt-floored dwelling was crudely furnished, but well kept all the same, revealing Sara's determined pride, despite her humble surroundings. Her children's faces were scrubbed clean, and the rags they wore were expertly mended.

"The tax collectors came again yesterday," Sara explained to Guinevere as the princess doled out thick loaves of crusty bread, setting them on the wooden table at the center of the hut. The children watched her with eager, hollow eyes. "What do they expect us to give, when the never-ending wars between the lords leave us with nothing but burned fields and no seed? We scarce have a bite to eat ourselves after we give Sir Ector his due."

"It's gotten terrible," Guinevere agreed as she went over to the cradle to coo at the new addition to the family. "All these tribal lords, fighting one another, all desperate to become high king. If only they could see what they are doing to their people." She pulled the baby from his crib and nuzzled him to her cheek.

"I shan't think they'd care much if they did," Sara replied bitterly. "The only thing that could possibly save us now is Merlin's promised hero. The one who will pull the sword from the stone."

Arthur helped spread out the food, handing a hunk of bread to each child, only half listening to the conversation. It was a story he'd heard a million times before. Of a legendary hero arriving and pulling the sword Excalibur from the stone that sat in Sir Ector's courtyard, becoming king, and uniting all of England under his reign. It didn't seem all that likely to him. But that didn't stop the knights from trying. After the big tournament today, they'd be sure to have another go at it, though most of the knights had already tried and failed many times before. The blade was stuck fast and likely would be forever.

He felt a sudden tug at his tunic and looked down. A scrawny redheaded boy looked up at him with an excited gleam in his big blue eyes. "Sir Arthur!" he cried. He was missing his two front teeth. "You promised me a sword lesson."

Arthur ruffled his hair. "And you shall get one!" he assured the boy. "Let's go outside so we don't disturb the ladies." He shot Guinevere a wink. She waved him off cheerfully.

The two boys headed outside, and Arthur collected two long sticks, handing one to Thom. "You ready?" he asked.

Thom nodded and Arthur began his lesson. But he hadn't gotten very far before he heard two familiar voices on approach. He cringed. Quickly, he ushered Thom inside and then joined him, yanking the cottage door shut. He turned to Guin and Sara.

"Hide the food!" he cried. "Now!"

Sara and the children sprang into action, scurrying to find hiding spots in the tiny home. Guinevere looked at Arthur questioningly.

"Sir Agravaine and Sir Kay," he said in explanation. "Looks like they found you after all."

Sure enough, a moment later, the door flew open and the two knights poked their heads inside. Sir Agravaine was in town for the big jousting tournament. He was a brutish knight from the Orkneys of the North who wasn't exactly known for his acts of chivalry.

"So, Princess, this is where you choose to spend your time?" Agravaine clucked, looking over the small cottage with disdain. "Down in the mud with the serfs?" His eyes locked on to Arthur, who stood protectively in front of the family and Guinevere, arms crossed over his chest. "And *this* your only escort?" He gave Arthur a scornful look. "I hardly think a scrawny little wart like him could properly serve and protect a royal princess."

"Go away, Agravaine," Arthur growled. "There's nothing for you here."

"Oh, I think I'll be the judge of that," Agravaine replied dismissively. He started trolling through the cabinets.

"Please, sir," Sara begged, stepping in front of him. "We have nothing. Your fellow knights have already been here and taken it all."

"Then you won't mind me searching around a bit," Agravaine said with a mean-spirited grin. "Kay, help me!" The two knights started scouring the hut, haphazardly throwing plates and pots around.

Arthur glanced over at Guinevere, who was looking back at him with troubled eyes.

"What are we going to do?" she whispered under her breath.

"They're knights," he whispered back. "There's nothing we can do." Under the current laws of the land, the knights had every right to take what they needed as "supplies" for the war campaigns. And if Arthur made any move against them, he'd be arrested and likely burned at the stake. And while at the moment he wouldn't mind taking that risk to protect the poor innocent family—not to mention Guinevere herself—he knew it would do no good in the end. The knights would burn the cottage down anyway, just for spite.

He scowled. Sometimes he just felt so helpless.

"Hey, look here, Agravaine!" Sir Kay, Arthur's older foster brother called out. He was just as mean as Agravaine, though not half as clever. He pulled out a long loaf of bread, hidden beneath the table. "Looks like the cow has been lying to us." Then he added a hunk of cheese. "Isn't this the same cheese we had at the banquet last night?"

"Where did you get this?" Agravaine demanded, grabbing Sara by the collar of her dress. She squealed in terror. "Did you steal it from your lord? You know what the punishment is for thievery, don't you?"

"Stop it!" A little voice suddenly rose above the din. Arthur realized Thom had stepped forward, his expression fierce. He glared at Agravaine. "Or Sir Arthur himself will strike you down."

"Sir Arthur?" Agravaine repeated, looking amused. He released Sara and made a big show of scanning the room. "And *who*, may I ask, is Sir Arthur?"

Uh-oh. Arthur bit his lower lip. *Please don't point me out. Please don't point me out.*

The little boy pointed directly at him. "Why, him of course," he replied in an indignant voice.

Agravaine arched an eyebrow. "Is he now?" He left the boy and approached Arthur. "I wonder if *Sir Arthur* knows," he continued, staring straight at him, "that it's a crime to impersonate a knight."

"He's not...he's not imperson-tating," Thom defended loyally. He looked at Arthur with confused eyes. "Tell him!"

Arthur wanted to. He really did. Instead he hung his head, feeling utterly useless. "You know we were just pretending, right, Thom? Remember I told you that?"

Thom nodded slowly, a look of disappointment clear on his face. "Oh. Right," he said, taking a step backward. "I forgot." He stuck his thumb in his mouth and looked at Arthur mournfully.

"Now, as I was saying," Agravaine said, turning back to Sara. But Guinevere was too quick, leaping into his path, her blue eyes flashing fire.

"I stole the food," she declared. "Take me away if you must. But leave these innocent people alone."

Agravaine's lip curled. "For shame, Princess," he sneered. "Your father ought to keep you on a tighter leash." He shook his head, as if disappointed in her. "Luckily, it's only a temporary situation. Once you're old enough to wed I'll find a lovely ivory tower to stash you in. That'll stop you from causing mischief."

"Keep dreaming, Agravaine!" Guinevere glared at him defiantly, and Arthur felt a thrill of pride seeing her bravery. Of course she, as a person of royal birth, could rightfully stand up to a knight. Though, as a woman, she probably wouldn't win. "You're a pig and a shame to knights everywhere. I'll never marry you."

"That's sweet, Princess, but I don't think you have a choice. You're nothing more than a mare on market day, to be sold to the highest bidder. And I, my darling, am bound to be the highest bidder on an insolent wretch like you."

Guinevere squeezed her hands into fists. She stepped forward, staring up at Agravaine with hatred in her eyes. "Why, you..."

"*Gods above*, come on, Agravaine," interjected Kay in a whiny voice. "This is boring. Let's go to the tilting yard. I want to practice for the tournament."

Agravaine shot Guin one last threatening look, then turned to his friend. "Oh, very well," he agreed. "If you insist." He turned back to give Guinevere one more sly smile. "I'll see you at the tournament, m'lady, where you will watch me pull the sword from the stone and be crowned king of all England."

"I can't wait," Guinevere muttered under her breath.

And with that, the two knights exited the cottage, mounted their horses, and headed down the field toward the village below. Guinevere breathed a sigh of relief.

"Oh, lady, lady," cried Sara, running to her and bowing at her feet. "Thank you for your kindness. They would have taken me away and burned the house down had you not stepped in."

Thom turned to Arthur, looking up at him with sad eyes. "I don't understand," he said, scowling. "Why can't you be a knight? You're better than all the others!"

Arthur gave him a rueful look. "Because I'm not a noble," he replied. "I'm a commoner, just like you. And the rule is, you have to be of noble birth to become a knight." *Or marry a princess like Guinevere*, he added to himself, giving a longing look in his friend's direction. If only he really could save her from a brute like Agravaine.

"Well, that's a stupid rule," Thom said with a scowl. "If I were king, I'd make you a knight and my mom a queen and we'd all live happily ever after."

Arthur ruffled his hair fondly. "I think you'd make a very good king, Thom. A very good king."

But he knew in his heart the chances of all that happening— of any of them living happily ever after—were about as likely as Arthur pulling the sword from the stone himself.

CHAPTER 3

Stuart Mallory stared down at his cell phone in dismay. He'd known Sophie would flip out when he told her about the pizza thing. That was why he hadn't wanted to tell her in the first place. Friday night was gaming night. It was sacred. No way was she just going to be cool with him skipping out on it—especially not in order to hang with the soccer team.

If only she knew how much he'd rather be gaming, too.

"Reality to Stu, come in, Stu."

Stu jerked away from the computer as he felt the punch to his shoulder. He made a face at his stepbrother, Lucas, who had walked into the bedroom and was now waving his hands obnoxiously in Stu's face.

"Do you mind?" he snapped with a little more force than he'd intended. After all, it wasn't his brother's fault he was in this mess. Well, not directly, anyway.

Lucas grinned. "Oh, good. I've managed to unplug you from the Matrix. Want to go kick the ball around? Or do you have a damsel in distress on the hook?"

Stu rolled his eyes. Typical Lucas. Never missing a chance to poke fun at Stu's obsession with all things online. Lucas sometimes dabbled in social media, mostly to upload videos of the amazing touchdowns he'd made on the football field, but he wouldn't be caught dead playing an actual video game.

Stu still found it hard to believe that the two of them were now officially brothers. Their parents had met in line at Pizza Cave two years ago and bonded over their sons' shared love of pepperoni-and-pineapple pizza. Suddenly, eight months later, they were married. And the school's resident golden boy was sharing a bedroom with the school's resident geek.

Today, Lucas was still the most popular kid in his ninth-grade class and probably the best-looking—with thick, wavy black hair, intense blue eyes, and a smile that lit up every room.

The only time Stu had ever lit up a room? In fourth grade when he accidentally set fire to the science lab. Which was fine by him. In his opinion? Popularity was way overrated. He had his video games. He had Sophie. That was all he needed.

Though now somehow he had soccer, too. He was still not entirely sure how that had happened.

"Dude, are you psyched about Friday or what?" Lucas asked. "I can't believe your dad's taking both teams to Pizza Cave. They're gonna, like, run out of pizza with all of us there."

"Yeah," Stu replied uneasily, staring down at his hands. He thought about Sophie again. Would she really go and find someone else to down Morgana with if he didn't sign in? "Though, I don't know. I may just go home after practice or whatever."

"What? Are you crazy?" Lucas cried. "Why would you go home? It's pizza! And minigolf. And the girls' field-hockey team is coming, too!" He narrowed his eyes. "What could possibly be better than that?"

Stu felt his face heat. He knew if he told Lucas the truth—that he wanted to play a video game—his stepbrother would laugh in his face. Lucas, like most normal people, could not understand that video-game outings could be just as important—and fun—as real-life ones.

"Is it Sophie?" Lucas demanded. "Did she say something?"

Stu cringed. Was he really that obvious? "Not exactly..."

"Dude! You cannot let some girl tell you what to do!"

Stu bit his lip, wanting to defend his friend. After all, Sophie wasn't just *some girl*. And she was way cooler than all the airhead girls Lucas spent his time with. The ones who only cared about clothes and makeup and shoes. (Seriously, why anyone needed more than two pairs of shoes Stu would never understand.)

Sometimes Stu could swear he felt his brain cells dying just from breathing the same air as some of them.

But Sophie—Sophie was different. She was smart and interesting and played real video games, too. Not just the karaoke dance ones all the other girls liked. Not to mention she thought zombies were cool, which pretty much sealed the deal for Stu.

He sighed. "I'll go, okay? I already told Dad I would."

"Awesome." Lucas jumped from the bed. "Now, you want to kick the ball around? I can help you practice. You've got your first game coming up. You need to be ready."

"Maybe later," he said, mostly just to get Lucas to leave. "I need to finish up here first."

Lucas groaned. "Seriously, sometimes I think you'd like it better if you could crawl into that game and live it in real life."

He grabbed his soccer ball and tossed it in Stu's direction. Stu tried to catch it, but missed by a mile. It crashed into the bookcase instead and knocked a few books off a shelf. Lucas shook his head and headed out of the room.

Stu watched him go, his stomach feeling as if it had been tied in knots. What had he gotten himself into? This whole soccer thing hadn't seemed like a big deal when he first tried out. He'd do a few practices, he'd play the games. Make his dad happy. Then go on with regular life.

But it wasn't turning out that way at all.

He sighed, trying to remind himself of the look on his

dad's face when he told him he'd made the team. He'd been so excited—you'd think Stu had gotten into college or something, the way he kept going on about it. Which wasn't surprising. His father loved sports. He went to all of Lucas's games. Even though he wasn't his real dad. And he was always bragging about Lucas's football skills to everyone he met. To hear him talk, it was like Lucas had already been drafted into the NFL.

He never bragged about Stu. Even when Stu won second prize in the regional robotics competition. Which everyone knew (well, except his dad, obviously) was a way bigger deal than scoring some dumb touchdown.

Stu turned back to the game. Signing out of his Lord Vanquish account, he selected one of his alternate characters and loaded her up. A few minutes later Lady Wolverine, his elf druid, smiled at him from behind the screen.

His shoulders relaxed as he maneuvered his character into the village to pick up supplies from the local shop. Life was so much easier here, inside the game. You never had to worry about being cool. Or impressing anyone. There were no surprises in the game. All the fights could be looked up online. You could look any way you wanted to look. Act any way you wanted to act.

Lucas wasn't wrong; sometimes Stu *did* wish he could live his life in a medieval-themed video game. He was positive things would be a whole lot simpler if he could.

CHAPTER 4

"By the moon and stars! It's like a thousand suns in here!" Princess Guinevere shielded her eyes with one hand as she attempted to follow Arthur into the home of his teacher, Merlin, later that morning. While she'd heard many tales over the years of the druid's legendary "Crystal Cave," she'd always thought them an exaggeration. Surely no cave could be made entirely out of multicolored gemstones, as the bards would sing of in taverns down in the village.

But sure enough, the rock walls before her did indeed appear to be encrusted with jewels—ruby reds, sapphire blues, clear diamonds—all exploding in a kaleidoscope of color as they caught the sunlight outside. The effect was breathtaking, beautiful, but a bit overwhelming, too. She wondered how Merlin could live here and not go blind.

A moment later, Arthur provided the answer, handing her a strangely shaped object with the word "Ray-Ban" written on the side. "Slide these shades over your eyes," he instructed, demonstrating with his own pair. "They'll help block out some of the light."

She followed his example, surprised and relieved to see how well they worked, dropping the brightness to a nonpainful level. Now, *there* was some magic! With these "Ray-Bans" she could actually see beyond the gemstones and into the cave itself, which, she had to admit, was a bit underwhelming after the brilliant entrance. In fact, the place looked as if a storm had blown in and knocked everything from its proper place. Overturned pots, discarded buckets with drops of water puddling the floor. Scraps of leather here, bits of feathers there. In the center of the room stood an iron cauldron, bubbling with some kind of unidentifiable green goop that Guinevere prayed the magician would not be serving at lunch.

"My apologies," Arthur said, giving her a rueful smile. "Merlin is not exactly a good housekeeper on the best of days."

She laughed, reaching down to pick up an overturned goblet, setting it down on a nearby table. "I'm just thankful to have a safe hideaway, no matter what its condition," she assured him.

After their run-in with Agravaine and Kay earlier that morning, she'd decided it was best to make herself scarce, at least until the afternoon's tournament. Out of sight, out of mind, as they said—and lately Guinevere had been on Agravaine's mind far too much for her liking. While she'd attempted to put on a brave face in front of Sara and the children, the knight's threats worried her more than she wanted to admit. Her father was at his wits' end, eager to get her matched with a future husband, and she'd already insulted half the nobles in the land. If Agravaine offered a large purse and a willingness to put up with her, she was sure her father would hand her over with a smile.

Arthur always spoke of being powerless, but sometimes Guinevere wondered who was actually worse off between them.

"I've seen Merlin attempt to clean this place only once," Arthur informed her, grabbing a plate off the floor and sticking it in a wash bucket. "When Viviane, the Lady of the Lake herself, was planning a visit." He laughed at the memory. "She came exactly one time and after that insisted that Merlin always come to visit her in Avalon instead. Evidently, his cleaning spells were not as effective as he'd hoped."

Guinevere giggled appreciatively. She'd heard many stories of the legendary Merlin—most of them terrifying. But when Arthur spoke of him it was different. The great and powerful magician—the one whom everyone feared—had taken an interest in the orphan boy when he was but a baby, taking him under his wing and becoming his teacher. He didn't care that Arthur's parents were likely commoners and that the boy had no chance of a real future beyond scrubbing dishes in the castle's kitchen. He treated him as if he were a crown prince. And the feeling was obviously mutual, judging from the sparkle in Arthur's eyes when he spoke of his mentor.

"Merlin?" he called out, looking around the cave. "Where are you? I've brought a friend."

"I'm in my chamber," a gruff old voice answered from behind a large wooden door located at the back of the cave. "I'll be out in a few."

Arthur turned back to Guinevere, rolling his eyes. "He must be on his magic box again," he explained.

"Magic box?" The princess cocked her head.

Arthur shrugged. "I don't know exactly what it does. But whatever it is, it takes up the majority of Merlin's time these days."

She watched as he walked to the other end of the cave, approaching a great wall of swords that she hadn't noticed before. She had to admit, the sorcerer had an incredible collection of blades. From heavy two-handed swords with ornately carved hilts depicting dragons and other fantastic beasts to jeweled daggers with razor-sharp tips. He even had a strange-looking curved sword at the very top of the wall, sheathed in an emerald-green case. A far cry from the rusty old practice blades she and Arthur had been sparring with earlier in the day.

Arthur grabbed one of the sheathed one-handed swords from the wall and tossed it in her direction. As she caught it, he pulled down another for himself. "Shall we rematch, my evil knight?" he asked, with a mischievous look in his eyes. "I would most enjoy besting you once and for all."

She looked down at her weapon doubtfully. It looked valuable. "Merlin won't mind us using his swords?"

"Of course not. He encourages it," Arthur explained, unsheathing his own blade from its scabbard and studying it with a critical eye. Even through her Ray-Bans Guinevere could see its sharp edges gleam. "He thinks I can be a great swordsman someday, if I practice enough." He looked at her, his eyes shining, and admiration rose inside of her. Here, in the Crystal Cave, he was no longer a scullery boy. An orphan of no importance. Here, he was as powerful as any knight. As noble as any king. His confidence was enchanting, and she had a wild thought about what a great leader he could have been, if only he had had the right pedigree.

"Very well," she agreed. "But this time I won't let you win."

"As if you ever do," he bantered back, skipping toward the cave's entrance gleefully.

She started to follow, then stopped as her eyes caught a flash of light from a workbench to her right. Turning to examine it, she discovered a breathtaking scabbard lying on the bench. A sheath of rich leather, encrusted with multicolored jewels.

She felt herself drawn to the object, involuntarily reaching out, picking it up, and sliding her sword inside of it, just to try it out. She turned it over in her hands, marveling at the fine embroidery winding through the gemstones, more intricate than any of her ladies could possibly have produced. As if it had been sewn by the fae folk themselves. Her eyes widened as she realized what the embroidery spelled out.

Pendragon.

She gasped. Could this really be the scabbard of legends? The one the bards sang about at banquets in the castle courts. The priceless artifact gifted to young Uther Pendragon by the druids of Avalon. A magical scabbard to hold his sword and ensure he would never bleed. To lead him to victory and rise to High King of Britain.

According to the tales, the scabbard had been stolen by the sorceress Morgana, who wanted revenge against Uther, who had killed her father and married her mother. With the scabbard lost, Uther also lost his invincibility and soon fell to a Saxon blade in battle, leaving Britain without an heir to the throne.

That was years ago. And as far as anyone knew, the scabbard had remained in Morgana's possession. Yet here it was. Out in the open and unprotected, in Merlin's Crystal Cave.

She had to show Arthur.

Pulling out her sword, she grabbed the scabbard and ran outside, removing her shades as she peered around the clearing, looking for her friend. "Arthur?" she cried. "Where are you?"

"Wouldn't you like to know, evil knight!" she heard him cry from somewhere beyond the bushes to her left.

Oh, so it was going to be like that, was it? Laughing, she dove into the brush, sheath and sword still in hand, clawing her way through the briars. Her silk dress caught and tore and she grimaced; her father would not be pleased if she arrived at the tournament in a muddy, torn dress, though it wouldn't be the first time. Maybe it would work out to her advantage—with Agravaine so horrified by her appearance that he'd withdraw his offer of marriage.

Yanking her dress free, she pushed through the remainder of foliage, catching a glimpse of movement and color ahead of her. There he was.

Leaping out of the bushes, she charged her opponent. But Arthur was ready for her, dodging at the last second and nearly sending her crashing into a small stone well just beyond the bushes. She dug in her heels, somehow managing to stop in her tracks. Unfortunately, the scabbard was not so lucky, flying free of her grip and straight down into the well.

Guinevere cried out in horror as she realized what she'd just done. She peered into the well, but saw nothing but blackness. This was not good.

"Making a wish won't help you," Arthur teased, coming up behind her and poking her in the back with his sword. "You're all mine, evil knight."

"Stop joking and help me!" she cried, grabbing the well's rope and pulling it with all her might. Maybe the scabbard had been caught by the bucket below. Maybe she could still retrieve it somehow. Her heart pounded fiercely in her chest and her hands shook.

"Don't get too close to that," Arthur warned, the joking look fading from his face.

She turned to him. "Why not? It's just a well."

"The Well of Dreams," he corrected. "Merlin uses it to see the future."

Guinevere winced. "It's a magical well?" she squeaked. This was getting worse and worse.

"What's wrong?" Arthur asked, crinkling his eyes in confusion. "Did you drop something in there? If it was that sword, don't worry about it. Merlin won't even miss—"

"It wasn't a sword," she admitted, her heart plummeting as the bucket rose to the top of the well with nothing but water. "It was a scabbard."

The most important treasure in the world, she didn't add. Merlin was going to have her head. Sure, he might be nice to Arthur, but he didn't know her. And she'd heard stories of what happened to people who wronged him. What had she been thinking, taking the artifact from the cave? She'd just been so excited to show Arthur.

"A scabbard?" Arthur repeated. "I don't under—"

"Arthur? Are you out here?" interrupted the same creaky old voice she'd heard back in the cave. The bushes shook and Guinevere took a step backward, scarcely able to breathe.

What would he do to her when he found out what she'd lost?

CHAPTER 5

The dishwasher was broken—which was probably why Dad had been so insistent Sophie be the one to clean up—and it took almost an hour before she put the last dried plate away. When Sophie finally walked through the living room on her way back upstairs, her father was putting on his shoes.

"I'm headed to the bowling alley with some of the guys," he said, reaching into the closet to grab his coat. "I'll be gone a few hours. Will you be okay by yourself?"

"Sure." Sophie nodded quickly. She appreciated the fact that her dad was okay with her staying home alone for a few hours in the afternoon, now that she'd turned twelve. "Have fun," she said, starting up the steps. She'd almost escaped when her father called out to her again.

"You don't want to . . . come with me, do you?" he asked, his voice hesitant.

Sophie paused. It would be nice to get out of the house for a bit, especially since she'd been barred from the computer for the rest of the afternoon. And the bowling alley was pretty fun. They had old-fashioned video games from the 1980s that took actual quarters and a snack bar with extra-salty popcorn.

"Who's going to be there?" she asked. Sometimes Stu's dad met up with them. And sometimes he brought Stu along, too. If Stu were there, she could apologize to him for their stupid fight earlier and then they could hang out in the game room while their dads bowled.

"You know. The usual guys . . ." He shuffled his feet. "And, uh, Cammy might stop by later, too. I don't know."

Cammy. As in Cameron Jones. As in the mother of Ashley Jones, her school's head cheerleader. As in the woman Sophie had only recently learned had been dating her dad.

"Sorry, I've got homework," she blurted, even though she'd done it all Saturday morning and was pretty sure her father knew it. Still, it was the only reasonable-sounding excuse she could come up with on the fly. Because there was no way she was going to hang out with her dad's new girlfriend, mother of her archenemy.

Without waiting for her father's reply, she ran up the rest of the stairs, taking them two at a time. She could feel her father's eyes burning a hole in her back as she reached the landing, and for a moment, she worried he'd call her back down to have a talk. Which was the very last thing she wanted to do.

But thankfully, all she heard was his sigh, followed by his heavy footsteps as he made his way to the front door, stepping out and pulling it shut behind him.

Leaving Sophie all alone.

She threw herself down on her bed, grabbing the ratty stuffed bear off her pillow and hugging it tightly to her chest. Then she rolled to her side and picked up a silver-framed photo from her nightstand. It was a portrait of her mother and father, taken at some kind of charity ball years before. Her mother looked so beautiful, in a long but simple silver gown. And her dad looked dashing in his tux. The two of them were ignoring the camera, gazing instead into each other's eyes, as if promising each other a happily ever after.

It was a beautiful picture. But it had been an empty promise. Mainly because five years ago, Sophie's mother had vanished without a trace and no one had heard from her since.

Sophie would never forget the last time she saw her mom. She'd been seven years old, curled up asleep in this very bed, when she'd felt a hand on her shoulder. She'd opened her eyes to find her mother leaning over her, her beautiful blue eyes filled with tears.

"Mom?" she'd asked, a little frightened.

"I'm sorry," her mother said in a choked voice. "I didn't mean to wake you."

"What's wrong?"

"Nothing. It's just that I have to go, my darling. And I don't know when I'll be able to come back."

Suddenly Sophie was wide-awake. "But why?" she asked, her heart pounding.

Her mother gave her a rueful smile. "I have to save the world," she said. Then she kissed her daughter's forehead and hushed her back to sleep.

When Sophie awoke the next morning, she wasn't sure if it had been a dream. But she liked to think it wasn't—that her mother was really out there, somewhere, saving the world.

While her father dated the head cheerleader's mom.

She tossed the photo back on the nightstand, feeling angry and sick. Then she rolled over to the other side of the bed, reaching for her cell phone. She had to call Stu and apologize. She had to admit, she'd been kind of a jerk earlier. If he wanted to play soccer, he should play soccer. After all, he never told her what she should or shouldn't do. Even that time she'd thought it would be a good idea to chop her hair and get bangs. (Which in hindsight had not been a good idea at all.)

Before she could dial, her phone started ringing. She smiled. Of course. Stu had an uncanny knack for that kind of thing.

"Hey," she said into the receiver.

"Hey yourself," he replied.

They both fell silent. *Okay ... awkward.* Sophie realized it was up to her to make the first move. "Listen, I—"

"About before—" Stu said at the same time.

They laughed and the tension broke between them. "Seriously, Stu. I acted like a jerk. I'm sorry. If you want to do the pizza-with-the-team thing, you totally should. Who knows, it might even be fun."

He sighed. "Yeah, sure. Fun."

Sophie picked at a loose thread on her mother's old quilt, wondering what was going on with her friend. Why were things suddenly weird between them? Everything had been so good for so long. She and Stu against the world. But now that wasn't enough for him. *She* wasn't enough.

It was like suddenly, out of the blue, he had this whole other life. A life that had nothing to do with her. Would Stu still want to hang out with her? Would he still have time for gaming? She knew some computer game wasn't technically as important as real life. But she couldn't help sometimes feeling like it was. She and Stu had a special bond through the game. As if their characters had a friendship all their own. If she lost that, it would be like losing part of herself. Which sounded so lame, but it was true.

"Um, Sophie?" Stu broke in over the line. "Are you still there?"

Oh. She blushed, coming back to earth. "Sorry," she said. "I was just . . . thinking."

"Look. If you want to play Friday night, I can skip the pizza thing. It's not a big deal."

She sat up in bed. "Don't be ridiculous. Like you said, Morgana isn't going anywhere."

"Really? So you really don't mind me going?"

His voice sounded so hopeful. Just like her dad when he'd asked her if she would be okay with him dating.

A lump formed in her throat.

"Of course not," she assured him, trying to swallow it back down. "Anyway, I gotta go. See you at lunch tomorrow?" she asked, holding her breath. Praying he wouldn't say he planned to sit with the team instead.

But she needn't have worried. "Absolutely!" he crowed. "It's pepperoni pizza day. I wouldn't miss it for the world."

Relief flooded her. "One of these days you're going to turn into pepperoni pizza," she teased, a smile lighting her face.

"You say that like it's a bad thing."

She snorted. "Okay, pizza boy. I'm hanging up. May the Merlin be with you," she added, quoting their favorite *Camelot's Honor* sign-off.

"And also with you," he chimed back, as was their custom. And suddenly things felt back to normal.

She pulled the phone from her ear and hit the end button. Then she snuggled back into her bed, telling herself everything would be okay. Soccer or no soccer, he was still Stu. Her best friend in the world. And just like the awesomeness of pepperoni pizza, that would never change.

CHAPTER 6

"There you are," Merlin exclaimed, popping his white-bearded head through the bushes, suspicious eyes leveling on Arthur. "What are you doing out here? And, more importantly, what"—his gaze roved to Guinevere, his mouth twisting into a disapproving frown—"is *she* doing here?"

Arthur gave Guinevere an apologetic look. For reasons he could not understand, his mentor had taken an extreme disliking to his friendship with the princess, even though he had never met her before. He was constantly telling him the girl was trouble and that Arthur was better off without her. Which seemed ridiculous to Arthur. If anything, his friendship with Guinevere had helped him survive and given him the only joy he had ever known. She was sweet, noble, brave, and true. And if there was something Merlin knew about her that Arthur didn't, well, he couldn't imagine what it could be.

"We had to hide out from some errant knights," he declared, stepping in front of the princess protectively. "I figured they wouldn't dare come looking here."

He watched, in relief, as Merlin's shoulders relaxed, his watery old eyes dancing with mirth. The magician knew, as well as anyone, how ignoble the knights of this realm could be. "Very well," he replied. "Come inside. I've whipped up a very lovely pea soup and..."

The magician trailed off, his smile fading as his gaze focused on something behind them. Arthur turned around slowly, his heart fluttering as he wondered what it could be.

His eyes bulged from his head. The once-calm waters of the well were now bubbling like a boiling cauldron, gushing over its stone sides as mists rose from the depths. Merlin pushed past Arthur and Guinevere, peering down into the well, ignoring the water splashing onto his robes. Then he looked back at Arthur, meeting his eyes with a furious look on his face.

"Did you try to use the Well of Dreams?" he demanded.

Guinevere opened her mouth to speak—to admit to what she'd dropped into the well—but Arthur realized suddenly that he couldn't let her take the blame. After all, he'd been the one messing around, causing her to drop the scabbard to begin with. And Merlin would likely take things easier on him than her.

"I dropped a scabbard into the well," he replied stoutly. "One I found in the Crystal Cave."

"A scabbard." Merlin's disbelief was clear on his face, his normally confident voice croaking in a mixture of fury and fear. "You don't happen to mean the jeweled scabbard that was sitting on my workbench, now, do you?"

Arthur stole a glance at Guinevere. Her white face gave him all the answers he needed. "Yes, that is the one," he replied uneasily. He'd never seen his teacher so upset before. "Why? Is it really valuable?"

"Valuable?" Merlin repeated with a scoffing laugh. "Valuable?" He fanned himself with his hands. "Arthur, that scabbard has the power to change the very history of this world."

Oh dear. Arthur let out a breath, his stomach swimming with nausea as he realized what he had to do. "Well, don't worry, I can go get it," he informed his teacher. "You could turn me into a fish or a sea turtle, perhaps. I could dive down into the well and find the scabbard. Then you can turn me into a bird and I can fly it back up." Merlin had taught him the power of shape-shifting as part of their lessons. He even had a special magical powder that could transform a person into any animal they wished to be. It was pretty fun and maybe would prove useful now. He just hoped the scabbard hadn't gotten damaged by the water.

But to his surprise, his teacher shook his head. "The Well of Dreams is no ordinary vessel. It serves as a portal to other times.

Anything or anyone dropped into its depths will be transported instantly before ever touching the bottom." The magician paced the ground, like a cat in a cage. "The scabbard is no longer in our world, my boy. And no fish or turtle could ever hope to bring it back."

"Well, then, where has it gone?" Guinevere piped in, her own voice quavering. "If not down in the well?"

Merlin stopped pacing. He fixed a glare on her, as if he suspected her involvement in this tragedy. "To twenty-first-century America," he replied matter-of-factly. "Massachusetts, to be precise."

Guinevere's jaw dropped.

"The twenty-first century," Arthur blurted. "You mean like the future?"

"I mean exactly the future." Merlin nodded glumly. "Before you arrived, I'd conjured up a time portal to connect to Wi-Fi. . . ."

"Wi-Fi?" Arthur repeated, baffled.

Merlin waved him off. "The point is, your timing couldn't have been worse. The Companion will be here at any moment to retrieve the scabbard and bring it to this afternoon's tournament. I do not know what her mistress, the Lady of the Lake, will do to me if she learns of its current fate."

"Wait!" Guinevere cried, her eyes lighting up. "You're bringing the Pendragon scabbard to the tournament? Does this mean you believe someone will pull the sword from the stone today? Will we be getting a new high king?"

Merlin gave her a nervous look, as if he'd said too much. But before she could press him, a giant black horse stepped into the clearing with a tall woman astride. The woman was dressed in plain white robes, her waist encircled by a simple silver chain. She slid off her horse and stepped toward them. Though she was largely unadorned, she radiated a beauty and glory that left Arthur awestruck.

"A Companion!" Guinevere hissed at Arthur. "Drop to your knee."

Arthur complied with no question. He'd never seen one of the Lady of the Lake's maidens before, but he'd heard many tales. They were warrior priestesses, serving and protecting the land. Descendants of the goddess of war, known as the Morrigan, who long ago brought victory to Britain over the invading Roman Empire.

In other words, no one you wanted to trifle with . . . or accidentally disrespect. Or, you know, lose the priceless artifact they were sent to retrieve.

The Companion had long blond hair and true-blue eyes and a face so ageless Arthur couldn't tell if she had lived a mere twenty summers or eighty. He watched, terrified, as she approached Merlin.

"M'lady," Merlin said, bowing low. "We are honored by your visit."

"I cannot stay long," she told him. "There is still much to do. I assume everything is in place for this afternoon?"

Arthur dared steal a peek and realized she was staring straight at him as she spoke. He felt his face heat under her intense gaze. "We are ready," Merlin told her. "Today is a great and glorious day. Finally the prophecy shall come to pass."

Guinevere gave Arthur an excited look. He knew what she was thinking. Would someone finally pull the sword from the stone? Could they have a new high king before the day was out? It was a thrilling idea, to say the least. He only hoped this new king—whoever he was—would be just and good. He didn't think the kingdom could take an Agravaine type.

"Very well," said the Companion. "Then give me the scabbard and I shall be on my way."

"Actually, there's been a change in plans," Merlin informed her smoothly, as if he wasn't lying through his teeth. "I am going to be bringing the scabbard to the ceremony myself."

The Companion's serene smile dipped. "That was not what we agreed to. You were only to keep the scabbard long enough to re-enchant it. The Lady wishes to be the one to gift the new king with his scabbard and sword."

"And she will!" Merlin exclaimed. "I'll give it to her the second I get to the castle. There's just one more thing I must do to . . . make it even more powerful."

The Companion was silent for a moment, pursing her lips. "Very well," she said at last. "I will let the Lady know. But I can assure you, she will not be pleased."

"She will be pleased soon enough!" Merlin insisted. "When she sees what this new and improved scabbard can do." He beamed at her with a confident whiskered grin. "Now, my dear, you've come all this way. Why don't you spend a moment at the well? I've got it all dialed in, just for you." He put a fatherly arm on her shoulder.

The Companion stiffened, and Arthur thought he caught a shadow of longing cross her elegant face. "I shouldn't tarry," she hedged. "I must get back to my Lady."

"Would your Lady begrudge you one moment of joy on this most joyous of days?" Merlin cajoled. "After all, you do not pass through this way often."

"You are right." The Companion walked slowly over to the well, but her face betrayed her eagerness. "Just a quick glimpse . . ."

Arthur and Guinevere watched as she peered into its depths. Hopefully the scabbard wouldn't pick that moment to bob to the surface. That would be a bit awkward, to say the least.

A moment later, a wistful smile spread across the Companion's face. It was as if whatever the well was showing her was both happy and sad. A moment later, she sighed deeply, forcing herself to straighten and turn away.

"Thank you," she said, bowing low to Merlin. "You are right. It is a vision I don't get to see often enough and one I love well."

Merlin patted the Companion on the back. "The Well of Dreams is always here for you when you need it," he told her. "But now I must ask a favor of you as well."

"Anything, m'lord."

"Will you escort this young lady back to the castle on your way to Avalon?" he asked, pointing to Guinevere. "She has been gone some time and I am sure her father has missed her by now."

Guinevere frowned. "I don't think that—" But Merlin's sharp look cut her off. She ducked her head, then followed the Companion to her horse.

"Bye, Arthur," she said with an apologetic wave.

Arthur wished they could have just a moment together alone to talk, but Merlin was evidently eager to be rid of the princess. And Arthur was in enough hot water already; he knew better than to protest.

"Till we meet again, my evil knight," he quipped instead.

"Indeed, my conquering hero," she quoted back, smiling widely.

Merlin rolled his eyes, mumbling something that sounded a lot like "stupid destiny." Then the Companion flicked the reins and the two women on horseback disappeared into the forest.

Once they were gone, Merlin turned to Arthur. "Don't think

I don't know what you just did," the wizard rebuked him. "Very chivalrous, but extremely misguided. That girl is no good, I've told you a thousand times. She'll break your heart and destroy everything we've worked to build."

"I'd rather my heart be broken a thousand times than spend one day without her," Arthur declared valiantly.

Merlin groaned. "I seriously don't know why I bother," he muttered under his breath. Then he turned his attention to the well. "Now, about that scabbard. We have to get it back somehow. It's bad enough that if I don't come up with a convincing knockoff by this afternoon, the Lady of the Lake will trap me in a tree for a thousand years. But if it were to get in the wrong hands—if Morgana were to learn it was just lying out there, unprotected . . ." He shook his head. "Normally I'd just go retrieve it from the twenty-first century myself, but I've already time-traveled three times this year and my old heart can't take another trip so soon."

Arthur drew in a breath, daring himself to speak. "You should send me instead," he declared. "I'll retrieve the scabbard from the future and bring it back to you. I'm young and . . . well, I'm expendable." He had been really looking forward to serving as Kay's squire at the tournament that afternoon, especially if the new high king was going to be chosen from the sword-and-the-stone ceremony. But he didn't like the idea of Merlin being in trouble on his account.

"Absolutely not," Merlin said. "You will go to the tournament, as planned, and serve as Kay's squire."

"Then who will go get the scabbard? Perhaps you could hire a knight?" After all, it was a quest of sorts.

"No. A knight would never do. If they learned of the scabbard's power, they might choose to sell it to the highest bidder. Or use it to become king themselves. I can't trust anyone from this time period. It's all too volatile." He stroked his beard. "If only I could use one of the Companions," he mused. "But they all report to the Lady, and then I'd have to admit..." He trailed off, his eyes widening as he stared down into the well, as if he could somehow read the answer in the water's depths.

"What?" Arthur asked, scrambling over to get his own peek, though he knew it was technically forbidden. Luckily, Merlin didn't shoo him away this time. Squinting down into the water, he tried to make out the vision below.

It was a girl. Blond and blue-eyed and about Arthur's age. She was lying on her bed, curled up with some kind of small, furry animal nestled in her arms. Arthur glanced at Merlin. His master was practically dancing with excitement.

"Of course!" Merlin cried. "Why didn't I think of her to begin with?" He clapped Arthur on the shoulder. "Come back to the cave with me, boy. All may not be lost after all."

CHAPTER 7

Sophie had just hung up with her father when her cell phone buzzed, notifying her of a text message. She glanced at the screen, first assuming it was Stu. Instead, the message had been sent from an unknown number.

** LIMITED TIME ONLY! UNLOCK THE MYSTERIES OF CAMELOT'S HONOR WITH THE CAMELOT CODE! WWW.CAMELOTCODE.COM **

She squinted. What was a Camelot Code? A cheat code for *Camelot's Honor*, maybe? A hack? She'd heard about these from Stu, who was all up on the latest illegal add-on programs that enabled you to duplicate rare items or give your character unlimited money. Of course, they were totally against the game's terms of service and could get your character deleted. Not to mention her dad would kill her if she just downloaded some random program from an unknown source.

She debated deleting the message, but curiosity got the better of her. It couldn't hurt to just take a quick peek at the website, could it? After all, it could be something really cool that Stu hadn't heard about yet. *She* could impress *him* for once, the little gaming know-it-all.

Dragging herself out of bed and over to her computer, she plopped down on her chair. Setting her phone next to her keyboard, she opened her browser and typed the URL into the top window.

Nothing happened.

At first she thought the website hadn't loaded—that their lame Wi-Fi was down again. But then she realized that wasn't the case. The page *had* loaded; it was simply blank. No words, no graphics, no video. Just a visitor counter all the way down at the bottom, which currently read 00001.

"Not a very popular website," she muttered, glancing at her phone to make sure she'd typed it in right. She had. Could the site have been recently shut down for offering illegal hacks, perhaps? It seemed possible, but if so, why would they still be sending out texts to players' cell phones?

Curious, Sophie clicked the web developer tools at the top of her browser to open up the page's source file, just in case there was any information embedded in the HTML code. Some clue as to who set up this page in the first place.

What the...?

She squinted at the screen, not sure what she was seeing. Amid a simple web-counter code sat a string of foreign-looking words that hadn't shown up on the website. Even odder, the words seemed to dance and sparkle on her computer screen, as if they were some kind of animated GIF.

```
Rex quondam, Rexque Futurus
```

She absently highlighted the words with her mouse, trying to puzzle out the mystery. Why were they there? Why didn't they show up on the website? She refreshed the page. Nothing, except now the counter read 00002.

Was this someone's idea of a joke? She switched back to the source code.

"*Rex quondam, Rexque Futurus,*" she read aloud.

And suddenly she found herself spinning into blackness.

CHAPTER 8

The pain! Sophie groaned and rolled over, clutching her head in her hands. It felt as if a thousand knives were boring into her skull all at once, each sharper than the last. Forcing her eyes open, she made a valiant attempt to pull herself upright and take in her surroundings.

Wait, what?

She rubbed her eyes and did a double take, but the scenery didn't change. What had moments ago been her cozy bedroom had now somehow transformed into a vast forest, with dark leafy trees stretching out in all directions.

Panicked, she racked her brain for the last thing she remembered. She'd been in her bedroom, that weird Camelot Code website pulled up on her screen. She'd blacked out. Was she dreaming? This didn't feel like any dream she'd had before. For one thing, the pain in her head seemed very, very real.

It was then she remembered the words. The ones in Latin she'd spoken aloud. Could they have been some kind of—

No, that was stupid. She'd obviously been playing too many video games. More likely she'd somehow passed out, fallen off her chair, and hit her head against the sharp corner of the desk. The pain from the fall was simply seeping into her dream. Soon she'd wake up and be back at home safe and sound. If she wasn't in some kind of weird coma.

A rustling in the bushes startled her and she whirled around. She relaxed when she saw it was just a small white bunny rabbit, emerging from a nearby bush. The creature raised itself on its hind legs and peered at her quizzically, with odd green eyes. It twitched its nose a few times, then, to Sophie's delight, dropped to all fours and hopped over to her. Enchanted, she reached down to pet its soft fur.

What a cool dream, she thought. With the exception of the headache, of course. She loved dreaming about furry animals, since she was allergic to them in real life. Dreamland was the one place she could get up close and personal, cuddling them without—

She sneezed.

The rabbit's ears perked up and its nose twitched. After

thumping its hind legs twice, it darted back into the bushes, disappearing from sight. At first Sophie thought her sneeze had startled it, but then she heard a thundering in the distance. Rising to her feet, she scanned the vicinity. Whatever the noise was, it seemed to be getting louder. And closer. Her eyes fell upon a cloud of dust barreling down the path.

What on earth . . . ?

Slam! A split second later, something solid smashed into her, violently knocking her to the ground and out of the path of what she now realized were riders on horseback, approaching at top speed. She cried out in a mixture of protest and pain as her palms skidded across the rocky ground and her knee collided with a stump. A moment later, she had a face full of dirt and a heavy something—make that some*one*—lying on top of her.

The horses charged past, battle-decked steeds, ridden by men in suits of chain mail, galloping full tilt. She swallowed hard; if she hadn't been pushed from the path they would have likely trampled her to death.

Her rescuer rolled off and pulled himself to his feet. Her eyes widened. It was a boy, probably around her own age, with short, messy chestnut-brown hair, flashing green eyes, and a strong face with a square jaw. Which seemed altogether normal until she noticed what he was wearing. A beige, belted tunic, tan leggings, and a pair of soft, mud-stained leather boots. Not exactly an ensemble you could purchase at your local Abercrombie.

First, knights on horseback, now, a guy who looked like he'd stepped off the screen of *Camelot's Honor*. This dream was getting stranger by the second.

She realized her rescuer was staring at her, so she scrambled to her feet. "Thanks for pushing me out of the way," she said, flashing him a grateful smile as she brushed off her now dirt-caked pants. "Those guys were definitely not looking where they were going."

The boy looked down at the road. "They never do," he muttered under his breath, so quietly she barely heard him. Then he looked back at her. "Anyway, come with me."

He grabbed at her hand. Startled, she yanked it back.

"Hang on," she cried. "I'm not going anywhere with you. I don't even know who you are."

"Merlin sent me to retrieve you," he replied impatiently. "Now come on. We have to get back to the cave as soon as possible before—"

A sudden whinny interrupted his words. Sophie whirled around to find that the group of armored men had circled back. Their horses snorted and pawed the ground as they surrounded her and the boy. Sophie crinkled her nose in disgust as the smell of manure flooded the air. This had to be the most realistic dream she'd ever had.

Unless, something inside of her warned, *it isn't a dream at all.*

She glanced back at the boy who'd rescued her. He'd lost his cocky swagger and was looking up at the knights with a blood-less face. *Uh-oh.*

"Well, well, what have we here?" asked the tallest of the group, a broad-shouldered man with a shock of ginger hair. He drew his sword from its scabbard and the metal caught the sun, forcing Sophie to shield her eyes. She took a wary step back; the blade looked way too real for comfort. Way too sharp.

"Looks like the *wart* has found himself another little friend," the second man jeered. He had bushy black hair and a matching beard in desperate need of a trim. "He's quite the ladies' man, this one."

Sophie startled, recognition suddenly tickling at her brain. *Wart?* Wasn't that the boyhood nickname of King Arthur in *Camelot's Honor*? And hadn't the boy just been talking about Merlin—another legendary Camelot character—before the knights showed up?

This was getting stranger by the second.

She turned questioningly to her new friend, who was wring-ing his hands and looking as if he was about to blow chunks. "You're Wart?" she asked, wanting to get this straight. "Like, King Arthur Wart?"

The black-haired knight broke into a full guffaw. "King Arthur Wart," he repeated to his companions, elbowing the redheaded one to his left. "That's a good one."

"First a knight and now a king," the redheaded guy chortled.

"Why, by nightfall, he'll have become emperor of Rome!" He kicked at the boy with a big black boot. "King, indeed. The most my foster brother here can ever hope for is to become my squire. Right, boy? And that's only if you behave yourself."

"Yes, Kay," the boy—Wart? Arthur?—replied dully. From the tone of his voice, she guessed this wasn't the first time he'd been smacked around by his foster brother. Poor guy. If only he knew about his illustrious destiny as England's greatest king. He wouldn't have to take grief from anyone.

But until then, it was evidently up to Sophie. After all, if she was going to dream about *Camelot's Honor*, she might as well be as tough as her game character.

"Why don't you go pick on someone your own size?" she demanded, stepping in front of Kay's horse, arms crossed over her chest. She gave him a critical once-over from head to toe. "Or is it too hard to find someone so ugly?"

Kay's friends burst out laughing, causing the knight's face to darken to match his carrot-colored hair. "Mind your tongue, wench," he growled.

"Hey! I like a girl who can speak her mind," protested the third knight, a blonde who had been quiet up until now. He winked at Sophie. "Come, girl. Leave this worthless wretch and take a turn with some real knights. We're on our way to the tournament. You can watch me pull the sword from the stone."

"Uh, spoiler alert? You will never pull the sword from the stone," Sophie scoffed. "You morons could try all day."

The knights stared at her, looks of utter disbelief on their faces. Disbelief and quite a bit of annoyance, too. Hmm. Maybe she should have kept her mouth shut on that last part. Or at least resisted calling them names . . .

"Do you dare insult us, girl?" the black-haired knight demanded, raising his sword again and urging his horse forward. Sophie had to stumble backward so as not to be stepped on. She glanced over at Arthur, hoping he'd know what to do.

"Run!" he whispered.

Right.

Sophie dove through the group of horses, her heart pounding as she tore down the path, fast as her legs could take her. Her feet slammed against the dirt road, keeping a frantic pace. She could hear the shouts behind her.

"She flees!"

"Don't let her get away!"

Soon they were hot on her heels. Of course she hadn't exactly gotten a huge head start, especially considering it was horse versus girl. She forced herself to pick up the pace, lungs burning as she dove off the path and into the underbrush, where she figured it would be harder for horses to follow. Branches whipped at her face, thorns slashed at her bare arms, but still she pressed onward, praying she'd wake up. Even though this was seeming less like a dream by the second.

Finally, she burst into a clearing, the sun beating down on her already sweaty skin. Her gaze darted from edge to edge, not sure in which direction she should go. The men would be here any second. She was a sitting duck.

As she plunged back into the forest, she unfortunately missed seeing the rotting log looming in front of her path. A moment later, she went flying, and her head slammed straight into a nearby tree.

For the second time that day, Sophie found herself swimming into blackness.

CHAPTER 9

Sophie woke sometime later, not sure how long she'd been out. She rubbed her eyes, which felt heavy and sticky from being closed so long. What a weird dream she'd had. Being back in time. Meeting King Arthur. Sir Kay. Being chased by a gang of knights...

She stretched her hands out lazily, reaching out and touching—

Straw?

She bolted upright, her heart pounding as she took in her surroundings. She was in a dark, circular cell with dim light filtering in through a small barred window across the room. And the bed she was lying on was nothing more than a bale of hay.

Not her bedroom. Not even close.

She leaped up in a panic. It hadn't been a dream at all. She was really here. Wherever here might be.

She ran to the door, harboring an insane hope that she might somehow be able to open it. But no luck. It was locked tight. Pounding on the solid wood with her fists, she shouted for help.

But there was no reply.

She sank down to the floor, head in her hands, too afraid to even cry. Those words—"the Camelot Code"—they must have brought her here. It seemed impossible, but what other explanation could there be?

But if that was true, no one knew where she was. Or even *when* she was. Which meant there'd be no one to rescue her. They'd try, of course. Gathering the dogs, searching the woods, putting out an Amber Alert. But in the end, they'd have to give up. They'd have to assume she was dead. Because really, who would ever believe she'd ended up in another millennium by reading some magic words off a website?

A flapping noise at the window startled her out of her panic. A small brown-speckled hawk was beating its wings against the bars. If she didn't know better, she'd say it was trying to enter her cell.

The bird screeched in apparent frustration while trying to push its way through the narrow bars. Sophie watched, fascinated and horrified at the same time, not sure what to do. Finally, the hawk managed to squeeze through and fly into the room.

And then, right before Sophie's amazed eyes, the hawk's wings began to stretch. To ... grow. Talons elongated, feathers fell away, claws morphed into ... feet?

A moment later the hawk had disappeared. And in its place stood none other than Arthur himself.

Sophie leaped to her feet.

"A-Arthur?" she cried, gaping. "How did you ... ? I mean ... did you just ... ?"

"Shape-shift from a bird?" he finished. "Yes. Isn't that great? I can do any animal. Dog, horse, fish, turtle. Even magical ones like unicorns, though those take a little extra powder."

"Shape-shift?" she repeated, her baffled brain trying to catch up. "You're telling me you can shape-shift?" It was a dumb question, she knew, seeing as she'd just witnessed him doing it. "But how?"

Arthur grinned, looking proud of himself. "Merlin taught me the secret. A little magic powder, a couple magic words ..."

Merlin. Of course. Sophie suddenly remembered that according to some of the legends, as well as that old Disney cartoon, the magician had taught young Arthur early life lessons by turning him into various forest creatures. She'd always thought that would be pretty cool.

There were other legends, too, she thought. One of which claimed Merlin was able to travel through time ...

She looked up, hope rising inside of her. "This Merlin," she ventured. "Is he . . . nearby, maybe?" She crossed her fingers. If anyone could help her get back, it'd be the greatest wizard of all time.

"Yes, of course. He's waiting for you in his Crystal Cave," Arthur replied, as if stating the obvious. "Didn't you receive the message he sent you? He told me he 'texted' you—whatever that means."

"*Merlin* texted me?" she repeated, now totally lost. Then she remembered. "That text about the Camelot Code was from *Merlin*?" Just when she thought none of this could get any stranger.

"I'm sure he'll explain everything when we get there. But we have to hurry. There's something he needs you to do and we're running out of time."

Sophie let out a relieved breath. Thank goodness, she was being rescued. Not only rescued, but brought to the one guy who could, hopefully, send her home.

"Great," she said, heading over to the door. "Where's the key?"

"The key?" Arthur chuckled. "We need no key."

"Uh, so you want to . . . break down the door, then?"

Arthur's eyes sparkled. "We don't need the door, either," he told her. "We're going to fly."

Sophie stared at Arthur, not quite sure she'd heard him right.

"Fly?" she repeated. "Maybe that's okay for you. I mean, you can shape-shift and everything. But there's no way I can..."

She trailed off as Arthur reached into a small leather bag hanging off of his belt. He pulled out a handful of what looked like glitter, brought it to his lips, and blew hard.

"What the—" she cried, but her question was cut short as she accidentally inhaled some of the glitter. She started coughing—hacking—and couldn't seem to catch her breath. Grabbing her throat with one hand, she made the universal choking sign while waving wildly at Arthur. Unfortunately, he seemed too busy glittering himself up to notice her desperate gestures.

Sophie felt a sudden tugging at her feet. Looking down, she watched in horror as her shoes crumbled away and her toenails began to elongate into long, curled talons. A moment later, her arms sprouted soft brown feathers and her fingers started webbing together.

She was turning into a bird. Just like in *Camelot's Honor*. And it was a lot more freaky when it happened in real life.

Sophie tried to scream, but it came out more like a screech. At least she'd found her breath, though that wasn't a huge comfort as she felt her body shrinking, literally collapsing in on itself. Sharp pain stabbed through her back as wings burst from her rib cage. Terrified, she bent a wing to touch her face. Her freckled little nose had grown into a Pinocchio-length beak.

"Calm yourself," Arthur instructed, his own transformation already complete. "Let the magic take hold. Struggling only makes it hurt more."

"Easy for you to say," she tried to retort. It came out more like, "Caw, ca-caw, caw, caw."

He laughed. "That's exactly what I said to Merlin my first time." She realized that he was cawing himself, yet she could completely understand every word out of his mouth—make that beak.

"Is this really necessary?" Sophie demanded. "I mean, you couldn't have brought a skeleton key or something to bust me out?"

He shrugged as well as a hawk could shrug and gestured at the window with his wing. "This seemed easier."

"Oh no!" she cried, shaking her little bird head as vehemently as she could. "I'm so not jumping out of some window. Just 'cause I've somehow miraculously developed wings doesn't mean I know how to fly."

"Flying is simple," Arthur replied, hopping onto the window-sill. "You just spread your wings and flap." He demonstrated with his own wings and was soon effortlessly hovering a few feet off the ground. "See?"

Sophie let out a frustrated breath, then gave a reluctant flap. Her little feathered body levitated almost immediately. She flapped a few more times, then a few more, feeling the air shifting through her feathers. Actually, this was pretty cool, as long as she didn't look—

She banged her head against the tower ceiling. Knocked off-balance, she struggled to right herself, but only managed to crash to the stone floor below.

"Are you all right?" Arthur flew over and studied her with his beady bird eyes.

"Urgh," she managed to spit out as she attempted to right herself. "I don't think this is going to work."

"It has to work," Arthur insisted. "Trust me, you don't want to be stuck here in the tower when Kay and Agravaine return."

"Couldn't you just have Mr. Merlin, I don't know, poof himself here or something?" Wizard house calls. That made so much more sense.

But Arthur shook his head. "Look, you're a bird. You have wings. Spread them and trust you will fly."

"But..." If only she could explain to him that it wasn't her wings she didn't trust, but her crazy bird brain and its paralyzing fear of heights.

"Watch me," Arthur said, flapping over to the windowsill. He pushed his way through the bars and proceeded to jump into the abyss. She watched as he glided gracefully through the sky, almost as if he'd been caught by a breeze and carried along like a surfer, cresting on a perfect wave. Every so often he'd flap his wings to gain a little altitude, then switch back to gliding.

Sophie resigned herself to her fate. She had to get out of the tower, after all, and it didn't seem like there was going to be any other way to do it. Maybe if she just forced herself to not look down.

She drew in a breath. It was simple, as Arthur had said. She had wings, therefore she could fly. Perfectly logical and no big deal.

After swallowing down a big gulp of fear, she pushed her body through the bars, closed her eyes, and jumped, spreading her wings, just as he'd instructed, trying to find the currents of air to carry her along. For a moment, she thought she actually had it as an updraft picked her up and thrust her forward. She glided smoothly, the breeze ruffling her feathers. Maybe this would be okay. Maybe it'd actually be fun.

Then she looked down.

Her stomach heaved. The ground was too far away. Losing her concentration, she tumbled through the sky, flapping her wings frantically, desperately trying to gain some kind of elevation. But gravity seemed to have other ideas. She was doing a nose dive—fast. In a few seconds she'd be splattered against a rock, nothing more than a stain on the medieval landscape.

"Help!" she croaked, her wing muscles burning from the nonstop flapping. *"Arthur!"*

She felt a sharp pain dig into her back and her body jerked upward. Daring to open her eyes, she saw that Arthur had swooped down and grabbed her in his talons, just in time to save her from becoming intimately acquainted with the forest floor below.

"Stop flapping!" he screeched. "You must *glide.* Let the wind take you."

"Just get me to solid ground!"

Rolling his little bird eyes, he carried her over to a nearby tree and set her down on a high branch. Not exactly the solid ground she'd asked for, but she supposed it was better than nothing. Digging her claws into the wood, searching for her center of gravity, she sucked a shaky breath. That had been close.

Arthur fluttered down onto the limb beside her. "You panicked," he said, as if that wasn't totally obvious. "You must trust that the winds will embrace you. Don't fight them."

"Come on," she pleaded. "We're out of the tower, right? Just pick me up again and put me down on the ground. We can walk to Merlin's place."

"But it'll take twice as long to get there."

"I don't care if it takes all day. As long as I don't have to fly."

"Look," Arthur said, sounding exasperated. "Flying's really not that hard once you get the hang of it. You were doing really well there for a moment."

She gritted her beak miserably. If only she could explain to him that she was really quite brave under most other circumstances. Those that took place on the ground, anyway.

"Come on," Arthur pleaded. "How about another try?"

"No!" she cried, realizing only after she spoke how angry she sounded. Mostly at herself, of course, and her patheticness. "Take me down to the ground this instant and turn me back into a human!"

Arthur flinched. "Very well." Grabbing her in his talons, he dragged her back down to the ground. A moment later, she felt solid earth under her feet once again.

Arthur waved his wings, poofing her, then himself, back into human form. (Thankfully their clothes and shoes reappearing as well.) She flexed her arms and legs, stamped down on the ground, then sighed in relief. "My hero."

To her surprise, he stopped short at her words, his formerly frustrated face morphing into one of pure pleasure. It was then she realized that for all her complaining, she hadn't properly thanked him for a pretty heroic rescue. Without him, she'd still be stuck in the tower, at the mercy of those disgusting knights.

"I'm sorry," she apologized. "Thank you for rescuing me. That was pretty great. Maybe I can try that bird thing again sometime. You know, starting from a lower perch."

"It was my honor to serve," he replied gallantly, bowing low. Then he straightened and beckoned her to the path in front of them. "When you're ready, m'lady."

She smiled. "Lead the way."

CHAPTER 10

"There you are," Merlin's voice boomed as Arthur turned the corner and stepped into the clearing outside his teacher's cave. The elderly magician hobbled toward him, leaning on his staff. "What took you so long?" he demanded. "I've been worried."

"We had a few . . . complications," Arthur admitted. "But I took care of them." No need to go into details. Like how he'd almost accidentally killed the girl he'd gone to rescue.

Merlin patted him on the shoulder. "Good boy. I knew I could count on you."

Arthur beamed at the praise. His master already seemed in a better mood. Perhaps this girl had brought him hope. Perhaps she'd be able to find the scabbard and everything would go back to normal.

"Hello? Arthur? Where did you go?"

Arthur and Merlin turned to see Sophie stumbling out of the bushes, her hair riddled with leaves and her face awash in a sheen of sweat. Her eyes fell upon Arthur's teacher.

"Merlin!" she cried, looking extremely relieved. "Are you really Merlin?"

"The one and only," the magician agreed with a smirk.

"Wow. Am I happy to see you. You don't even know. You see, I somehow found myself here and—"

Merlin waved her off. "All in good time, my dear," he said. "But first, come inside with me and we'll have a little talk. And maybe you'd like some water? I think I have a bottle of Evian somewhere. Maybe some San Pellegrino?"

"At this point, I'd drink from the castle moat."

Merlin laughed. "I'm sure we can do better than that. Come along." He started leading her toward the cave, then stopped, turning back to Arthur and glancing at the strange metal bracelet he always wore on his wrist. The one with the numbers on it.

"You'd better get going. The tournament's set to begin soon. You don't want to incur your foster brother's wrath, now, do you?"

Arthur definitely did not. He'd already angered Kay far too much for one day. "I'm on my way," he said with a bow. "Good luck with the scabbard!"

Merlin gave him a small salute before he and Sophie disappeared into the cave.

Arthur turned to start down the path back toward the castle, but an odd sound made him pause: a high-pitched humming, coming from the other side of the cave. He frowned. Was the Well of Dreams acting up again? Worried, he switched direction, walking around the cave and pushing through the bushes to investigate.

As he came across the well, the sound stopped abruptly and the placid waters began to bubble and boil again. Arthur peered inside, mesmerized, as they shifted to reveal a large green field, painted with some kind of numbers and lines and surrounded by stands made of metal.

Strange. But not dangerous-looking. Arthur shrugged and turned to walk away; he'd already messed with the well enough. But then a glint of light caught his eye and he found himself looking back again. It appeared the field wasn't so empty after all.

The scabbard was there. Lying on the grass, just waiting to be picked up. Arthur groaned. It looked so close. As if he could just reach down and grab it through the strands of time.

Perhaps he could.

Arthur leaned down into the well, heart in his throat. Holding on to a nearby vine, he stretched his right hand out, down into the waters, trying to grab the sheath. At first he felt nothing. Just water. Then his hands brushed across something solid.

He could feel the jewels at his fingertips. He just had to lean in a little bit more to wrap his hand around it and—

Suddenly the waters swirled. The vine he'd been holding broke.

And Arthur found himself tumbling headfirst into the Well of Dreams.

CHAPTER 11

"Wow!" Sophie exclaimed as she entered the cave and was greeted by a blinding mosaic of emeralds, rubies, sapphires, and diamonds. She was more than a bit grateful when Merlin handed her a pair of Ray-Bans, though she did wonder where he'd bought them—a medieval Sunglass Hut?

"It's a bit...bright in here, I know," he admitted.

"It's incredible," she corrected, looking around in awe. It was still hard to believe she was really here. In medieval times. In Merlin's legendary Crystal Cave! This was, like, the coolest thing ever, now that she was done being scared. "I've never seen anything like it. Stu would be so jealous right now!"

"Oh, Sophie," Merlin cried suddenly. To her surprise, the

magician threw his arms around her and squeezed her into a bearlike hug. "It's so good to meet you in real life."

"What?" She pulled away from the hug, looking at him, confused. "I don't understand. What do you mean 'real life'? Do I know you?"

But Merlin only chuckled. "Melvin-Oh-One of *Camelot's Honor*, at your service," he replied, dropping to a grand bow.

Her mouth gaped. "What? But you're not...I mean...You couldn't be."

Was it possible? Could she and Stu have, all this time, been playing *Camelot's Honor* with someone actually from Camelot?

"I thought you were a surfer from California."

"I apologize for not telling you the truth. But would you have believed me if I had?"

He had a point. "So you *are* the one who sent me the Camelot Code?"

Merlin nodded.

"But...why?"

The magician's smile faltered. He gestured for her to have a seat at a small wooden table. "Because I need your help. There was an accident. A very valuable relic of Avalon was lost."

And so he told her the tale. How the Companions had entrusted him with the scabbard. How Arthur—or maybe Guinevere—had dropped it into the Well of Dreams.

"If it were to fall into the wrong hands, the results could be catastrophic," he finished gravely. "Morgana isn't just a villain in a video game. She's very real and she's very interested in the scabbard's power."

"What does she want with it?" Sophie asked, still a little blown away by the whole story. After all it wasn't every day you were told your video-game nemesis was actually a living, breathing baddie out to destroy the world.

"The scabbard is very powerful," Merlin explained. "He or she who wears it can never bleed and never be killed. It was meant to be gifted to Arthur as a sheath for the sword Excalibur once he pulled the sword from the stone. Without it, he remains vulnerable to attack. I've shielded him this far—hiding him away through spells and misdirection. But once he becomes king, he'll need a great power to protect him."

"But why me?" she asked. "I'm no one. Just some kid."

Merlin chuckled. "You may think that. But it's far from the truth." He stroked his white beard thoughtfully. "I've been watching you, Sophie. I know you'll prove worthy of this quest."

"Watching me?"

"I made a promise to your mother that I would."

Sophie almost fell out of her chair. "M-my mother?" she stammered. "How on earth do you know my mother? Do you know where she is?"

Please don't say dead. Please don't say dead. Please don't say—

"I am not at liberty to say." Merlin's tone was apologetic. "But

I can assure you that she is alive and well and misses you very much." He stroked his beard again. "Perhaps I could arrange a meeting when you get back from your errand."

Sophie felt like her heart was going to pound its way out of her chest. The idea of seeing her mother again . . . Suddenly this mission impossible didn't seem like that big a deal.

"Where do I sign up?" she asked. "And where do I start looking? I mean, no offense, but 'somewhere in the twenty-first century' doesn't exactly narrow the search."

"Oh. Well, that's easy," Merlin replied. "To get online, I need a twenty-first-century internet connection. I use the one from your school."

She raised her eyebrows. "You steal Wi-Fi from Sacred Mary's?"

Merlin cleared his throat. "I prefer the term 'borrow.' In any case, when the scabbard was dropped into the well, I was in the middle of playing *Camelot's Honor.* Therefore the Well of Dreams would have been keyed in to the general vicinity of the school. If I were you, I'd start my search there."

Okay, well, at least it wasn't in the Antarctic or something. But still . . . "And if I find it? Then what?"

"Then you just repeat the Camelot Code and return here. That should also give me enough time to arrange a meeting with your mother."

Sophie's hands shook. It was almost too good to be true. To

see her mother again. To hug her and hold her close. To tell her all the things that had been going on in her life. To find out where she'd been . . . and why she'd left.

"Well, then, what are we waiting for?"

Merlin reached across the table and squeezed her hand, his eyes sparkling as he looked at her. "Not a thing. There's a portal out back that will take you there in the blink of an eye."

Sophie followed him out of the cave, trying to focus her whirling thoughts. Once outside, she looked around for Arthur, but there was no sign of him. Too bad. She'd wanted to thank him again for rescuing her—and apologize for being such a wimp about the flying thing. Maybe she would see him when she got back with the scabbard.

"The well is right through . . ." Merlin disappeared into the bushes, his voice trailing off. She hastened to catch up. Pushing through, she found the magician standing in front of a small stone structure, his face drained of color.

"What's wrong?" she asked, tilting her head.

Merlin drew in a slow breath. "The well," he murmured. "It's been . . . used."

"What do you mean, *used*?"

"See the swirling water?"

Sophie peered down into the well's depth. Something caught her eye. "Um, Merlin?" she said, reaching in and pulling out a small object floating on the surface. A leather shoe.

"By the gods," Merlin whispered. "He did it. He actually did it."

"Wait—who did what?" Whatever it was, from the look on Merlin's face, it wasn't good.

"Arthur," the magician said solemnly. "He went to retrieve the scabbard himself."

CHAPTER 12

"Why would he do this?" Merlin muttered. "To jump to the future—alone, without a plan, or even an iPhone? Have I taught the boy nothing over the years?"

"So wait," Sophie interjected, wanting to get this right. "You're saying King Arthur just time-traveled to the twenty-first century?" she asked, incredulous. "To my school?"

"And the timing couldn't be worse; the tournament is this afternoon. If the boy fails to show up for his date with destiny..." Merlin motioned for Sophie to follow him back through the brush and into the Crystal Cave. "How familiar are you with Arthurian legend?"

"I'm a level seventy-nine *Camelot's Honor* druid. What do you think?"

"Then you know the story of the sword in the stone," Merlin replied. "And the prophecy."

Sophie nodded. "Of course. *Whoso can draw forth this sword is rightful King of Britain born*," she quoted. She knew it by heart, after Stu had quoted it to her a thousand times. "I remember in the game we had to ward off all these tribal kings who wanted to kill Arthur and become king in his place. It took three tries for us to beat them."

"Yes, well, unfortunately in real life there are no do-overs," Merlin said solemnly. "And Arthur is scheduled to pull the sword from the stone at the tournament this afternoon. If he doesn't, he will lose his chance to become king."

"Then why would he just take off like that?" she asked. "I mean, no offense, but it seems a bit shortsighted to be time-traveling just hours before you're scheduled to meet your destiny."

"He doesn't know," Merlin explained. "He knows of the sword in the stone of course, but not that he is the one who will pull it."

"You didn't think to give him a heads-up on that?"

Merlin stared down at his hands. "The prophecies forbade it."

Of course they did. "Well, does it have to be *this* tournament?" Sophie asked, knowing she was probably grasping at straws. But her gaming partner just looked so upset, she felt she had to say something. "I mean, they have these things all the time, right? Couldn't he just do the sword/stone miracle thing at the next one?"

"No. I have consulted the prophecies extensively," Merlin replied. "If Arthur does not become king of England and establish peace at this very moment in history, the Saxons will invade and take over the land. Many will die and history will spiral off onto an alternative track. One in which the future—your future—may no longer exist." He turned to Sophie, meeting her questioning eyes with his own. "Meaning, *you* may not exist. And if Arthur is still there, in the twenty-first century, when this happens, he may no longer exist, either."

O-kay, then. "So what are you going to do?" Sophie asked, her voice hoarse.

"I don't know," Merlin admitted. "Even if we knew exactly where he is at this moment, there would be no time to go back and retrieve him. And I can't text him like I did you."

"I don't mean to sound stupid, but we are talking about time travel, right? Couldn't you just order up some extra time to go get him?"

"Sadly, it doesn't work like that," Merlin replied. "Time travel is a very delicate thing. You start messing around with it too much and all sorts of things can get mucked up."

Sophie pursed her lips. To think this morning her only worry was killing a video-game Morgana...

"What we really need is some kind of pinch hitter," Merlin added. "A stand-in King Arthur to do the big dog-and-pony show. That would, at least, buy us some time to go back to the future and retrieve our errant king."

"But I thought it was Arthur's magical destiny," Sophie argued. "How can anyone else do it for him?"

"Actually there's no magic involved whatsoever," Merlin told her. "I myself rigged the sword and the stone years ago and made up the legend to impress the locals. Anyone who knows the secret of how it's wedged in could manage to get it out." He stroked his beard miserably. "Problem is, I can't trust anyone with that knowledge. If they betrayed me—told the tribal lords it was a trick—they'd never accept Arthur as king once he got back." He looked up at Sophie. "And he must be king. The world as we know it depends on it."

"So you need a trustworthy stand-in," she mused. "A guy who understands how important the quest is, but won't spill the secret to his friends."

"Aye," Merlin agreed. "But where will we find someone like that? And on such short notice, too?"

Suddenly Merlin's computer pinged, signaling the arrival of a private message. Sophie couldn't help but glance at the screen, and was surprised to see it was from Stu.

>>StuartMallory: Hey Melvin, any chance you could run one of my alts through the sword and the stone quest after school tomorrow? We could knock it out before Lady Bella gets online.

Merlin slowly looked up at Sophie, and she knew they were thinking the same thing:

Maybe there was hope for them yet.

CHAPTER 13

Stuart opened his eyes and looked around, wondering what on earth had just happened. Moments ago, he'd been on his computer, checking out some video-game cheat code Melvin01 had sent him. Now he was standing in some kind of grassy clearing, surrounded by woods in every direction—not a bedroom or computer in sight. Which made no sense at all. Except—

His eyes fell on Sophie, walking toward him with hurried steps. Which was odd in and of itself. But even weirder? She wasn't wearing her normal, everyday jeans and T-shirt combo. Instead, she had on some kind of long, fancy dress. Like something straight out of *Camelot's Honor*.

"What's going on here?" he demanded. "Am I dreaming?"

"It's not a dream," she replied. "We're really here."

"Here?" He looked around. "Where's here? 'Cause this so does not look like Massachusetts."

A crazy thought suddenly occurred to him. Maybe he'd actually been sucked into *Camelot's Honor* somehow. Like what happened in that movie *Jumanji* where they go into the video game in real life. After all, he'd just been thinking how much easier life would be inside the game. Maybe his wish had come true.

He grinned. Now *that* would be the ultimate cheat code.

"Okay," Sophie said. "This is going to sound super crazy. But I know you've read all the Harry Potter books. Not to mention your ongoing obsession with Doctor Who. It's obvious you want to believe—"

"Believe what?" he interrupted. "Sophie, stop with the riddles. Where on earth are we?"

"The question isn't *where*," she said quietly. "It's . . . *when*."

He stared at her. "What?"

"We're back in time," she blurted out. "To the days of King Arthur. Well, technically right before the days of King Arthur. In fact today's the day he's supposed to pull the sword from the stone. Just like in our video game."

Stu gaped at her.

"That Camelot Code Melvin sent you?" she added. "It's actually a time-travel spell."

"Yeah, right," he retorted. "You really expect me to believe that?" He scanned the woods for some kind of hidden camera. Something—anything—to prove this was all some stupid joke. A new reality show, maybe. Because there was no way that they'd actually gone back in time. That was even crazier than being sucked into a video game.

"You'd better not be planning to put this on YouTube," he warned. "Or I'm so uploading that one video I have of you in that Pikachu costume."

Sophie let out a frustrated breath. She glanced up at the oak tree above her. "I told you he wouldn't buy it," she shouted up at a branch. "You'd better come down and tell him yourself."

What? Stu watched in amazement as, a moment later, a large spotted owl floated down from the branch and settled on Sophie's shoulder.

"Who?" the owl said to Stu, large yellow eyes drilling into him.

"Um, Stu?" he replied, realizing too late that he was, in fact, introducing himself to a large bird.

"He knows who you are," Sophie said impatiently. "Come on, Merlin, transform already. We don't have much time, remember? Also, your claws are totally digging into my shoulder."

Stu blinked as a puff of smoke surrounded him. When the air cleared, the owl was gone, and, to Stu's amazement, in its place stood an elderly man with a long white beard and blue robe, leaning on a gnarled wooden cane.

Merlin. A real-life Merlin.

It was all Stu could do not to fall over backward.

"Hey, Lord Vanquish," the wrinkled sorcerer greeted him with a toothy grin. "It's good to meet you in real life at last. I'm Merlin," he said, holding out a hand. "Aka Melvin-Oh-One, your epic healer from *Camelot's Honor*."

"Uh..." Stu stammered. "Uh..."

Merlin dropped his hand. "He's much more eloquent in video-game chat, isn't he?" he remarked casually to Sophie.

"Well, you've got to admit, it *is* a lot to take in."

"True." Merlin turned back to Stu. "Sorry about the whole Camelot Code pretense. It's just that... well, as Sophie said, time grows short and I had to ensure you'd come."

"Come?" Stu repeated. He couldn't be more lost if he tried. "Come for what?"

Merlin ran a wrinkled hand through his shock of white hair. "You know that sword-in-the-stone quest you wanted me to run your character through?" he asked. "What if we... well... what if we did a real-life run-through instead?"

CHAPTER 14

"**G**et out of the road, you idiot!"

Arthur leaped back, horrified, as a metal monster roared past him at frightening speed. He gasped for breath, watching the monster's glowing red tails stream down the road and disappear around a bend. He shuddered. The beast would have trampled him to his death had he not stepped out of the way. What a dangerous world, this twenty-first-century future was. He felt completely unprepared.

After falling into the Well of Dreams, Arthur had found himself in the same large, deserted field he'd seen in the waters. It was not unlike a jousting tiltyard back home—except for the lines and numbers painted onto the grass. The metal stands on either side were apparently meant for seating an audience. And though it was night, the place was lit by strange yellow glowing orbs set atop tall wooden poles.

At least there was one thing he recognized. The scabbard had been lying only a few feet away from where he'd landed. He'd grabbed it and tied it securely to his belt, not wanting to lose it again.

But how to get back home? He'd already searched the area for a second Well of Dreams, but found only a puddle of mud. After jumping in it a few times, he only succeeded in dirtying his leather breeches and soaking his feet, so he decided to follow the line of lighted poles to see where they led. At the very least, he needed to find shelter till morning.

He came across a road coated in some kind of hardened black substance. But instead of horses and wagons, this road was alive with more of the strange metal creatures, and they howled at him angrily when he attempted to cross the road. He resigned himself to walk alongside it instead, on a smaller side path that paralleled the monsters' domain, praying they would not jump the barrier.

It wasn't until a few monsters had passed, and one had shouted at him, that he realized they were not monsters at all, but strange horseless carriages with humans sitting in their glass bellies. He felt stupid for being afraid.

Eventually he entered a sort of a town with a number of buildings, each offering unfamiliar wares like "donuts," "tires," and "ATMs." While none of them seemed to be particularly fine establishments, even the most decrepit had real glass in their windows, which impressed Arthur quite a bit. Even more impressive? The smells drifting from some of them. Particularly the one called Pizza Cave.

It was then that he saw it. A castle—a real castle—rising high and mighty on the side of the road with white stone walls, stained-glass windows, and brightly colored flags waving from multiple turrets. Arthur rubbed his eyes before daring to take a second look, thinking perhaps his exhaustion was making him see things. But the beautiful building was still there when he opened them again, standing tall and proud, its drawbridge lying open, as if welcoming him home.

Arthur approached cautiously, still feeling as if there must be some kind of trick at play. What was a castle doing in twenty-first-century America, a place where Merlin had insisted there were no kings and queens? And why was it sitting here of all places, on the side of a common road, with no gate or moat to protect it from siege? A sign affixed to a metal pole proclaimed it MEDIEVAL MANOR, and Arthur prayed Lord Medieval would be a kind man who would agree to take him in for the night.

A guard, surprisingly dressed in a simple tunic and tights

instead of proper chain mail, stood at the far end of the draw-bridge, eyeing him curiously. "Are you the new guy?" he asked, giving Arthur a disapproving once-over. "A little young, aren't you? And what happened to your other shoe?"

"I am Arthur," he introduced himself, forcing his voice to sound as noble and confident as possible. "A stranger to these lands. Do you think your lord would be kind enough to grant me shelter and a bite to eat?"

To Arthur's surprise, the guard rolled his eyes. "Oh, you're one of *those*," he said with a snort.

"I beg your pardon?"

"Look, dude, just 'cause I'm stuck working here doesn't mean I'm into the whole LARPing thing," he replied. "But hey, what-ever floats your boat." He waved Arthur through the doorway. "Last show's going on now, but I'm sure Mr. Applebaum will get you started on the paperwork as soon as the crowd clears out."

"Show?" Arthur asked, more confused than ever.

"Yeah, feel free to check it out if you want. We're not a full house tonight, so sit wherever you find a spot. It's down the hall, through the blue curtain. You can't miss it."

"Very well." Arthur turned to go, then remembered his man-ners. He pivoted and bowed low to the guard. "Thank you, good sir. You are gracious to show such kindness to a stranger."

"Sure, dude," the guard replied, shaking his head as he turned back to his post. "I knew I should have taken that job at Pizza Cave," he muttered under his breath.

Arthur walked inside the castle and down the hall as the guard had instructed. He found the curtain and ducked behind it, entering the castle's great hall. His eyes widened as he took in the scene.

It was perhaps the biggest room he'd ever seen—an indoor tiltyard, set up for a jousting tournament. Horses dressed in colorful tack pranced around the sandy field, ridden by knights in full armor. Surrounding the field were risers, stretching up to the ceiling and filled with people feasting behind long row tables. At the very end of the field, high above on a dais, an old man sat on a throne, crowned with gold and draped in purple. Lord Medieval himself? Beside him stood a beautiful maiden with long, flowing black hair. His queen? His daughter?

As Arthur watched in excitement, a knight, dressed in a green-and-yellow tabard, tapped lances with another, dressed in red and blue. The two men got into position, then charged down the barrier, lances out and shields held tightly to their chests. A moment later, the lances each struck their opposing shields and splintered, the impact causing the blue knight to fly from his horse and roll onto the ground. Oddly, to Arthur, it almost appeared as if he'd jumped on purpose. He must be new to jousting.

"Hey, are you the new dishwasher?" A blond woman in a long

red peasant dress and apron approached Arthur, shoving a tub of dirty pewter plates and mugs into his arms. "Get a move on. We're piling up out here."

Arthur opened his mouth to protest but the woman had already turned and continued down the aisle. He looked down at the bin of dishes and sighed. It seemed as if he was doomed to live out the same destiny, no matter what time period he found himself in. Still, he supposed, he *was* asking for food and shelter from Lord Medieval—cleaning a few dishes would indeed be fair trade.

He followed a lad carrying a similar load down the hall, through a doorway, and into a large kitchen. Unlike the main jousting hall, where the trappings seemed mostly familiar, here Arthur found a confusing array of unrecognizable shiny metal gadgets. He searched the area, trying to locate something that made sense, and finally discovered a large tub of soapy water. Perfect. He set his bin down on a nearby side table and grabbed his first dish.

"No, no, you don't do them by hand!"

Arthur looked up from the soapsuds. His eyes fell on a tall, black-haired boy around his own age. "I don't?"

"Please. You'd be here all night," the boy scoffed. "Come 'ere, I'll show you the washer." He grabbed Arthur's bin of dishes and carried it over to one of the large metal machines. Arthur watched, fascinated, as he pulled open a door and stacked the dishes inside. "Now just close the door and hit start," he instructed, pressing a big red button. The machine roared to life, causing Arthur to take a wary step backward.

"The machine washes dishes?" he asked, fascinated.

The boy laughed. "Of course. Give it ten minutes and it'll have those suckers shiny and new. I'm Lucas, by the way."

"Arthur. And you are a dishwasher, too?"

"Nah. I'm too busy with football to have an after-school job," Lucas explained. "But my uncle trains the knights, so I know the drill. Tonight I'm just here looking for my stepbrother. He didn't show up for dinner and isn't answering his cell, so Mom's freaking out. I told her he probably just came here to catch a show—my uncle hooks him up with free tickets—so she told me to come get him." He shrugged. "Want to help me look?"

Arthur nodded. Though he admittedly only understood about a quarter of what Lucas had said in his strange accent, he didn't want to be rude. "I will help," he agreed.

"Cool," Lucas pronounced, though in Arthur's humble opinion the room was actually quite warm. In any case, he dutifully followed Lucas out into the main jousting hall. "He's got brown hair and glasses," Lucas told him. "He'll be by himself most likely. Unless he has a blond girl with him. That'd be Sophie."

Arthur's eyes widened. "Sophie?" he repeated, his heart beating fast. But she was still with Merlin, right? Or maybe she was back. Maybe she could help him get home. He had to find her!

"Yeah. Blond curly hair. Blue eyes. Kind of cute, though a bit too obsessed with video games if you ask me."

But Arthur was no longer listening. He was scanning the room, praying for a glimpse of Sophie. Instead, his eyes stopped at the jousting field. The knights were currently competing in some kind of game of skill, attempting to free a circlet hanging from a length of cloth as they rode by on horseback, using only their lances.

"Pretty cool, huh?" Lucas said again. The boy was clearly obsessed with the room's temperature. "Stu is dying to become a knight someday. It's not really my thing, to be honest. But I suppose the knights do get all the girls."

"They do back home, too," Arthur agreed, wondering for a moment about Guinevere and how she was making out at the tournament. Was Agravaine bothering her again? He hated that he wasn't there to protect her. Not that his princess wasn't able to take care of herself.

"Where's home?" Lucas asked curiously.

"Uh . . ." Arthur paused, his mind searching for an acceptable answer. Obviously, mentioning time travel was out. "I'm here from a faraway land called Britain," he replied at last, praying there was still an island known as Britain in the twenty-first century.

"Oh, are you like a foreign exchange student?"

"Yes?" Arthur ventured.

"I guess I should have figured that from your accent," Lucas replied. "Anyway, I'm going to go take the top two rows. You do the bottom two, okay?"

Arthur nodded and the boys split up. As he walked the rows, peering at the audience, he couldn't help but glance back to the action on the field. The blue knight had just been knocked off his horse by the green knight and his squire had tossed him a sword. Still on his mount, the green knight swung a dangerous-looking mace as he galloped toward his opponent.

Arthur watched, enraptured, forgetting he was supposed to be looking for Lucas's brother. There was nothing more exciting than a joust.

The blue knight struck the green and managed to unmount him, and now they were both on the ground, circling each other, armed and ready to strike. Arthur's heart pounded with excitement. The two knights seemed very evenly matched. Who would win?

The blue knight's sword crashed into the green knight's shield and sparks flew at the impact. The green knight fell backward, dropping his mace. The blue knight took his advantage and a split second later the tip of his sword was at the green knight's throat.

The crowd went wild.

The knight set down his sword and approached the dais,

bowing low to his master. Lord Medieval rose from his throne and declared him victor of the evening. Everyone cheered.

But suddenly, to Arthur's horror, the green knight rose to his feet, grabbed the discarded sword, and unceremoniously drove it into the blue knight's back.

Arthur gasped along with the crowd at this display of treachery. The blue knight staggered for a moment, his expression shocked and horrified as he fell to the sand.

What had once been a friendly tournament had now become a murder scene. The blue knight's men took the field, armed with maces, swords, and poles. But the green knight dispatched them quickly—slaying each and every one of them where they stood.

Arthur steamed with fury. The evil knight should not be allowed to get away with this. But what could he do?

It was then he noticed movement from the blue knight. His heart fluttered with excitement: the man was attempting to stagger to his feet. Arthur looked around, praying someone would notice and help him—give him a weapon to defend himself before the green knight realized he lived. But no one came. They were all on the field. Dead.

It was up to Arthur. The only trained squire left in the place.

Without regard for his own safety, he jumped the barrier, grabbing the nearest sword from the sidelines and diving onto the field. The green knight turned, a shocked look on his face, but Arthur nimbly dodged him and headed straight for the blue knight. Another knight tried to stop him, but he darted away. Finally he reached the blue knight and thrust the sword in his direction.

"Use this!" he cried, panting heavily from his run. "Defend us from the evil that plagues this hall."

Arthur waited for the knight to take the sword—to smite his enemy where he stood.

"Dude, what are you doing?" the knight whispered instead.

Arthur cocked his head in confusion. *What?* He tried again to give the sword to the knight. "Take it. He will kill you otherwise!"

The knight awkwardly took the sword, an uncertain expression on his face. "Um," he stammered. "Hey, Steve, did George change the choreography and forget to tell me again?"

To Arthur's shock, the green knight pulled off his helmet and dropped his sword. "Of course not," he replied, shooting Arthur an annoyed look. "Man, they really need to start background-checking the dishwashers. Keep us from getting these guys with delusions of knighthood."

"No, no!" Arthur protested, desperately trying to make sense of it all. "I am no knight. I simply meant to help right a wrong as any good squire would do. . . ."

"Whatever, dork," the blue knight replied, rolling his eyes.

"Hey, can we get some bouncers out here?" he shouted toward the sidelines.

Arthur squared his shoulders, staring down the approaching men. "I apologize," he said, bowing his head low. "I did not mean to overstep my bounds."

But it did no good, and a moment later Arthur found himself tackled by three burly guards and yanked unceremoniously off the tiltyard. He could hear the audience booing as they dragged him down a hall and tossed him headfirst out the back of the castle into a big pile of smelly mud.

"And don't come back!" they cried, before slamming the door closed behind them.

Bruised and still confused, Arthur picked himself out of the mud and brushed himself off as best he could, his mind spinning as he tried to figure out what had just happened. He'd only meant to help. To bring justice to the great hall. Did this world not value honor? Did they not live by the code of chivalry?

He swallowed down the lump in his throat as he surveyed his surroundings. A trash-strewn alleyway, surrounded by chain fences. The temperature had dropped and his hunger had grown. And now he had no bed and no food, and no prospects of finding any, either.

He trudged back down the street and toward the field where he'd first landed in the future. Maybe it was best to make camp there for the night. After all, Merlin had always told him that if he were lost, he should stay where he was so people could find him.

But as he arrived back at the field, rain began to fall. He sighed. His luck, it seemed, refused to turn.

Eventually he managed to find an overhang in the doorway of a large building just up the hill from the field, and crawled beneath it. At least here he'd be dry. Hugging his legs to his chest, he leaned his head against the brick wall, praying tomorrow would be a better day.

CHAPTER 15

"Your brother, m'lady!" the young priestess cried as she burst into Morgana's solar without remembering to knock. Her light gray eyes flickered with excitement as she hastily bowed to her mistress. "The spring has revealed him to us at long last."

"What? Are you certain?" Morgana looked up from her weaving, her voice trembling. Goddess help the girl if she were playing at something.

But the maiden looked completely serious. Excited, even. "Aye, lady. Alys checked twice."

"Show me. Quickly!"

The maiden turned and Morgana followed her down the stone hallway, trying to still her pounding heart. She had been waiting for this moment for nearly fourteen years and had begun to believe it would never come to pass. Still, every day, without fail, she instructed her women to consult the sacred spring, praying it would reveal Arthur's whereabouts.

They stepped into the courtyard. Morgana's dwelling had been constructed around the sacred spring to protect it from others seeking to use its gifts. Three maidens circled it now, hands clasped as they chanted in low voices.

The sorceress approached the water, blinking twice before daring to peer down into its depths.

She drew in a breath. Her brother. There could be no mistaking him. Even though the last time she had seen him, he had been a baby.

"Ah, Merlin, you thought you could hide him from me," she murmured, dipping her fingers into the cool water. "But I have found your precious prince at last."

She'd never forget the cold, winter day the wicked magician had swept into Tintagel, her mother's castle in Cornwall. Morgana had only been nine years old, a mere child herself, but had often served as Arthur's caretaker. Her mother, Queen Igrainne, was too busy with her new husband, High King Uther Pendragon, whom she married after Morgana's father was slain in battle.

Morgana didn't mind taking care of her baby brother; in fact, she quite enjoyed it. Singing him songs, rocking him to sleep, playing silly games. That night she'd been feeding Arthur some ground-up herbs mixed with milk and barley. The wise woman of the nearby village had brought them to her, promising they would make the boy grow strong and healthy and shield him from any sickness.

Unfortunately, all the herbs in the world could not protect young Arthur from the evil Merlin, who showed up that night in a swirl of black smoke and demanded Morgana hand over the boy, claiming King Uther had traded him before he was even born in exchange for Igrainne's love.

"But he is my brother," Morgana had argued meekly, frightened by the wild, white-bearded man who towered over her.

"Aye," Merlin had replied, his voice deep and threatening. "But your brother has a larger destiny than this. He will grow to rule all of England, uniting the tribes and ushering in a new era of peace for this battle-torn land."

She looked down at the babe in her arms. He smiled happily, gurgling and blowing a bubble. It was hard to imagine such a little child growing up to become a great king.

"Mayhap you speak true," she said, forcing herself to be strong. "But he is yet a babe, who has not lived through his first summer. Destiny can wait until he is grown."

"Nay," Merlin corrected. "I must prepare him while he is still young. Give me the child."

"No!" Morgana scrambled to her feet. "You shan't take him."

She ran from the room, clutching Arthur to her chest. Frightened at the sudden movement, the baby let out a loud wail.

As she ran through the twisting castle passageways, her slippered feet padded against the stone floors. Finally she burst into the great hall, where King Uther and her mother sat on their thrones, holding hands.

They looked over in surprise at her sudden intrusion. "What is the meaning of this, Morgana?" her mother demanded. "And why is the child wailing so?"

"It is Merlin," she managed to reply, her breath still trapped in her throat. "He has come to take Arthur away."

A shadow of fear flickered across her mother's face. But Uther placed a large hand on her shoulder. "You know, he has a right to the child," he chided, confirming Morgana's worst fear.

"Mother," she pleaded, "don't let him do this! Don't let him give my brother—your son—to this man! Arthur must carry on my father's bloodline and become Duke of Cornwall. He is the only one left!" She thought of her wonderful, kind father. Of his unkempt beard and loud belly laugh. There wasn't a day that went by she didn't miss him.

But her mother had just turned her head, refusing to meet her daughter's desperate eyes. It was Uther who spoke instead.

"Silly girl," he scolded her. "Do you really think Arthur is the son of a mere duke? Look at him! He clearly has Pendragon blood running through his veins. And someday he will take over my throne, becoming High King of Britain!"

Morgana stared at him in shock. Could it be true? Could her mother have betrayed her father before he had died, and borne a son to Uther?

"You killed my father!" she blurted, hardly daring to believe it. "So you could marry my mother." Suddenly it all seemed so clear . . . and so horrifying. She felt as if she'd be sick.

Uther smirked. "Your father fell in battle," he said simply. "I can assure you it was not by my hand."

Maybe not. But it was by his order, Morgana knew that now for sure. And her mother—her mother had gone along with it all.

At that moment, Merlin burst into the hall, ripping Arthur from her arms. This time Morgana didn't protest. "Do what you will with him," she spit out. "He is no brother of mine." Just looking at him now made her stomach turn. To know that Uther's poisonous Pendragon blood ran through his little veins. That her father's bloodline was gone forever.

"I promise you, Father," she had whispered as she watched Merlin sweep the child away, "I will not rest until your murder has been avenged."

And she hadn't. She'd worked for years to bring down Uther. To make him suffer as her father had suffered. And now all that was left was his only son. The last of the Pendragon bloodline.

If only she'd killed him back then, as a baby. Of course back then she'd been too young, too innocent, to think of such things.

But she was not innocent now.

"Where is he?" she demanded of Alys, her head priestess. "Why does the spring reveal him to us now?" After taking the boy years ago, Merlin had cloaked him with thick magical spells so no one could find him and do him harm.

Alys squinted down into the waters, her serene eyes widening in shock. "Why," she replied, "it appears he's traveled to the future...the twenty-first century, to be precise. Far enough, I suppose, to shed Merlin's protective veil."

Morgana grinned widely. This was better than she could have hoped for. Arthur was far from Merlin's touch. Far from any protection. She could swoop down on him and kill him with no effort at all. It was almost too good to be true.

"Thank you, Alys," she replied. Then she turned to the novices. "Ready my things. I shall leave immediately."

"Oh, Father," she murmured as she dipped a finger into the pool. "Finally you will have your revenge."

CHAPTER 16

"Hey you, get up!"

Arthur groaned and rolled over. Was Mistress McCready harassing him about the dishes again? He'd had such a strange dream last night, it felt as if he'd barely gotten any rest at all. Traveling to the future to find a magical scabbard. Being chased out of a castle after defending injustice at a joust. Falling asleep outside a...

"I said get up!" This time, the voice was accompanied by a swift kick in the direction of his leg. Reluctantly Arthur sat up and rubbed his eyes. Then he opened them and saw, to his surprise, not Mistress McCready at all, but a craggy-faced man, tunic tucked and belted, standing above him with a stormy frown.

"You kids. Staying up all night, playing your blasted video games. Can't even stay awake for school." The man crossed his arms over his chest. "Now get up and get inside. First bell's already rung. If you don't make it to homeroom in time for the second, I'm going to give you detention."

Arthur stared at him, horrified. So it wasn't a dream. He was still here in the future, the scabbard still tied to his belt. He scrambled to his feet, wondering what on earth he was going to do.

"Sir, could you please tell me where I am?" he asked the man. Perhaps he could help him locate a Well of Dreams so he could return home.

"Oh, that's cute. Real cute. What, do you have...*amnesia*? Do you need to see the school nurse?"

Arthur scratched his head, trying to figure out what the man was saying. He was pretty sure he was speaking English—but he had no idea what he was going on about.

Deciding it was perhaps best to just walk away from this hostile adversary, Arthur stepped to the right to move past him. But his opponent sidestepped him quickly, effectively blocking his path. "Where do you think you're going?" he demanded. "I told you—get to homeroom now."

He grabbed Arthur by the shoulders and started hurtling him toward the building. Arthur wrestled away, jumping back and holding up his hands, ready to defend himself against this crazy man. If only he'd brought a sword.

The man's eyes flashed his fury. "Why, you little—"

"Art! There you are!"

Both Arthur and his attacker whirled around to find Lucas standing in the doorway of the building. He strolled down the steps and grabbed Arthur by the arm. "I was looking all over for you!" he exclaimed, giving Arthur's attacker an apologetic look.

"You know this student?" Arthur's enemy demanded.

"Yes, Mr. Mooney," Lucas replied. "Art here is from England. He's transferring to our school and I'm supposed to show him around." He paused, then added with a big smile, "My stepdad said it was okay."

The man narrowed his eyes, glaring at Arthur, then at Lucas. He let out a frustrated breath. "Fine," he growled at last. "I guess if Mr. Mallory says it's okay, then it's okay. But get him to home-room. I don't care what they do at those English schools. Here in the United States of America we don't go around taking naps on the school steps."

"Of course, of course," Lucas replied breezily. "Come on, Art. Let's go." And with that, he grabbed Arthur by the tunic and started dragging him toward the building.

"Hold on a minute," Mr. Mooney called out suddenly. "Stop right there!"

Lucas's shoulders slumped and he turned around again. "What?" he asked in an exasperated voice.

Mr. Mooney pointed to the scabbard tied to Arthur's waist. "What is the meaning of *that*?" he demanded.

"It's nothing," Arthur stammered. "Just a scabbard."

Mr. Mooney looked at Lucas, then at Arthur, his face turning a distinct shade of purple. "I don't know what they let you kids in *England* get away with," he snarled, taking a menacing step forward. "But here at Sacred Mary's we have a zero-tolerance policy on weapons at school."

"But it's not—"

"I ought to call the police. Have you arrested."

"Dude!" Lucas interrupted quickly. "I mean, Mr. Mooney! It's just a prop. From the drama department." He reached for the scabbard. Arthur tried to grab it back, not wanting the priceless relic to leave his side, but Lucas shot him a warning look. "Trust me," he mouthed. Against his better judgment, Arthur allowed him to take it, praying that Lucas knew what he was doing.

"See?" Lucas said, holding out the scabbard. "It's just a sword holder. Not an actual sword."

Mr. Mooney grudgingly took the artifact and turned it over in his hands, examining it closely. He picked at one of the large rubies on the side and Arthur held his breath.

"Well, whatever it is, you don't need to be bringing it to

school." He stuffed it under his meaty arm, then looked up at the boys again. "You can have it back at the end of the day."

Arthur's eyes widened in horror. "But I—"

Lucas stomped on his foot. Mr. Mooney gave the two of them a self-satisfied smirk. "Now get to class," he ordered. "Or I'll ensure you spend your entire visit to America in detention."

"Yes, Mr. Mooney. Thank you, Mr. Mooney," Lucas replied as he hurried Arthur up the steps and into the building. Arthur glanced back at the man, wondering if he'd done the right thing just giving the scabbard away like that. If Merlin knew he'd lost it again . . .

"Seriously, let it go," Lucas told him. "It's not worth fighting over. You'll get it back at the end of the day, I promise. Mooney's a jerk, but he does keep his word."

Arthur sighed and reluctantly followed Lucas into the building and along a narrow corridor lined with skinny red doors. The floors were made out of some kind of impossibly smooth, shiny material, while white squares above illuminated the chamber with an unearthly light. All around them boys and girls, dressed in the strangest clothing Arthur had ever seen, bustled around, opening the red doors and pulling out books, each seeming to be in a big hurry to get wherever it was they were going.

"Welcome to Sacred Mary's," Lucas said with a grin. "You know, I looked for you after you got kicked out of Medieval Manor. That was some awesome stuff, by the way! The way you dodged them—you oughta play football." He grinned. "Anyway, I couldn't find you anywhere, so I figured you went home. But you're still in your uniform." He gestured to Arthur's tunic, which was, at this point, covered in grime.

Arthur hung his head. "I slept outside last night," he confessed. "I had nowhere to go."

"Don't you have, like, a host family?" Lucas asked, looking confused.

Arthur bit his lower lip, wondering how much he should tell Lucas. He didn't like lying, but at the same time, he didn't want to scare off his only friend here with a wild story of time-travel adventure.

"They died!" he blurted out at last.

"They *died*?" Lucas repeated, looking even more incredulous now.

"It was a terrible accident..." Arthur stumbled on, making the story up as he went. "Very sudden. They're going to give me a new family, of course. But until then..." He trailed off, shrugging both shoulders.

"Sorry, man. I didn't realize," Lucas said. "I would have invited you to sleep at my place. We even had a spare bed. Turns out my brother, Stu—the one I was looking for at Medieval Manor? He ended up staying at his mom's last night. My stepdad got the text while I was out looking for him. I think he's crashing there tonight, too, if you want to come over after school."

Arthur nodded doubtfully, not sure why Lucas seemed so happy about his brother "crashing"—something that sounded quite painful to him. But he was relieved at the idea of not having to spend another night sleeping outside by himself.

"So did your host family actually enroll you in school before they died?" Lucas asked.

"I don't know," Arthur said with a shrug. Though, of course he did know. Seeing as there was no family to begin with, it seemed quite unlikely they had done any sort of enrolling, whatever that might be.

"Right. Well, let's go to the computer lab, then. I'll get you in the system to back up the whole transfer-student thing in case Mr. Mooney goes and checks." Lucas pulled him down an adjoining corridor. "Luckily for you, my stepdad's the principal and I know his password."

Arthur had no idea what Lucas was talking about, but followed him into a small, dark room. Lucas closed the door and pressed a button and suddenly the white squares above them started illuminating. Arthur's eyes widened as he realized the room was full of magic boxes, just like Merlin's room back in the Crystal Cave. Lucas sat down at one of them and began what Merlin called "typing" furiously.

A few moments later, Lucas rose from his seat, a proud smile on his face. "There. You are now an official transfer student at Sacred Mary's. And you're in all my classes, too!"

"Um, thanks?" Arthur replied.

Lucas laughed. "I know, exciting, right?" He headed for the door. "Next up, we need to get you showered and changed. No offense, but you totally stink."

Arthur followed Lucas down the hall and into a small room filled with benches and more red boxes. Lucas rummaged through one of them and pulled out a white tunic with a blue number two on it. He handed it to Arthur, along with a pair of breeches and some white shoes, tied together with string.

"This should work until tonight. Then you can come over to my house and I'll let you borrow some real clothes." Lucas walked over to a tiny room, draped with a white curtain. "You can take a shower here."

Reaching into the room, he turned a small knob. To Arthur's amazement, water started raining down from the room's ceiling.

"An indoor waterfall!" he cried before he could help himself. After catching Lucas's confused look, he forced himself to laugh. "Just kidding," he added as he'd heard Merlin say in the past.

"You're a weird guy. Anyone ever tell you that?" Lucas grabbed his bag. "Take your time. We'll miss first period, but I have some hall passes I stole from my stepdad's office." And with that, he exited the room.

Arthur quickly stripped his clothes and walked into the waterfall room. He started laughing in delight as the water cascaded over him. It was so warm! If they had these *showers* back home, why, he'd even be willing to bathe as often as twice a year.

He finished cleaning himself, then got dressed and hurried out to meet Lucas.

"All right," his friend said, nodding at his outfit. "*Now* you look like a real knight."

Arthur frowned, remembering something Agravaine had said the day before. "Is it not a crime to impersonate a knight?" he asked, not wanting to break any more laws his second day in the twenty-first century.

"What are you talking about?"

"I am . . . a peasant. An orphan of no importance," he confessed, feeling his face heat. "To be a knight you must be noble-born."

Lucas made a face. "Um, I don't know what it's like back in England, but here in America we're all created equal." He grinned. "It even says so in the Constitution. Orphan or no— you have the inalienable right to play football or anything else you want to do."

Arthur stared at him in disbelief. "Everyone's equal here?" he repeated, not sure he was understanding right. "Even the serfs?"

"Sure. Even surfers," Lucas agreed. He made a gesture with his hand and fingers. "Hang tight, dude!" he quipped, and laughed. "Now come on. Let's get to class."

Arthur followed Lucas out of the room and around a corner,

managing to slam headfirst into a gaggle of women loitering in the hallway. They were all wearing matching short skirts and tops, the same color as the clothes Lucas had given him to wear.

One of the girls stepped forward, her eyes resting on Arthur. She had long auburn hair and sparkling green eyes. Almost as pretty as Guinevere herself.

Guinevere. Arthur's heart panged as he thought of the princess. By this time, he'd surely missed the tournament. Had Agravaine somehow managed to pull the sword from the stone? Had he convinced Guin's father to grant him her hand?

Would Arthur ever see her again?

He realized the girl before him was speaking. "Who's your friend, Lucas?" She dragged her green eyes from Arthur's shoes to his shirt. "There's no way you're on the football team. I totally would have noticed!"

Her ladies tittered, causing Arthur to blush again.

"Art, meet Ashley Jones," Lucas said. "Head cheerleader and pretty much the hottest girl in school."

"Oh, shut up!" Ashley groaned, playfully shoving Lucas in the shoulder. But she looked pleased all the same. Then she fixed her gaze on Arthur. "So are you new? Where are you from?"

"England," Arthur replied. "I'm . . ." He strained to remember what Lucas had told him. "I'm a new student."

"England?" Ashley's eyes danced with excitement. "I love England. My parents are English. Our ancestors came over on the *Mayflower*, you know. Direct descendants of Miles Standish and Priscilla." She stuck out her hand. "Anyway, it's awesome to meet you. It's about time we had a hot *guy* at this school." She gave Lucas a smirk. He rolled his eyes.

As any real knight would do, Arthur reached out and took her hand in his. Then he bowed low, pressing his lips against her fingers. "I am honored to make your acquaintance, Lady Ashley," he murmured in his best chivalrous tone.

The ladies broke out into excited giggles. Arthur beamed. He was finally getting the hang of this future thing.

"I'll see you guys at the game tonight!" Ashley said, before walking away with her ladies.

Once she had gone, Lucas turned to Arthur, eyes shining.

"I think she likes you!" he teased. "Maybe you should ask her out."

Arthur blushed. "I hardly think her father would approve of me."

"Trust me. Ashley doesn't give a rat's butt what her father thinks."

"Maybe so," Arthur protested. "But I'm just—"

Lucas slapped him on the back. "Equal," he finished for him. "We're all equal."

Arthur nodded, a big smile crossing his face. He had to admit, he was starting to like it here.

CHAPTER 17

"Lords and ladies of the joust, may I have your attention please?"

The roar of the crowd dulled to a low murmur as all eyes lifted to the wooden stage high above. Merlin stood there, dressed in rich purple robes trimmed with ermine. He'd even bathed and brushed his beard, Stu noticed, removing the twigs that had tangled in his snow-white hair during their recent journey to Sir Ector's castle. The joust had just finished and now the sword-in-the-stone competition was about to begin.

"For ten years—since the tragic death of High King Uther Pendragon—Britain has gone without a true leader," the sorcerer continued. "Ambitious lords have assaulted our land, drowning the kingdom in bloodshed and civil war—all while barbaric Saxons hungrily lap at our shores."

Stu shifted from foot to foot, trying to pay attention to the history lesson all the while feeling itchy and uncomfortable in his new body. Arthur's body, to be precise. Just after they'd arrived, Merlin had done his magic thing, transforming his twenty-first-century gamer geek self into the spitting image (at least according to Sophie) of the once and future king. Stu was still trying to get used to the insta-muscles and had already tripped over Arthur's large feet three times.

"We must find a ruler to lead us," Merlin proclaimed. "Rid the land of invaders and usher in a new time of peace and prosperity." He scanned the crowd. "Who here thinks he could be that man?"

"Or woman," Sophie muttered. "Why couldn't it be a woman?"

"Shh," Stu scolded. Mostly so he wouldn't giggle. This was so weird, he was having difficulty staying in character. Also, it was a little frightening. What if he couldn't pull it off?

When Sophie and Merlin had first proposed that he stand in for King Arthur, it had seemed like an awesome idea—a once-in-a-lifetime opportunity to literally step into the shoes of a legend.

But now that he was here, in Arthur's shoes, he was starting to get nervous. What if something went wrong? What if there was a battle and he got wounded? And what if his wound got infected? He was pretty sure penicillin had not yet been invented.

He shook his head. *Get a grip, Stu.*

The crowd erupted in excited discussion and men started stepping forward. It appeared quite a few of them were down with becoming King of England. But Merlin cut them off with a simple wave of his wooden staff.

"Now, now, you all know the prophecy as well as I," he scolded. "Only he who can pull the sword from this stone can be crowned king."

He made a sweeping gesture to the sword in question, embedded in a large boulder in the center of the courtyard. The audience oohed and aahed as light shone down from the sky, illuminating the weapon with an otherworldly glow.

Excalibur. Stu drew in a breath. The legendary blade of King Arthur himself. The sword looked even more majestic in real life than it had looked in the video game.

"Who shall be first to try their luck?" Merlin asked the crowd. "Perhaps meet their destiny this day?" Stu caught a glint in the old man's eyes as the eager knights stepped over one another fighting to be first in line. The sorcerer was nothing if not a showman.

"Allow me!" A giant of a knight, dressed in a bright yellow

surcoat, successfully made his way into the circle. "I am Sir Sagramore," he said. "Your humble servant, Lord Merlin."

Merlin nodded curtly. "Very well, Sir Sagramore, please go ahead."

The crowd watched as the knight stepped up to the sword, wrapping his meaty hands around the steel hilt. Anchoring his foot against the base of the stone, he drew in a large breath and pulled.

The sword stuck fast.

He pulled again. Then again. Still nothing.

The crowd started to jeer. "Give it up, man!" cried one.

"Let someone else have a go!" cried another.

Finally, defeated, Sir Sagramore released the sword, an angry scowl on his face. He kicked the stone bitterly before disappearing back into the crowd.

Sir Kay—Arthur's foster brother—tried next and was equally unsuccessful. He was followed by Sir Percival, Sir Agravaine, and Sir Lamorak. Knight after knight, lord after lord. Big, strong, muscular men—yet none of them able to budge the sword even a single inch. The crowd was going crazy.

"How am I supposed to do this?" Stu whispered to Sophie. "I mean, look at these guys. I may have Arthur's muscles, but these are trained knights."

"But you have something they don't have," Sophie whispered back. "Merlin's secret."

"Yeah." Stu kicked a small stone by his feet. "I suppose." The idea didn't make him feel a whole lot better. After all, it was one thing to try and maybe fail. Quite another to make a fool of himself in front of an entire kingdom. Especially when the future of the world was at stake.

"Is there anyone else?" Merlin called to the crowd after the last knight stormed off the field. "Would anyone *else* care to attempt to pull the sword from the stone?" He made a big show of searching the crowd, a small smile playing at the corner of his mouth.

This was it. His cue. Stu willed himself to step forward. Unfortunately, his feet suddenly seemed glued to the ground and wouldn't budge.

"Anyone?" Merlin repeated, now staring directly at Stu. "Would *anyone* here like to give it a go?"

Sophie shoved him forward. "You're up!"

Unfortunately, what was meant to be an encouraging push caused Stu to completely lose his balance and stumble forward, headfirst, into the circle. His palms smacked the ground, immediately followed by his face, which landed in a puddle of mud that reeked of horse manure. The crowd roared with laughter as Stu looked up. Merlin shook his head in disappointment. Probably not the grand entrance he'd been imagining for Arthur.

Well, beggars couldn't be choosers, now, could they?

Face blazing, Stu managed to pull himself upright, swiping

the mud from his face. He glanced back at Sophie, who mouthed, "Sorry!"

"Well, well, what have we here?" jeered one of the knights—Sir Agravaine, if Stu remembered right. The knight strutted into the circle, giving Stu a comical once-over. "Ah yes, the peasant boy with delusions of grandeur." He burst out laughing. "Shall we bow to you, lad? Lay down our lives to serve you?" He then proceeded to bow mockingly, so low his nose almost touched the ground. Stu had half a mind to kick him into the mud. But he knew from experience what provoking a bully would do. He had a mission and he couldn't be distracted. If Merlin was right, Sir Agravaine—and the rest—would be bowing for real soon enough.

"Hey, Kay, we've found your squire!" called another knight, Sir Percival. "You should keep a tighter leash on your servant."

The redheaded knight—Arthur's foster brother—pushed his way through the crowd, a scowl clear on his red, zit-covered face. "Where the devil have you been, Arthur?" he demanded, grabbing Stu by his ear and yanking him hard. Stu couldn't help a small squeal of pain as the knight's ragged fingernails dug into his skin. "I've been looking for you all afternoon." He shoved Stu so hard he almost ended up in a mud pile again. "Now get lost, and let the real men here compete for the prize." He stepped up to the sword and stone, evidently ready for a second go himself.

"Halt!" a young knight dressed in green cried in a loud voice.

Sir Gawain, Stu remembered. According to legends, the guy became one of the best Knights of the Round Table, second only to Lancelot himself. "Let the boy have a turn if he wishes one."

"Come now, brother!" Agravaine growled. "Look at his scrawny arms. If one of us cannot free the sword from the stone, surely he has no chance to do so."

"Maybe not," Gawain agreed. "But what harm could come from his attempt?" He turned to Stu and beckoned him to come forward. His eyes were kind. "Come, lad," he said, "and try your luck."

Sir Kay reluctantly stepped back, giving Stu room to approach. The crowd fell silent, all eyes on the new challenger. All waiting for him to fail. Stu gritted his teeth. And here he thought soccer tryouts had been intense. The sword and stone looked bigger this close up, the blade shining brilliantly in the afternoon sun.

Not just any blade, he reminded himself. *Excalibur itself.*

Trying to ignore his impatient audience, Stu circled the stone slowly, checking it out from all angles. Then he reached up, carefully wrapping his fingers around the ornate hilt.

Closing his eyes, he went over Merlin's instructions in his head. The secret to pulling the sword from the stone. He twisted the blade slightly to the left, then to the right, then forward and back. He squeezed the hilt and yanked the sword as hard as he could.

It didn't budge.

He tried again, carefully working his way through the intricate puzzle before giving it a second hard pull. Still nothing. He opened his eyes and stared down at the sword in frustration. Why wasn't this working?

The crowd was getting restless and lobbing insults in his direction. Insults and a filthy leather boot that nearly hit him in the head. He had to figure out a way to do this before they dragged him off and he lost his chance forever. The future of the world was at stake. He couldn't let the world down.

Worried, he searched for Sophie, needing a familiar face to calm his nerves. She was over to one side, her intense eyes glued on him, concentrating so hard he could almost hear her thoughts echoing through his brain.

You can do it. You can do it. You can do it.

Suddenly a strange, cold wind whipped through the courtyard, pebbling his skin with goose bumps. Stu shivered as electricity seemed to crack through him, as if a storm were approaching.

You can do it. You can do it. You can do it.

He looked around to see if anyone else had noticed the sudden change of weather. But no. Whatever this magic was, it was happening to him alone.

You can do it. You can do it. You can do it.

He squinted at Sophie. Her lips still weren't moving, but he could hear her thoughts as clear as if she were shouting them across the courtyard. And suddenly he could see himself from her perspective, sliding the sword from the stone as if it were no challenge at all.

You can do it. You can do it. You can do it.

He reached down and grabbed the sword—not bothering with Merlin's instructions this time. To his surprise, the blade easily slipped from the rock, causing him to tumble backward from the excess force he'd used to yank it free. He could hear the crowd gasp as he attempted to scramble to his feet, Excalibur now firmly in hand.

Holy epic win, Batman.

He looked down at the sword, scarcely able to believe what had just happened. He'd done it. He, Stuart Mallory, had succeeded where all the other knights had failed. He flashed an excited grin at Sophie, then raised the weapon triumphantly in the air. The sun caught the blade's metal, scattering rainbows of light across the courtyard.

Excalibur. The sword of legend was in his grasp. And she was beautiful.

She was also really heavy. His muscles buckled and he quickly lowered the weapon before he accidentally dropped it onto the ground.

Luckily, Merlin took that as his cue. "Behold," he cried in his grand voice. "The prophecy has been fulfilled at last. This lad—the long-lost son of Uther Pendragon—has pulled the sword from the stone. Ladies and gentlemen, I give you your king."

The cheers that followed were almost deafening as the crowd rushed the circle, surrounding him in excitement. Lords and ladies got down on their knees, pledging their eternal allegiance. Even the knights who had jeered at him moments before gave him respectful nods. Well, all except Agravaine. He still looked a little mad.

Stu scanned the mob, finally finding Sophie, stuck in the middle. He gave her a little wave. She raised her hand in victory, a big grin spreading across her face.

I knew you could do it, she seemed to be saying.

Stu gave her a thumbs-up. *You were totally right.*

CHAPTER 18

"Arthur, Arthur!" Guinevere shoved through the crowd, feeling as if her heart would burst from her chest. She couldn't believe it. She'd just seen it with her own eyes, but she still couldn't believe it. Arthur—her best friend, Arthur—had done the impossible. What all the knights in all the land had tried and failed to do.

"Stand back!"

A burly guard shoved her backward, almost knocking her into the mud. She struggled to regain her balance, shooting him an indignant look. "Stand aside, sir. I need to see Arthur." She rose to her tiptoes, trying to peer over the throng to catch a glimpse of her friend.

"As does half the kingdom," growled the guard. "You'll have to wait your turn."

Guinevere let out a frustrated breath. She began circling the outer edges of the mob, looking for a place to slip through, all the while scanning for Arthur. At last she caught his eye from across the courtyard. Leaping up, she waved both arms frantically. "Arthur!" she cried. "I'm over here! I can't get through."

She waited for him to wave back—to demand that the guards retrieve her and bring her to him or even push through the crowd himself to reach her. But to her surprise, Arthur just turned and looked away. As if he hadn't even recognized her. Her heart plummeted. Had he not seen her? No, she was sure he had. Was he angry at her for dropping the scabbard into the well? Now that he knew the scabbard was supposed to belong to him?

"Come now, Guinevere, don't traipse through the mud like a common serf!"

Guin whirled around to see her father coming up behind her, a scowl written on his battle-scarred face. "You are a princess of the Summer Country. It's high time you start acting like one."

"But Arthur..." she tried, not holding out much hope. Her father had never approved of their friendship.

"You'll see the king soon enough. I've petitioned Merlin to consider you a royal suitor." Her father rubbed his hands together with glee. "Imagine what a match this will be! My daughter.

The High Queen of Britain. Why, you'll be the most powerful woman in all the land."

Guinevere stared at him in disbelief, her heart suddenly pounding. Sure, she and Arthur had joked about getting married, but they'd both known it would never come to pass. But now everything had been turned upside down and she didn't know quite what to think.

Only that she needed to get Arthur alone. And fast.

CHAPTER 19

*T*he brave and noble knights lined the field, preparing for battle, as the dreaded Celts from the North scurried to stop them. The afternoon sun had long abandoned the fight and now only small globes of light illuminated the battlefield below. Peasants from both sides had gathered on the sidelines, shouting their support, but in the end, the knights knew they were on their own.

Suddenly the battlefield erupted in activity—both sides exploding out over the ground. The knights pushed forward, determined to gain ground while the Celts worked to knock them back.

Sir Garrett remained behind his men, secure in a pocket as he searched for an opening. Finally, his eyes alighted on Sir Lucas, who was trying to get down the field while being chased by two Celts.

Garrett raised his arm and readied his throw, waiting for the perfect moment to—

"What's he doing?" cried the coach. "Lucas! Get down the field!"

But before Lucas could comply, one of the Celts tackled Garrett to the ground, hard. The referee blew his whistle. The cheerleaders stopped waving their pom-poms. The audience booed.

"That's a penalty!" the coach yelled. "Ref! Are you blind?" He stormed out onto the field.

Arthur watched him go, his heart still beating wildly in his chest. He had to admit, this "football" they played here in the twenty-first century was more thrilling than any jousting match. Sure, the rules were confusing at first, but the other players had been patiently explaining everything to him, play by play (assuming that, since Arthur was from England, he was more familiar with something called "soccer"). By the fourth quarter, Arthur felt that he was really starting to get it.

He headed over to Lucas, who was now sitting on the bench rubbing his knee. "What happened?" he asked worriedly. His new friend did not look good.

Lucas grimaced. "I think I messed up my knee on that last play," he said in a dejected voice. "It's killing me." He grabbed a fistful of ice from an orange barrel labeled GATORADE and held it against his knee, which, Arthur noticed, had already started to swell.

"Dude, you can't go back out on that," Garrett cried, walking over and checking out his teammate's injury. "No way."

Lucas looked pained. "But I have to," he protested. "The high school coach is here, scouting for the varsity team. I'm not going to blow my chance to play next year."

"So you'll blow out your knee instead?" Garrett replied, reaching down to stretch Lucas's leg. The receiver winced. "End up in surgery like my cousin?"

"We have no choice. Jon's already out. You want to put Morty in there for the last play of the game?"

Everyone turned and looked down to the very last spot on the bench where a brown-haired, blotchy-faced kid sat, his nose buried in a book. He looked up, his face brightening with hope.

"You need me?" he asked. "You want me to go in?"

"We might as well forfeit the game now if we do that," Garrett muttered.

Out on the field, a linebacker tackled the opposing team's tight end, sparking a burst of applause from the home-team fans. The players on the sidelines looked at one another worriedly. "We'll be up in a few minutes," remarked Tristan, one of the offensive linemen. "We have to make a decision. Now."

Connor glanced at the score clock. "We don't have enough time to run the ball. So either Lucas or Mortimer goes in and tries to make the catch."

"Unless..." Lucas looked up. He waved for Arthur to join the huddle.

"You all met Arthur, right? He just transferred here from England." He slapped Arthur on the back. "Guy's fast as lightning and can dodge like you wouldn't believe. You should have seen him last night at Medieval Manor." He paused, then added dramatically, "What if we sent *him* out there in my place?"

Arthur looked at Lucas with astonishment. They wanted him to play? To become a knight and join the team for real? Hands shaking, he dared pipe in, "I can catch, too." He certainly had had enough practice back home with his abusive brother and his friends always lobbing things at his head.

"It's not a bad idea..." Garrett mused.

"But what about the rules?" Tristan piped in. "He's not on the team. They'd never let him play. Especially not midgame."

The others nodded glumly.

"What if they didn't know it was him?" Lucas asked. "I mean, he and I are pretty similar in height and weight, right? With a helmet on, who would know?"

The players seemed to consider this. "The high school coach is sitting over on the Celts' side," Lucas added. "And our coach is occupied with the ref." He motioned to the teacher, who was, sure enough, still screaming at the man in black and white stripes.

Graham and Garrett looked at each other. "You sure he's good?" Graham asked. "I do *not* want to lose this game."

"He's amazing," Lucas assured him. "Besides, what choice do we have?" he added, gesturing to Mortimer. The other players sighed.

"Okay, team, let's huddle up." Garrett called the players over. When everyone was assembled in a tight circle, he ushered Lucas and Arthur into the middle. "Change jerseys quickly," he instructed. "Before Coach comes to check on us."

The boys did as instructed and a moment later they emerged from the huddle, Arthur now wearing Lucas's uniform and helmet and Lucas wearing Arthur's jersey and a baseball cap pulled low over his face. The whistle blew and the defense started coming off the field.

Arthur drew in a breath. This was it.

"Make me look good," Lucas said with a twinkle in his eyes. "My future depends on it."

"I will," Arthur assured him, the enormity of the situation suddenly hitting him hard and fast. For the first time in his life, he'd been asked to do something important. Something that mattered.

"Come on, boys!" Garrett cried, grinning under his helmet. "Let's win ourselves a football game."

And that was how, a few moments later, Arthur found himself standing in the field, surrounded by tall boys in uniform, as the final play of the game began. As Tristan hiked the ball to Garrett, Arthur ran down the sideline, got into position, and waited for the quarterback's throw. For a moment, standing on the field, he felt paralyzed. Could he really do this? Could he really catch the ball and win the game?

His foster brother Kay's jeering face appeared in his mind, telling him there was no way he'd pull this off. No way a nobody like Arthur could ever hope to save the day. He might as well not even try.

But just as Arthur began to despair, his ears picked up another sound, drowning out his brother's taunts. Cheering and clapping from the crowd in the bleachers. It was louder than any jousting match and twice as exciting.

Because this time they were cheering for him.

"You can do it!" Lucas screamed.

Here, no one knew of his past or his humble birth. They didn't know he was the whipping boy of every knight. They only knew that Lucas believed in him. And they believed in him, too. Believed in him enough to rest the entire outcome of the game on his shoulders.

Here, everyone was equal. Here, he could be anything he wanted to be.

And right now he wanted to be a football player.

As the ball spiraled through the air, Arthur dove for it with all his might—channeling the lessons in agility he'd learned when he'd shape-shifted into a dog—and the ball fell into his hands.

He caught it.

He grinned, clutching the pigskin against his chest as Lucas had told him to do. Then he started off down the field, running as fast as he could toward the end zone, using the speed techniques he'd learned as a rabbit. Dodging the first Celt coming after him, then the second, then a third—he imagined himself a skittery mouse, winding through the bushes to escape the castle cat. The wind whipped at his face through his helmet and his heart slammed against his chest as he ran and ran and ran, desperate to reach his goal.

But just as he was about to cross the white line and win the game for his team, he was yanked backward by his ankles. Flailing, he lost his balance and started falling forward.

"No!" he cried. He couldn't fail now. Not when he was so close.

Then he remembered—he only had to get the ball over the line, not himself. As he fell to the ground, he stretched his arm out as far as he could—a frog capturing a fly on its tongue—mere seconds before the rest of his body slammed down onto the grass with a hard thump.

For a moment, the world went still. Then Arthur lifted his face from the dirt and forced himself to take a look. The ball had crossed the line.

Touchdown.

CHAPTER 20

"Excuse me, could I get some food over here?"

Sophie grabbed a servant boy by his tunic and pointed to her empty plate. The coronation after-party had been going on for about an hour now and she still hadn't managed to score a bite to eat. Probably didn't help that she was stuck at the back table, about as far away from the guest of honor—aka the newly crowned King Arthur/Stu—as possible.

She was dying to talk to him, to find out how things were going, but no one would let her near him. Most likely because Merlin had insisted she play the role of some lowly priestess-in-training from Avalon—which basically meant glorified nun—rather than the beautiful and powerful visiting princess she had told him she'd like to be.

Sophie rose to her feet. If she wasn't going to eat, she at least needed to breathe some fresh air. The overwhelming smells of the hall—burned meat and body odor—were making her queasy.

She made her way across the cavernous room, weaving through a series of long wooden tables, packed with rowdy knights and nobles shoveling handfuls of stringy meat into their mouths. (Sophie had quickly realized this was strictly a "bring your own knife" type of time period.) Pretty, young servant girls pushed past her, arms laden with heaping trays of fruits and cheeses that they set down on the already overflowing tables.

She pulled up her skirts to step over a steaming pile of dog poop no one had bothered to pick up. The mangy mutt responsible for the mess was nearby, contentedly scratching his fleas. Sophie wrinkled her nose and kept moving. To think that once upon a time she'd imagined a medieval castle to be romantic. In reality, it was as rowdy as a state fair and twice as smelly.

She finally made it to the front door. But just as she was about to open it and taste some blessed fresh air, the door burst open from the other side, clipping her hip and sending her sprawling to the ground. She looked up to see a tall figure wearing chain mail under a sash of plaid stepping over the threshold. He had broad shoulders, wild black hair, and a fierce scowl written on his scarred, bearded face.

A hush fell over the once-jovial crowd. Sophie scanned the

room, noting the frightened eyes of each and every noble. The servant girls quickly retreated to the kitchen. Even the dog had crawled under a nearby table. Whoever this guy was, he was definitely bad news.

The man clomped forward in heavy black boots, almost stepping on Sophie as he passed. She scooted back quickly, only to smack into Sir Gawain, who had come up behind her.

"I apologize for my father's ill manners, lady," Sir Gawain murmured as he helped her back to her feet. "Far north in the Orkney lands even kings can be found lacking in chivalry."

"Your father?" Sophie raised an eyebrow. It was hard to imagine this guy as anyone's dear old dad.

Gawain's face flushed. "King Lot. But I can assure you, madam, it is but by birth, not choice, that I claim him as kin."

Sophie gulped. She knew from playing *Camelot's Honor* that Lot was one of the major villains in the King Arthur story. Right up there with Morgana herself. Ruthless, power-hungry, and prepared to stop at nothing to gain the throne of England.

"Will he try to hurt...Arthur?" she asked, casting a worried look at Stu. It was unlikely that this legendary bad guy had just shown up for the all-you-can-eat coronation buffet.

Gawain gnawed at his lower lip, eyes not leaving his father for a second. "I do not know," he admitted. "But he's had his sights set on the lowlands since Uther died, believing that without a proper heir, they're ripe for conquering. And you won't find him taking much stock in magical prophecies that would crown an unknown boy king."

Guilt and worry warred inside Sophie. It'd seemed like such a simple thing when she'd first come up with the plan for Stu to fill in for Arthur. How had she not realized how dangerous it could be?

"Where's Lord Merlin?" Gawain asked her. "After all, he is the one who gave Arthur the throne."

"He's not here," Sophie replied, with rising panic. Merlin had gone to spread the word of the sword-and-stone miracle, neglecting to mention that while he was gone, an evil knight might be swinging by with intentions to kick Stu's butt.

Her kingdom for an iPhone.

"Where can I find this legendary king they sing of in the streets tonight?" Lot asked, his sarcastic tone echoing through the stone hall. "This mighty King Arthur, destined to save us all?"

The crowd was silent, all eyes turned toward Stu. He rose slowly from his seat and Sophie could see his trembling fingers and white face. But he held his head high as he addressed the intruder with a clear, strong voice.

"I am the one you seek. State your business with the court, sir. Do you come to pledge your allegiance?"

Sophie grimaced.

Lot burst out laughing. "To you?" he asked incredulously. "You're just a boy. Not even grown your first beard, I'd wager."

"Beards do not make a king," Stu replied, not missing a beat. "I am the son of Uther Pendragon and rightful heir to the throne of England." Sophie had to admit all those video games were paying off. Stu had his lines down pat.

Lot's eyes narrowed. "I knew your father," he growled. "We fought side by side for years, slaughtering the barbaric Saxons who dared breach our shores. You, my boy, with your scrawny legs and unscarred face, are not your father. In fact, I would wager a year's crops you have never spent a day in battle."

"I have proven my birthright by pulling the sword from the stone," Stu countered. "As many in this room have witnessed." He gestured to the crowd, most of whom, Sophie noted, suddenly seemed extremely fascinated by the food in front of them. So much for backup.

"My lord, I've no doubt you pulled a blade from a rock," Lot replied smoothly. "What I wonder is, do you know how to wield it?"

A flicker of fear passed over Stu's face, but he recovered quickly. "You obviously came here with a proposition," he managed to say, his voice a little less steady than before. "I suggest you make it now."

"Why, how astute of you, my lord," Lot said mockingly. "Yes, I have indeed come to offer you ... a proposition. A chance to prove your claim to the throne once and for all. One-on-one, you and I, man-to-man." He paused dramatically, then added, "If you win, I promise to bow down to you and call you master."

"And if I lose?"

"I'll call you a hairy son of a sheepherder's wench." Lot shrugged. "But you'll be too dead to care."

Ugh. Sophie dug her fingernails into her palms, not knowing what to do. Stu couldn't fight this guy. He could barely lift his sword. And even with Arthur's more muscular frame, he was still a shrimp compared to this battle-scarred knight.

Just say no! she begged him silently. *Say you're busy. The dog ate your sword. Run and hide under the freaking Round Table if you must.* Something—anything—to get out of a fight to the death with a well-trained medieval knight.

Stu paused for a moment, and it seemed the whole kingdom was collectively holding its breath. Then, "I accept your challenge," he told Lot. "Name your place and weapon."

Sophie stared at him, eyes wide in horror. Was he utterly insane? This was going to be a slaughter of epic proportions. She should never have brought him here to begin with. Never asked him to pull the sword from the stone.

Lot smiled a slow, lazy smile. "The courtyard," he named. "Tomorrow when the sun is highest. And as for weapon, it matters not what you bring. A sword, a mace, a magical staff gifted to you from the gods themselves . . . Please. I could cut you down with a serving wench's knife and use it to eat dinner when I'm through."

"You certainly can try," Stu replied with a casual shrug. "Though that doesn't sound very sanitary to me."

Don't antagonize him! was Sophie's first thought. Until she realized the banquet hall had erupted in laughter, Stu's bravado evidently emboldening them. For the first time since he'd arrived, Lot seemed to lose his cool. His face darkened as he turned to address the jeering audience. "Laugh now," he growled in his gravelly voice, "for your tears will fill a river once I cut down your useless boy king and take this land for my own."

And with that delightful prediction, the Orkney king turned and stormed out of the hall, knocking Sophie over a second time as he swung the doors back open and disappeared into the night. The banqueters erupted into excited conversation. This was better than reality TV.

Sophie scrambled to her feet and dove through the crowd, desperate to get to Stu. She almost made it, too, before she was grabbed roughly by a guard and yanked backward.

"Let me go!" she cried, trying to squirm free. "I have to talk to Arthur!"

"You will not bother the king," the guard replied, pinning her arm behind her back. *Ow*, that hurt. She turned her head, ready to spit in his face.

"Let me go! Or I swear to—"

"It's all right, Brutus," Stu said, rising to his feet. He approached Sophie. Reluctantly, the guard let go of her arm. "Lady Sophie is a wise and powerful druid—arrived this day from the island of Avalon to counsel me."

"Yeah, I'm wise and powerful, you jerk," Sophie agreed, giving Brutus a dirty look. "And I have a message to deliver to . . . m'lord." She paused, then added, "For his ears only."

Brutus shook his head disapprovingly, but allowed Sophie to lead Stu into an adjoining room. She shut the heavy wooden doors behind her and bolted them, then turned to her friend, hands on her hips.

"Are you out of your freaking mind?" she demanded.

Stu looked defensive. "What?"

"Agreeing to a duel? A fight to the death?"

"He challenged me in front of everyone! What was I supposed to do?"

She ran a hand through her hair in frustration. "I don't know. Anything but that. After all, he's a trained knight. You're a twenty-first-century kid. The only battles you have half a chance to win are the ones played over Xbox Live. And even I can beat you at most of those."

"Wow. Thanks for the vote of confidence."

"It's common freaking sense," she countered. "You shouldn't be fighting battles. You should be keeping a low profile until we can get the real Arthur back where he belongs."

Stu winced. "Sophie, don't you see? In this time and place they believe *might* makes *right*. The guy with the biggest sword gets to rule. If I hadn't accepted his challenge, all the tribal lords out there who pledged their allegiance earlier would have turned against me. I might as well have never pulled the sword from the stone to begin with."

She groaned, hating that he was making sense.

"Look, you wanted me to play King Arthur," he reminded her. "Well, unfortunately, this is part of the gig."

"I know but..." She trailed off, anguished. "It's just that... I mean, I just...I don't want to see you die, okay?" she blurted out angrily, feeling like an idiot for having to say it out loud.

Stu laughed. "Come on, Sophie. You really think I'm going to let some dumb medieval meathead get the best of me?"

He was so confident. It made her almost believe him. Still...

"No," she said. "But let's look at the facts here. This guy's probably wielded a sword since before you were born. How can you possibly believe you'll be able to best him?"

"Easy," Stu said with a smile. "'Cause unlike him, I'm not gonna bring a sword to a sword fight."

CHAPTER 21

Stu peeked out the arched castle window at the throng that had gathered in the courtyard below. And here he thought the sword-and-the-stone thing had drawn a big crowd. Word spread quickly about Lot's challenge, and the entire kingdom had turned out to watch their new king beat the stuffing out of the upstart. Or the other way around. When Stu had passed through the marketplace earlier that morning to retrieve his package from the blacksmith, he'd overheard a few bets being made—with odds decidedly not in his favor.

He didn't blame the gamblers. Lot was a legendary bad guy. And Stu was a kid with only one trick up his sleeve. If it backfired (figuratively or literally) he was doomed. He tried to remind himself that either way this was a great adventure, but truth be told, no matter what brave face he gave Sophie, he was scared out of his freaking mind.

A knock forced his eyes from the window. "Come in," he said. The door opened and Sophie walked in, wearing a yellow silk gown embroidered at the neck and sleeves, with matching ribbons tying up her hair. Merlin had certainly hooked her up with a great wardrobe before he took off.

Stu let out a sigh of relief. He'd been so worried she'd go home last night—back to find Arthur and the missing scabbard. But thankfully she told him Arthur could wait one extra day; there was no way she was going to leave him here to fend for himself, alone against an evil knight.

"You okay?" she asked, joining him at the window. "Wow, there are a ton of people down there, huh?"

"All anxiously waiting to watch me bleed," he agreed.

"But you have a plan, right? And it's going to work, no problem. Right?"

"Um, right. Sure." He nodded. But his bravado sounded thin even to his own ears.

"Just be careful, okay?" she urged. "I need you back in the twenty-first century in one piece." She arranged her nervous face into a smile. "*Camelot's Honor* won't just beat itself, you know."

He snorted. It was funny. A few days ago beating *Camelot's Honor* was pretty much all he thought about. Now it seemed kind of lame. After all, with time and research, anyone could beat a video game. But there were no wiki boards to learn the secrets of battling an evil Scottish knight IRL. And it was bound to be tougher than that soccer game he was missing, too.

He reached down to the bed and carefully picked up his makeshift gun. "Help me attach this to my arm?"

Sophie obliged, taking the twelve-inch hollowed-out metal tube from him and placing it on top of his forearm. Then she attached the thick leather straps around his arm to keep it in place.

"This sure doesn't look like any gun I've ever seen," she observed.

"Yeah, well, they were a bit short on assault rifles in the medieval armory."

"How does it even work? There's no trigger."

"It's technically more like a cannon than a gun," Stu said. "I put my gunpowder inside here." He pointed to the back end of the weapon.

"Gunpowder?"

"Well, sort of. You wouldn't believe the random ingredients you can mix together to make an explosion."

"Does one of these ingredients happen to be cow dung?" Sophie asked, wrinkling her nose.

Stu nodded proudly. "Lucas and I used to use manure back home, but this should work just as well," he explained. "And I used rocks as my bullets. All I have to do is light the wick." He pointed to the wick at the back end of the tube. "Which will ignite the explosives inside. And kaboom! The explosion catapults the rocks out the front end and it's sayonara, King Lot."

"Or adios to your forearm," Sophie said, looking at the gun doubtfully. "If it backfires."

"Nah, the iron casing is really strong," Stu replied. "The blacksmith assured me it would withstand a ton of force."

Sophie didn't look entirely convinced, but to her credit she didn't try to argue. "Oh, I almost forgot," she said while reaching up into her hair. "They do this thing here where a lady gifts her knight with a small favor to wear during battle." She freed one of her yellow ribbons, then dropped it into his hand, closing his fingers around it.

"Dumb, I know," she said, her face a bit flushed. "But when in Rome—or medieval England, in this case."

"Thank you," he said. "I'll wear it with pride." He started to put it in his own hair.

"No!" Sophie burst out laughing. "You put it on your weapon. Not in your hair."

"Oh!" He blushed. "That makes way more sense." He tied the ribbon around his gun, securing it with a knot.

Sophie watched, her laughter fading. "Be careful, Stu," she said. "Don't try anything stupid. If the gun doesn't work right, you have to run. It's better to lose than to die."

"Yes, Mom," he quipped, trying to break the seriousness of

the moment. He was already well aware that this was a crazy plan. He didn't need her to freak him out further.

Thankfully, before Sophie could say anything else, Gawain stepped into the room. "They're ready for you, m'lord," the knight said, bowing low. Then he turned to Sophie. "Come, m'lady. I will show you to the best seat in the house."

"Thanks, Gawain," she said, heading to the door. "Good luck, *Arthur*!" And with that, the two of them headed down the stairs, leaving Stu to his destiny.

Or would it be his doom?

"Up here, m'lady." Gawain helped Sophie step onto the make-shift wooden staircase, leading her to the stage high above the courtyard. The VIP section, she realized as she stepped onto the platform. The wooden planks were covered with soft, luxurious furs and the chairs were hand-carved with swirling dragons, accented with glittering multicolored jewels and soft silk pillows. A purple canopy shaded the entire platform, and nobles lucky enough to be on the guest list mixed and mingled and drank amber-colored liquid from pewter goblets.

Sophie sank down into one of the chairs, but found she couldn't relax. She didn't like being up here, seated in the lap of medieval luxury, while her best friend was down in the pit, ready to fight to the death like some kind of Roman gladiator. Her heart pounded as she peered down into the ring, praying for some last-minute intervention. But she knew in her heart the chances were slim to none. In a few moments Stu would be fighting Lot. And gun/cannon or not, she didn't know how he was going to win.

The trumpets blew, forcing her to turn her attention to the ring below. Sir Gawain stepped into the center, addressing the crowd in a gallant voice.

"Today we gather to witness a fight to the death," he proclaimed. "In this corner we have King Lot, ruler of the Orkney Lands of the North."

Lot stepped forward dressed in a full suit of armor and carrying a heavy sword and shield. The crowd went wild, clapping and cheering. But Lot simply scowled and waved them all off, pulling his helmet over his head. To them this might be a game, Sophie realized. But he was taking it very seriously.

"And in this corner, we have your king—Arthur, son of Uther Pendragon," Gawain continued. "And rightful ruler of Britain."

Stu stepped forward, raising his arms to the crowd, urging on their applause like a rock star at a concert. But the audience stayed silent, save for a polite spattering of claps near the back. Stu's face fell and he lowered his hands.

"Why's no one cheering?" Sophie worried aloud.

"They don't want to show public support," a nearby courtier informed her. "In case Lot wins and takes over as king."

Sophie made a face. Talk about fair-weather friends. Rising

to her feet, she let out a huge "Whooo!" at the top of her lungs, jumping up and down. "Go, Arthur!" she screamed. "Kick his big old medieval butt!" Everyone turned to look at her in shock.

"Control yourself, lady!" the courtier cried, horrified. "You'll bring down the entire platform."

But Sophie didn't care. She'd made her point and at least Stu would go into the fight knowing someone had his back.

Gawain stepped away from the ring and the trumpets blew, signaling the start of the fight. Stu—who was wearing just a light leather tunic rather than a full suit of armor—leaped backward, grabbing the torch his servant held out to him, ready to light the gun's wick and get this party started. Meanwhile Lot, in full armor that probably weighed sixty pounds, lumbered forward. Sophie inched to the edge of her seat, worried that Stu's makeshift ammo wouldn't be able to penetrate the steel of Lot's chestplate.

Come on, Stu! You can do it!

But Stu was having difficulty, and suddenly Sophie realized why. When he'd waved his hands to rally the crowd, the wick must have fallen out of his gun and was now lying on the ground, a few yards away. And when he made a move to reach for it, Lot raised his sword and brought it crashing down in his direction. Stu barely had enough time to block the blow with his shield.

"This is likely to be a short battle." A girl to her right yawned.

"Not like the one I saw last summer with Lancelot du Lac. Now, *there's* a knight."

Sophie shot her a glare. The girl shrugged. "I'm Elaine," she added. "I don't think I've seen you around here before."

"I'm, um, a visiting priestess from Avalon," Sophie mumbled, trying to turn her attention back to the fight. She didn't have time to chitchat! Stu's life was at stake.

"Avalon?" Elaine cried. "Why, I trained at Avalon under the Lady of the Lake!" She frowned. "I don't remember seeing you there...."

Sophie inwardly winced. Of course. Of all the people to sit next to, she had to end up near someone who could totally blow her cover.

"You do look familiar, though." The girl squinted at her. "In fact you look a lot like—"

"Do you mind? I'm trying to watch the fight!" Sophie snapped.

Elaine huffed. "Fine. There's no need to be rude."

Sophie ignored her, forcing her attention back to the pit. Lot had raised his blade again, prepared for another charge. But this time Stu was ready. As the large knight launched at him, he dodged to the right, easily sidestepping the blow. Sophie let out a cheer. Elaine rolled her eyes.

Once out of harm's way, Stu tried to dive forward for the wick. But Lot stepped into his path, readying another blow.

Stu managed to block it, but the force threw him backward and Sophie cringed as his body bounced against a stone wall. At first she thought the force might have knocked him out, but thankfully he scrambled back to his feet—a move that clearly took a lot of effort. He was already tiring, she realized with dismay, and Lot was just warming up.

"By the gods, do something!" Elaine shouted down at Stu. "I've got thirty pieces of silver wagered on you!" Sophie had to fight the urge to do something herself. Like punch the girl in the head.

Lot had Stu pinned now, back against the courtyard wall. Stu couldn't do anything but hold the shield in front of his face. The crowd was deathly silent and Sophie thought she could hear laughter coming from behind the evil knight's black helmet. She couldn't breathe.

Could this be it? The death of her best friend? Tears sprang to her eyes and she squeezed them shut, unable to watch. This was all her fault. She'd brought him here. She'd let Merlin use him for his own gain. And now...if he died...

Please, Stu, don't give up, she begged silently. *Knock him back, knock him back, KNOCK HIM BACK!*

Suddenly a cold wind whipped through the courtyard and she felt her arms prickle, the hairs standing on end. Her eyes flew open, just in time to see Stu shove Lot backward. The Scottish knight stumbled over his own feet as he fought to keep upright. Stu raised his arms in triumph and the audience cheered.

Sophie stared in disbelief. But that was impossible. It was almost as if . . .

Lot charged again, barreling forward, sword high in the air as he let out an angry yell.

Block it, block it, block it!

"Block it!" she screamed out loud.

Stu blocked the blow, this time his shield seeming to effortlessly match Lot's sword and push it away. He danced to the far side of the field, rallying for the next round.

Sophie looked down and saw that her arms were covered in goose bumps. Was she really somehow affecting the fight? It seemed impossible, but she didn't know how else to explain what was happening. Stu had been exhausted, almost ready to give up. Now he looked energized.

Suddenly she remembered the sword sliding out of the stone. At the exact moment she'd wished it to. Had she made that happen as well?

Something niggled at the back of her brain. A thousand memories resurfacing. Times her mother had also wished for something and it had come true. A traffic light turning green, just as they approached. A last-minute touchdown for her favorite team. A narrow miss during a fall on the ski slopes—avoiding a looming tree. Her dad used to joke he'd married the luckiest woman in the world.

Suddenly the conversation with Merlin came roaring back to her. *I'm no one, just some kid*, she'd said.

You may think that, Merlin replied. *But it's far from the truth.*

She closed her eyes, concentrating as hard as she could, visualizing Lot tripping over something and giving Stu a chance to grab the wick and light his gun.

A moment later, the crowd burst into laughter. Sophie opened her eyes to find Lot facedown in a puddle of mud.

It was all the advantage Stu needed. He threw himself forward, somersaulting past Lot like a character in a video game. Grabbing the wick, he stuffed it back into the gun, then motioned to his servant, who threw him the torch.

Stu lit the gun, aimed at Lot, who had just managed to stand up, and...

BOOM!

The explosion was no louder than a couple of Black Cat firecrackers, but to a medieval crowd who'd never seen a gunfight, it might as well have been a nuclear blast. They watched in awe as fire shot through the front of the gun and Stu's stones came barreling out, smashing into their target's chest. The force threw Lot backward and he slammed into the courtyard wall, his body sliding to the ground like a character out of a SpongeBob cartoon. He didn't get up.

The crowd roared. Everyone was on their feet now, whooping and applauding their king. Stu pulled off his helmet and Sophie could see he was blushing with pride. Gawain knelt down beside Lot's prostrate body, removing his own helmet and putting his ear to Lot's mouth.

He turned to Stu. "He lives! You must finish him."

"No thanks," Stu said. "Just take him to the dungeon. He can live to fight another day, this time on my side." He turned to the crowd. "From this day forward," he said, "there will be no more fighting to settle your arguments. If someone breaks the law, they'll be tried peacefully in a court of their peers."

Sophie couldn't believe it. Not only had Stu just shown them the first-ever display of makeshift gunpowder in medieval England, he'd thrown in a lesson on the American judicial system to boot.

Who would have thought Stuart the geek would turn out to be such a medieval rock star?

CHAPTER 22

Stu was practically dancing with excitement when Sophie waved to him from across the courtyard. She pushed her way through the crowd and threw her arms around him. "You did it!" she cried. "You were amazing!"

"Told you," he teased. "Obviously you totally underestimated Sally, my *boomstick*." He held up the makeshift gun, now blackened and broken. A one-shot deal, but it'd done its job well. "She's totally *Army of Darkness*, right?"

"Not to mention a little *Raiders of the Lost Ark*."

Stu laughed. "With a little *Star Trek* thrown in. Season one, episode eighteen. Kirk against the Gorn."

"Geek!" she taunted playfully. But he could tell she meant it as a compliment.

"Oh, I almost forgot." He pulled the ribbon from the gun. "Here's your favor. In one piece, as promised. If you don't mind a little black soot."

She took it and pinned her hair back up. "My hero," she joked, beaming at him.

He rolled his eyes. "Yeah, yeah. Wanna go grab some food? All this saving the day has made me super hungry."

"Actually I'd better get back to the present," she said regretfully. "Find that once and future king and get him back here where he belongs."

"Right. It's your turn to save the day," he quipped, suddenly feeling a bit envious. She got to go back home while he was stuck here. By himself. "I wonder if anyone's noticed we're gone yet."

"Well, Merlin did send our parents those texts," she reminded him. "Saying you're staying at your mom's and I'm sleeping at my aunt's."

"Yeah, but what about school? Not to mention soccer practice. If I'm not back for the game on Friday..." He kicked at the ground with the toe of his boot. "I hope they don't kick me off the team."

"Yeah, wouldn't want *that* to happen," Sophie muttered under her breath.

He looked up. "Are you mad at me for playing soccer?" he blurted out before he could stop himself. After all, this was so not the time or the place. But still...she kept making these comments....

Sophie screwed up her face, but didn't, he noticed, meet his eyes. "Why would I even care?"

"That's what I'm trying to figure out."

For a moment, she said nothing and Stu thought she wasn't going to answer. Then she looked up. "I just think it's a little weird, that's all. I mean, the Stu I know is a geek. A gamer."

"Soccer is a game."

"You know what I mean."

"Come on, Soph. It's one after-school activity. It doesn't change who I am."

"I guess we'll have to see."

Stu bit his lower lip, indecision swirling inside of him. Should he tell her the truth? Why he had really joined the team? Would she understand if he told her about his father not showing up to his robotics competition? About how he never stopped bragging about Lucas, even though he wasn't even really his kid? About how proud he'd looked when Stu announced he'd made the team?

But that all sounded so stupid. And he didn't want Sophie to know how pathetic he really was. Still, it killed him to see the hurt in her eyes. By trying to impress his father, had he somehow let his best friend down?

"Do you want me to quit the team?" he asked quietly. "'Cause I will. If you want me to."

Her eyes widened. He could tell everything inside of her wanted to say yes. But at the same time, of course she wouldn't. She couldn't. Because that would be selfish.

"Why would I want that?" she said instead, with a fake barking laugh. "You want to play soccer? You should play soccer. Now let me get back to the present and fix history so you don't miss your pizza party."

And with that she turned on her heel and stalked out of the courtyard. Stu watched her go, his stomach tying in knots.

"May the Merlin be with you . . ." he called after her.

She didn't reply.

CHAPTER 23

I f Sophie had thought it would be at all difficult to find the once and future king back in the twenty-first century, she quickly learned otherwise. By the time she returned to school the next day, Arthur was literally a legend. Everyone was talking about him—and the rumors grew more unbelievable the more she heard. He was visiting royalty from England. A runway model for Calvin Klein. A James Bond–like spy under a witness protection program. Sole heir to the Post-it fortune.

At lunch he held court at the popular kids' table in the center of the cafeteria (ironically the only round table in the place), surrounded by football players, cheerleaders, and other high school royalty while others looked on with fascination and envy.

"He's so cute," Sophie overheard one girl say from the next table over. "He looks like he should be in a boy band or something."

"And so cool!" Her friend sighed. "Did you hear he single-handedly won the football game last night?"

Sophie tried not to make a face. Truth be told, the whole scene was making her kind of mad. Here Stu was risking his life to stand in for this twerp, while the twerp in question was having a blast hanging out at her school, not a care in the world. She tried to remind herself that he didn't know what he was doing; he thought he was just a peasant boy of no importance. He had no idea what this little time-travel trip had set in motion.

And he certainly didn't know how much she was already missing her best friend.

She thought back to her last conversation with Stu. Why had she been such a jerk? Why had she walked off without even saying good-bye? Was she so pathetically jealous that she couldn't even let him have one thing without her? What a terrible friend!

Worse . . . she'd left him all alone. Without anyone there to help him if things went wrong. What if another King Lot type showed up? Or something even worse? What if something happened to him? What if he was killed? What if she never saw him again? What if she never got a chance to say she was sorry?

She shook her head. This had gone on long enough. Time

to get both boys back where each of them belonged, before it was too late.

She stormed over to the round table. Everyone looked up at her approach. She cleared her throat. "Arthur," she said. "We need to talk."

Arthur looked up. When he saw her, his face lit up with excitement. He scrambled to his feet. "Sophie!" he cried. "Where have you been? I've been looking everywhere for you!"

"It's, uh, a long story." She could feel the other kids watching her curiously. Clearly she and Arthur couldn't talk here. She grabbed Arthur's arm and dragged him to the other side of the caf, out of earshot.

Once they were alone, Arthur turned to her, his eyes shining with excitement. "Sophie, this place is amazing!" he cried. "No wonder you like it here! I've been staying with Lucas and his family and you wouldn't believe all I've learned. Turns out the world isn't flat, but round, like a ball, and it revolves around the sun. Of course, the teacher had no idea of the real purpose of Stonehenge. So I let him know that it was once used for—"

"Arthur!" she cried, waving her hands in front of his face. "You need to listen!"

He shut up and stared at her with a confused expression.

"Look, I know the twenty-first century is great," she assured him. "But Merlin's freaking out. He needs you back, like yesterday. It's really important. You need to come with me. I can show you how to get home."

Arthur dropped his eyes to the floor. "I don't know about that," he replied slowly. "To be honest, I was . . . thinking of staying here."

Sophie's stomach twisted. "Wait—what do you mean, stay here? You can't stay here."

"Why not?" Arthur asked stormily. "What have I got to return to? An empty life as a kitchen boy? The girl I love marrying another man?"

"But—"

"Look, you can have the scabbard back. I'll give it to you after school—before I head to football practice."

Sophie's jaw dropped open. Football? He was here two days and he was already on the football team?

She had to tell him the truth, and now. Despite the whole prophecy thing. "Look, Arthur, there's a lot you don't know—"

"Hey, Arthur!"

Sophie whirled around, her eyes widening as they fell upon Ashley Jones, skipping toward them. The head cheerleader swept in, slinging a possessive arm around Arthur's waist. Sophie bristled. Football and cheerleaders? She had to hand it to the guy; he'd accomplished more in two days than most people did in their entire junior-high-school experience.

"Hey, girl! I see you've met Arthur!" To Sophie's surprise, Ashley leaned in to kiss him on the cheek. "Isn't he just too adorable?" she cooed. "Arthur, this is my bestie, Sophie Sawyer."

What?

It was all Sophie could do to stop her mouth from dropping open. Bestie? As in best friends? Her and Ashley Jones, daughter of her dad's new girlfriend? Was this some kind of crazy joke?

Ashley didn't wait for an answer. "He's going to come with us to the pizza party on Friday," she added. "What time should we pick you up?"

Sophie opened her mouth to reply, but nothing came out. And who could blame her? Something seriously crazy was going on here.

"Please, Arthur. You have to listen to me," she begged.

Arthur gave a wary glance at Ashley, then shrugged. "Sorry, Sophie," he said apologetically. "But what you're asking me to do . . . well, I just can't."

Before Sophie could reply, the bell rang, signaling the end of lunch. Ashley started pulling Arthur toward the exit, giving Sophie a friendly good-bye wave.

"Later, girl!" she cried.

Sophie ignored her. "Arthur!" she pleaded. "You have to go back! You don't understand what's at stake!" She realized people were staring at her, but she no longer cared. This might be her last chance to save Stu. "You're supposed to be king! You're supposed to pull the sword from the stone!"

But she was too late. Ashley had whisked Arthur out of earshot and her cries were in vain. Sophie tried to follow them, but when she finally got to the hallway, they were nowhere to be seen.

Suddenly a tall figure stepped into her path. She stopped seconds before slamming into him, looking up in surprise. It was Lucas, Stu's stepbrother.

"Sophie! There you are! I've been looking everywhere for you."

Oh, great. He was going to ask where Stu was. How was she going to explain why his brother was missing—at least without Lucas thinking she was completely insane?

"Look," she tried. "I know what you're probably thinking. But it's okay. Stu is fine. He's safe and not hurt. I can't explain where he is, but I promise you that—"

"Who's Stu?" Lucas asked with a puzzled expression.

"Um ... your stepbrother?"

"What?" Lucas narrowed his eyes. "I don't have a stepbrother. You know that."

"What are you talking about?" Sophie's heart began to pound.

"I'm talking about the fact that my parents are still married to each other and I'm an only child." He looked at her as if she'd suddenly sprouted three heads.

Oh no. First Ashley Jones's weird behavior and now this. Something was seriously wrong.

"So you…don't know anyone named Stu?" she asked, her voice quavering as Merlin's words came racing back to her.

History will spiral off onto an alternative track.

Was it already happening? Had placing Stu on the throne as a fill-in for Arthur not been enough to satisfy the historical record? Had he done something wrong? Stepped on a bug he shouldn't have stepped on, thus setting off a crazy chain reaction that led to a future where she was best friends with a cheerleader and Stu's own brother didn't know him from a hole in the wall?

A horrible thought struck her cold. What if Stu was really gone? What if, in this new world, he didn't exist? If, for some reason, he'd never been born? Her throat tightened at the thought. She'd already lost her mother. She could not bear to lose her best friend, too.

She realized Lucas was speaking. "Well, there's Stu Mallory, of course," he replied. "The seventh-grade class president? That's the only one I know of, and I can promise you, he's not my stepbrother."

Sophie blinked. Okay. So Stu still existed in this crazy new reality. That was something, at least. And it sounded like he was doing quite well, being class president and all. But the thought didn't make her feel a whole lot better. Sure, these changes were small—almost inconsequential—but she knew that these slight

ripples of change could soon turn into tidal waves of epic propor-
tion if she didn't get Arthur back where he belonged, and soon.

*The future—your future—may no longer exist. Meaning you may
no longer exist.*

She realized Lucas was still staring at her. "Um, right, sorry.
I must have been confused," she stammered, not knowing what
else to say. She started back down the hall, wanting to be alone
with her thoughts. To try to figure out a game plan.

But, to her surprise, Lucas put a hand on her shoulder, pre-
venting her escape. "You haven't answered me yet. What I asked
you about Friday?"

She stared at him blankly. *What now?*

"About the pizza party," he reminded her. "Did you want
to go? Ashley's going with Arthur. So we could all hang out
together...."

It was all she could do not to fall over backward. The pizza
party! Of all things to stay the same in this weird new world,
it had to be that stupid pizza party. And now she was the one
with the invite? It was like the world was literally changing right
before her eyes.

What would tomorrow bring, if she couldn't find a way to
send Arthur back? Would she suddenly find herself voted home-
coming queen? Or become the victim of a worldwide zombie
apocalypse? For all she knew, it could pretty much go either way.

She realized Lucas was waiting for an answer.

THE ONCE AND FUTURE GEEK

"I'm . . . I'm not sure if I can go or not," she stammered. "Can I let you know tomorrow?" Maybe by then she'd have figured this whole thing out, gotten Arthur back to where he belonged, and set history straight once and for all.

Lucas actually looked disappointed. Which was just insane. Before now, the guy had only thought of her as his brother's geeky little friend, always hogging the computer and playing their dumb medieval-themed video games.

Wait! That was it! The idea struck her like a lightning bolt. The proof she needed to show Arthur his future was all in *Camelot's Honor*. If he played the game, he'd learn everything he needed to know about his illustrious destiny. His rise to fame, his legendary battles, his beautiful wife. Surely then he'd be willing to go home. Once he knew his future went far beyond scrubbing dishes in the castle kitchen.

"Listen, Lucas, can you do me a favor?" she asked, her breath in her throat.

"Sure, what's up?"

"Um, Arthur's staying with you, right?"

"Yeah . . ."

"Do you think you could show him how to play *Camelot's Honor*?"

Lucas stared at her. "Um, what?"

"The video game?" she replied hopefully. Maybe he didn't

have it, now that Stu wasn't living at his house. For all she knew, the game no longer existed in this world.

"I know what it is," Lucas replied. "But I didn't think you did. The only video game I've ever seen you play is *Karaoke Jam*."

Sophie tried not to react. Seriously, the new "her" was so lame. Stu would be appalled.

"Well, yeah . . ." She stumbled over her words, thinking fast. "I just thought Arthur might like it. I heard he's really into the whole medieval thing."

Lucas laughed knowingly. "You can say that again!" he agreed. "You should have seen what he was wearing when I first met him."

Sophie let out a sigh of relief. Maybe this would work after all. "Exactly," she agreed. "So can you show him the game tonight?"

Lucas smiled smugly. "Under one condition. You tell me tomorrow afternoon whether you'll go to the pizza party with me. No more excuses."

"It's a deal," she replied firmly, throwing him her most confident grin. After all, if things went according to plan, by then everything would be back to normal and she'd never have to have that conversation. "Tomorrow afternoon it is."

Lucas grinned. "Till then, m'lady," he said with a small bow. Evidently Arthur's chivalry was rubbing off on him. And with that, he turned and headed down the hall. Sophie watched him go, her heart still pounding in her chest. Praying he'd keep his promise to show Arthur the game. Praying that Arthur would recognize himself in the game and realize his destiny.

All before the world, as they knew it, changed forever.

CHAPTER 24

Morgana leaned against an oak tree in twenty-first-century America, exhausted. Time-travel spells were brutally complicated and physically exhausting, and she was now suffering the after-effects of her major cast. In fact, at the moment, she was so drained of magical energy, she barely had enough spark left to even cast the tracking spell on her brother, to help pinpoint his exact location.

She knew she couldn't afford to rest, though it might take her a week to fully recharge her magic, and she didn't have time to spare. If she didn't find Arthur soon—if she didn't manage to kill him before he went back to his own time and back to Merlin's protection—she would lose her opportunity altogether.

And she wasn't about to let that happen.

Where was he? The tracking spell had led her here, into some kind of large building surrounded by a black field of metal carriages, but it couldn't pinpoint her brother in the crowd, and now she was on her own. The sign read SACRED MARY JUNIOR HIGH, which led her to believe it was a monastery or nunnery of some sort. Yet she saw no priests or nuns—only oddly dressed children walking to and fro. Perhaps some kind of religious orphanage?

Morgana knew about orphanages. She'd been sent to live in one by her stepfather, Uther, after Merlin took baby Arthur away. She'd tried to protest, insisting her place was by her mother's side in their Cornwall castle of Tintagel by the sea. But Uther was on a mission—to rid the castle of any reminder of his wife's first marriage, and that included her daughter. And her mother, so in love with her new husband, refused to speak out in her defense.

So Morgana was sent away—to live in poverty and squalor—while her mother took the throne as high queen of the land. Each night, as her mother curled up in a great bed piled with sumptuous furs, Morgana would shiver in her cold, dark cell, vowing revenge on the man who killed her father and took her mother away.

And now she would finally have it. She had killed Uther and now she would kill his son—before he ever had a chance to rise to his father's throne. Arthur Pendragon, son of Uther, would not pull the sword from the stone and take his father's place as high king. Instead, he would die here, a stranger in a strange land. Ending the Pendragon lineage forever and tearing Britain apart.

Morgana cackled to herself, imagining Merlin's face when he realized his promised child, the one he'd been training all these years, had perished at her hand. Only then would he realize her true power and finally bow down before her, begging for mercy.

She turned her attention back to the orphanage. She'd done her best to fit in, casting a glamour on herself in order to appear as one of them. Now she wore the same short plaid skirt the other girls wore, along with a stiff white tunic top and woolen socks pulled to her knees.

Now to find Arthur. Though that was easier said than done. She hadn't seen her brother since he was a baby, other than in a flicker in the sacred spring. How was she going to recognize him amid such a crowd?

Suddenly her ears picked up on a familiar tune. She whirled around to see a tall, lanky blond boy turn the corner and begin strolling casually in her direction, whistling as he walked.

It was a tune she knew well. After all, she'd sung it to her brother when he was a baby.

She slid behind the tree, studying the boy as he approached, her heart pounding. It was him! It was really him! She could practically see her own face reflected in his.

Arthur. Her brother.

Her hand trembled as she pulled out the knife.

He stopped to address a group of students, laughing and patting one of them on the back. He looked so relaxed, so happy, and for a moment she felt a pang of guilt and actually considered abandoning her mission. To let this poor boy go free, and not punish him for his father's sins.

But no, she couldn't do that. He might look innocent now, but he had Uther's blood running through his veins. And if given the chance to rise to power—to take his father's throne—who knew what he would eventually do? *No, he must be destroyed. His tainted blood must be spilled. Uther's line must end here.*

Arthur said good-bye to his friends and moved on. She waited, tense, until the last second, then stepped onto his path, the knife pressed firmly at her side. As they slammed into each other, she thrust the blade forward as hard as she could.

But instead of sliding easily into willing flesh, the dagger bounced off Arthur harmlessly, knocking her off-balance and onto the ground. She shrieked in a mixture of pain and surprise.

"Are you all right?" Arthur asked, a horrified look on his face. He reached out his hand and helped her to her feet. She slid the knife into her pocket unseen.

"Sorry," she muttered. "I . . . wasn't looking where I was going." Why hadn't she been able to stab him? It was as if he had some kind of invisible force field around him. But she could sense nothing.

She realized Arthur was looking at her with curious eyes. "Do I know you?"

"No, no, I don't think so," she replied quickly, lowering her face to obscure it from view. She muttered a spell of scanning under her breath, trying to determine what had made him immune to her weapon.

And that was when she saw it. The scabbard of power. The same one she had managed to steal from Uther in order to bring him down. The one the Companions had stolen back after Uther's death and had planned to present to Arthur at his crowning.

How could he have it in his possession already? That wasn't part of the plan!

"I'm sure I've seen your face before," Arthur insisted, still staring at her.

"I am . . . new here," she said, her mind racing quickly. "And, well, I've heard that you own a very valuable relic. I was wondering if you'd let me see it."

Arthur frowned. "I'm not really supposed to be carrying it around. Some people think it's a weapon and I don't want anyone to take it away again."

"I don't want to take it," she lied quickly. "I just want to see it. I heard it was beautiful."

Reluctantly, Arthur reached into his pack and pulled out the scabbard. Morgana's heart thudded. It was almost too good to be true! If she could get rid of Arthur and acquire the scabbard once again, she would become unstoppable!

She reached out with hungry fingers, but Arthur snatched the artifact away a split second too soon. "Sorry," he said apologetically. "It's really old. I'd rather just hold on to it, if you don't mind."

Morgana tried casting a possession spell, but to no avail. Her magic was weakened and the scabbard seemed bound to its master. She realized Arthur would have to drop it or willingly give it away if she was ever to be able to claim it. Something he didn't seem very likely to do, even if he didn't understand its power.

"I must go," Arthur said, stuffing the scabbard back into his bag. "I'm sorry again for bumping into you."

And with that, he headed down the path, whistling the same tune as before. Morgana watched him go, plotting her next move. She had to get that scabbard away from him, no matter what. Otherwise all would be lost.

It was then that she noticed she wasn't the only one with eyes on her brother. A tall, gawky-looking boy was walking in the opposite direction, staring at Arthur with eyes full of hate. As Arthur passed him, he stopped as if to greet the boy. Morgana couldn't hear what they were saying from that distance, but she could see the boy's expression twist into rage before he pushed past Arthur, knocking his shoulder against her brother's before continuing on his way.

Morgana smiled. Any enemy of her brother's was definitely a friend of hers.

"Hello," she purred, stepping into his path. He looked up, startled.

"W-who are you?" he stammered.

"My name is Morgana. And you are . . . ?"

He blushed bright red. "Um, I'm, I'm Mortimer."

"May I ask you a question, Mortimer?" she asked. "That boy you were just talking to . . ." Morgana nodded in Arthur's direction. "Who is he?"

Mortimer made a face. "You mean Arthur?" He spit out the name like he was expelling poison. Perfect.

"I take it you two are not friends?"

"Friends? No freaking way. He stole my spot on the team! It should have been me making that touchdown, not him!" The story tumbled from his lips. Morgana only understood half of it, but she got the idea.

"And now everyone loves him and I'm still as invisible as I've ever been," he finished, scowling.

"Poor, poor boy," she murmured, reaching out to stroke his hair. "If I were you, I'd be very angry. In fact, I'd want revenge."

"Yeah, right," he said. "What am I supposed to do to him? I'm no one and he's already the most popular kid in school. Completely untouchable."

"Come now, Mortimer," Morgana scolded, "everyone has their weaknesses. Even Arthur. You just have to figure out what they are."

"But how—"

"It's simple," she said, keeping her voice even. "You must become his shadow. Watch his every move. Find out what he cares about. What makes him happy. What makes him angry."

"And then what?"

"Then return to me," she replied firmly. "And I shall tell you what to do next."

Mortimer shuffled from foot to foot. Obviously trying to decide if this was a good idea. Then he looked up.

"Why do you care?" he asked at last. "I mean, you've got to have better things to do than worry about my pathetic life."

Morgana paused for a moment. "Let's just say I have my own issues with Arthur," she said at last. "And I have been looking for a friend who feels the same."

"Okay. I guess I can try," he said reluctantly.

"Excellent," Morgana said. "Meet me here tomorrow at the same time and tell me what you've learned." Her expression shifted and her voice dropped to a serious tone. "And Mortimer? Don't disappoint me."

CHAPTER 25

"Hey, Mom, we're home!"

Arthur followed Lucas into the house, feeling as if it were his home, too. It was hard not to. Lucas's house was warm and cozy and dry—unlike the drafty, leaky castle he was used to back in his own time. Not to mention Lucas's mom was a terrific cook and there was always plenty of food to go around. Perhaps if he made himself useful, they'd invite him to stay permanently, at least as a servant. He'd be more than happy to do dishes in exchange for dinner and a bed.

"Hi, darling. Hi, Arthur," Lucas's mother said. She was in the next room over, sitting in front of her magic mirror. A TV, Lucas had called it. "Come here for a second."

"What's up?" Lucas asked. Arthur followed, a little nervous. Lucas's mom had been suspicious about his "dead host family" story and had promised to call around to various foreign-exchange agencies to figure out where Arthur belonged. Had she found a way to get rid of him?

But when they stepped into the room, Lucas's mother only gestured to the screen. "They're talking about that missing kid from your school again. Do you know him?"

Arthur stole a peek at the TV and saw a reflection of a boy around his own age with messy brown hair and glasses. A moment later the screen cut to a man sitting behind a desk. "Twelve-year-old Stuart Mallory was last seen in his room Sunday afternoon in the Park Heights neighborhood," the man said. "If you have any information as to his whereabouts, please call the police tip line."

Arthur scratched his head. *Stuart Mallory.* The name sounded very familiar . . .

"That's your brother!" he exclaimed to Lucas, surprised. "He's still missing?"

In all the craziness of the past couple days, he'd all but forgotten that Lucas had been searching for his brother when he'd first met him at Medieval Manor. At the time, Lucas had been worried. Yet he hadn't mentioned him since. And why was his mother asking if Lucas knew him? Something wasn't adding up.

Lucas gave him a confused look. "What are you talking about?"

Arthur bit his lower lip, trying to remember the details. "You were looking for him. That's why you were at Medieval Manor to begin with. When I first met you..." Was he somehow mixing things up? No, he was positive he was right.

But Lucas just shook his head. "What the heck is a Medieval Manor? I met you outside of school yesterday, remember? Arguing with Mr. Mooney?" Arthur's friend gave a dry chuckle. "Jeez, first Sophie, now you. Is this Play a Joke on Lucas Day or something?"

Arthur's heart panged guiltily at the mention of Sophie's name, all thoughts of the mysterious Stu fading from his mind. He'd tried to find her after school, to give her the scabbard to take to Merlin, but didn't know where she'd gone. He felt bad about earlier—he hadn't meant to disappoint her and he truly didn't want to make Merlin worry. If only they could understand why he'd decided to stay. Why life here was so much better.

The TV picture flickered and a man with red-rimmed eyes appeared on the screen. "If anyone has seen my son, please let me know," he begged in a choked voice. "We love him and just want to know he's safe. We're offering a reward for any information."

Lucas's mother observed the crying man thoughtfully. "You know, I met him once," she remarked, "in line at Pizza Cave.

He was very nice." She paused, then grinned. "Of course there's no one for me but your father."

Lucas made a face. "Gross."

His mother laughed and said something in reply, but Arthur could barely hear her. He was too busy staring at the screen, watching images of people searching for the missing boy out in the woods. A thought suddenly struck him: Was anyone searching for *him* back home? After all, he'd been gone for a couple days, too. And here, they'd already sent out a search party. Had anyone back home even realized Arthur was gone? Well, besides Mistress McCready, that was, who was probably only noticing the unwashed dishes piling up in the castle kitchen.

His mind flashed to Guinevere. *She* had to be worried, right? After all, he'd promised to meet her at the tournament. What did she think when he didn't show? Was she, right now, as worried about him as this father was about his son? Did she think he'd abandoned her? Left her to fend for herself against knights like Agravaine?

Something churned in his stomach. Maybe this had been a mistake. Was he selfish to just walk away and leave her behind? She was his best friend—his true love—even if the laws of the land said they could never be together. How could he content himself to live in a world where Guinevere had been dead a thousand years?

He couldn't.

"Where's Sophie?" he blurted out. Now that he'd made up his mind, there was no time to waste. He'd find her and beg her for a second chance. Hopefully she wouldn't be too angry to show him the way back home.

Lucas looked at him strangely. "Sophie Sawyer?" he repeated. "I have no idea." Then he brightened. "Though she did want me to show you something! I almost forgot."

Arthur's pulse kicked up a notch. Sophie wanted Lucas to show him something. Maybe it was the way to go home. Maybe he could do it tonight and get back before dawn. Return the scabbard to Merlin, find Guinevere and apologize, even get a head start on the dishes!

"Show me," he said.

Lucas nodded and the two boys headed up the stairs, into the large bedroom they'd been sharing. Lucas sat down at his magic box and started typing away. "Sophie was insisting that I show you how to play *Camelot's Honor* tonight," he said as he typed. "Are you into video games or something?"

Arthur shook his head, not quite sure what his friend was saying. All he knew was that if Sophie wanted him to see it, it had to be important.

The magic box flipped pictures, revealing a knight, dressed in a full set of chain mail and carrying a large sword and shield. "That's my character," Lucas explained. "I'm level seventy-nine.

But don't worry, we'll make you your own. Do you want to do single player or online?"

"Uh…"

Lucas waved him off. "Single player is probably best to start. You get more of the story that way." He pressed a few more buttons. The box whirred and the next thing Arthur knew, the knight had disappeared and in his place stood a tall, scrawny boy, dressed only in a tunic and tights, much like Arthur himself normally was. In fact, he even looked a little like Arthur—with straw-blond hair, blue eyes, and gangly legs and arms that seemed too long for his body.

"Don't worry—as you play, you get more armor and weapons and stuff. Right now you're still a peasant boy, working at the castle of Sir Ector."

Arthur started. "Sir Ector?"

"Hmm." Lucas considered him. "Maybe you should watch the intro first. It's pretty cool cinematics actually, and this way you'll get the whole story line." He rose from the chair and beckoned for Arthur to sit down. "It's like five minutes long. I'll get us a snack while you watch."

Arthur sat down in front of the box. He could almost feel the magic radiating from its core, and his hands began to tremble in anticipation. As Lucas exited the room, the screen went black and music started to swell. A moment later, a large, ornate sword, stuck in a stone, flashed on screen. Funny—it looked a lot like Excalibur from back home. He wondered fleetingly if anyone had managed to pull it from the stone while he'd been gone.

"I AM MERLIN!"

Arthur leaped to his feet, knocking his chair backward. He stared at the screen, his heart in his throat. "M-Merlin?" he whispered, looking around the room for the wizard. "Where are you?"

Silence. Then, "You are Arthur, a young orphan boy of no regard," Merlin's disembodied voice continued. The screen dissolved, revealing the blond boy again, practicing swordcraft against an old tree, much as Arthur had been doing back home just days before.

"You dream of becoming a great knight," Merlin rebuked him, "but instead you spend most of your days working as a servant in your foster family's castle. Until now."

Arthur stood, transfixed. It was obvious Merlin was furious at him for falling into the Well of Dreams. "I'm sorry," he apologized to the sorcerer. "I was trying to get to the tournament but I heard this sound and—"

Merlin ignored him. "Your simple life is about to change—as you begin to discover your great and wondrous destiny."

Arthur cocked his head in confusion. "Wait. Destiny...?" he repeated. "What destiny?"

"The sword in the stone," Merlin replied, surprising him

with his answer. "Only you have the power to free the mighty Excalibur from its rocky prison."

"But I can't pull the sword from the stone," he protested. "They'd never even let me try."

"Good luck, Arthur. The next time I see you, all will be bowing down to you and calling you . . . king!"

And with that, triumphant music rose and the window faded to black. Merlin's voice fell into the ether.

"Wait! Come back!" Arthur cried. "I need to know more!"

"Need to know more what?" Lucas asked, pushing the door open, balancing a plate of cookies. He set it down on a large chest and came over to sit next to Arthur.

Arthur pointed a shaky finger at the box. "Merlin was there. And he was telling me my destiny."

"Oh, right," Lucas said, not sounding at all surprised. "Well, you've got to play the game to find out the rest. But really it follows the King Arthur story pretty faithfully."

"King . . . Arthur?" Arthur repeated carefully.

"Yeah, you know. Sword in the stone, Knights of the Round Table, quest for the Holy Grail?" At Arthur's blank face, he added. "Lancelot, Guinevere? None of this rings a bell?"

Arthur shook his head, confusion washing over him in waves. King Arthur. How could he be King Arthur? And how did Lucas know about Guinevere?

Lucas shrugged. "Weird. I would have thought everyone knew the story." He reached over and grabbed a small black device beside the magic box. A *mouse*, Arthur remembered, though it looked like no rodent he'd ever seen. A moment later the screen changed—now displaying one large word, in big colorful letters.

GOO-GLE?

Lucas grinned. "The answer to all of life's mysteries at the touch of a button." He typed KING ARTHUR and a moment later a list of text scrolled down the window. He selected one, then leaned back, allowing Arthur to see. "Here you go, the legend of King Arthur," he proclaimed. "For your reading pleasure." He rose from his seat. "Want a cookie?"

Arthur shook his head, no longer hungry. His heart thudded as he tried to focus on the words in front of him. A legend that might be true. Of a young boy who pulled the sword from the stone and became king of all England. A boy named Arthur.

He leaned back in his chair, stunned. Could he really be destined to be King of England? Was this what Merlin had been training him for all these years? He'd always wondered in the back of his mind why the great and powerful sorcerer bothered with an orphan like him. Had Merlin known his true heritage all along?

He smiled, imagining the look on his foster brother's face

as he took the throne—subjects far and wide, on their knees, paying their respects. Kay would have to bow, too. He'd have to beg forgiveness for all the wrongs he'd committed against Arthur year after year.

And then there was Guinevere. Beautiful, sweet Guinevere. She'd no longer be stuck with Agravaine or some other brutal lord who would lock her away in a tower for the rest of her life. He could marry her. They could do all they dreamed about—feeding the hungry, righting wrongs ...

"What else do you know about this King Arthur?" he asked his friend, his mouth stuck in a self-conscious grin. He couldn't wait to hear about his exploits. All the good he brought to the land. How the people loved him.

"Well, he was kind of a wimp," Lucas replied. "And he managed to mess everything up in the end."

Arthur's smile faded. "Um, what?"

"Like, first it starts out really good," Lucas explained. "He has all these awesome battles to unite England and stuff. But as soon as you think he has it all, he totally falls apart. Over a girl, nonetheless."

"What do you mean?"

"Well, he's married to this girl named Guinevere, right? But then she starts hanging out with his best friend, Sir Lancelot, behind his back. Nice friend, right?" Lucas made a face. "And

Arthur totally knows it's going on the whole time—but he's so in love with Guinevere he doesn't say anything. Completely whipped, let me tell you."

Arthur stared at him in horror. Guinevere betrays him? With his best friend, no less? That couldn't be true. Could it?

But Lucas wasn't finished. "Then this knight Mordred, who is dying to take over as king, finds out and sees his chance," he continued. "He catches Lancelot and Guinevere together and tells all the other knights. So then, of course, Arthur's forced to make a move—or he looks like a total butt-head."

Arthur didn't know what a butt-head was, but he was pretty sure from Lucas's tone he didn't want to look like one.

"So now it's Lancelot versus Arthur in this big civil war. All over a freaking chick." Lucas shook his head. "Ridiculous if you ask me."

Arthur swallowed hard. "So what happens then?"

"You know, the usual. Kingdom destroyed. Loyal subjects murdered. It's ugly, dude. Mordred ends up killing Arthur on the battlefield and taking over the throne, just like he planned to all along." Lucas shook his head. "Seriously, if Arthur had known what was in store for him, he probably never would have pulled the sword from the stone in the first place."

Arthur stared at him, having no idea what to say and no longer having a voice to say it, even if he did.

Lucas shrugged. "Listen, man, I've got a ton of homework to

do. You're welcome to keep playing or whatever." He pulled out a large book from his sack and lay back in bed, cracking it open.

Arthur nodded absently, his eyes still glued to the box's window, reading the stories one by one, each more horrifying than the next. And all the while he read, his friend's words continued to burn in his ears.

If Arthur had known what was in store for him, he probably never would have pulled the sword from the stone in the first place.

CHAPTER 26

A flash of lightning lit the battlefield, a crack of thunder hot on its heels. The skies opened and hail the size of rocks rained down, pelting King Arthur's armor relentlessly. But the king ignored the weather, head held high as he urged his steed forward, across bloody Camlann, searching for any still living after the massacre that afternoon.

The air grew thick as he approached the lake and he could barely see his hand in front of his face. It was no real surprise, then, when a fiery spear from some hidden enemy pierced through the mists, barreling straight into his horse's flanks. The mare, already spooked by the suffocating stench of death, whinnied in a mixture of pain and terror, rearing on her hind legs. The king crashed to the ground, the muddy field breaking his fall. As he scrambled to his feet, he watched in dismay as the wounded animal galloped away, disappearing into the mists.

With no choice but to press on, the king made his way on foot, careful to step over the corpses littering the field. Good men, he thought as he nodded in respect to each as he passed. Brave farmers, loyal townspeople, those who had remained faithful to the crown until the very end. But these common folk were no match for their enemy—the king's own companions. The infamous Knights of the Round Table, now turned traitors to the crown in this violent civil war.

Would all he fought for in his life now be for naught?

If only Lancelot hadn't had eyes for Queen Guinevere. Arthur should have accused them both of treason the first time he got wind of their affair, sending them to fiery deaths at the stake in a public display of power. But no, he'd turned a blind eye, not having the heart to strike down the two people he loved more than anything, even if they loved each other more.

He'd shown himself to be soft. Ripe for a takeover by Mordred, who called him out, saying he was a stupid, blind man, unable to rule over his own household, never mind the kingdom at large. Mordred called for war, and the knights, disgusted by Arthur's weakness, joined the revolution.

"Arthur! Turn and face me like a man!"

The king whirled around, his eyes rising to a dark knight, high *above him, astride a coal-black steed. He'd know that bloodred tab-ard anywhere.*

"Surrender, Arthur," Mordred commanded in a steely voice, draw-ing his blade from its sheath. "For it is over. Your men are dead. Your kingdom is mine."

"You may as well try to kill me, then," Arthur said, suddenly weary of the fight. "For while there is still breath in my body, I shall never give up Camelot."

Mordred brought his sword down, giving Arthur barely any time to parry the blow with his own blade. He leaped back, but Mordred was on him in an instant, striking again and again, wearing Arthur out with each blow.

Hot pain seared Arthur's side, the last blow finding the seam in his armor, slicing through the unprotected skin and bone beneath. When Mordred pulled back the blade, the king saw the steel was dripping with blood.

The world spun and Arthur found himself falling to the ground, agony stealing his final breaths. From above, his spotty vision caught his son removing his helmet, looking down at him with pitying eyes.

"If only you had made another choice."

Arthur woke with a start, drenched in a pool of sweat, the night-mare still pounding at his brain. No, not merely a nightmare. Nightmares faded with the dawn, but this horror was not so easily shaken. He clutched his side, reliving the phantom ache where Mordred's blade had sliced him open. A painful reminder of the mortal wound he'd one day suffer in real life, according to about a hundred googled texts.

The perfect life turned into a perfect nightmare. Gaining the world, only to lose it all in the end. Like everything else in Arthur's life, his future would just rack up another failure.

And then there was Guinevere. Could she really do what they said she did?

He couldn't bear to think about it.

Perhaps a short walk would ease his mind. Slipping out of bed, he tiptoed to the door, tossing the magic box a reproachful look as he passed. Not that it was the box's fault; it had only revealed the truth.

If only Merlin knew what a lousy king Arthur would become. The magician had done everything in his power to help Arthur succeed. How disappointed he would be when he found out that his protégé would fail when it mattered most. Fail and destroy the lives of all those around him.

It would be much better if he didn't pull the sword from the stone to begin with.

Arthur slipped downstairs and was surprised to see a light in the kitchen. Someone must be up. Not wanting to disturb whomever it was, he touched the handle of the front door, attempting to pull it open quietly. But the hinges squeaked in protest and a moment later Lucas's mother appeared from the kitchen.

"Who's there?" she called in a worried voice. Her expression softened as she stepped closer. "Oh, Arthur," she said. "Sorry. I'm jumping at ghosts tonight."

"I didn't mean to scare you," Arthur replied. "I just couldn't sleep. I thought I might take some air."

She smiled sympathetically. "I know the feeling. Do you want some warm milk? That always helps Lucas when he can't sleep." She beckoned for him to follow her into the small, cozy kitchen. He slipped into a chair and she bustled about, pulling two glasses from the cupboard and setting a pan on the stovetop. Then she busied herself emptying milk into the pan and sprinkling something from a box labeled CINNAMON.

"My secret sleeping draft," she said, looking over at Arthur with a wink. "Works every time." She stirred the mixture, humming softly to herself. Arthur watched her, the terror of his dream fading at last. She was so nice. Just like he'd always imagined his own mother would be.

"I . . . I had a bad dream," he said.

She gave him a sympathetic look. "That makes two of us," she told him as she brought a mug of frothy white liquid over to the table and set it down before him. Steam rose from the cup, evaporating quickly in the air. "I dreamed that the missing boy on TV—Stuart Mallory—was my own son. Strange, huh? I was frantically worried, searching the town, wondering where he could be. Somehow I knew he was in trouble and it was killing me that I couldn't reach him." She gave a half laugh. "Silly, now that I'm awake, I guess. But it felt so real. What about your dream?"

Arthur took a sip of his milk. It was warm, creamy, and delicious. "I can't really remember it all," he lied. "But I was afraid if I fell back asleep the dream would return."

"How about you stay up and keep me company, then?" Lucas's mother suggested. "I don't think I can go back to sleep after my dream, either."

Relieved, Arthur set his mug down, looking up at her with grateful eyes. "That sounds wonderful."

"Come on," she said, rising to her feet, her own mug clasped in her hands. "Do you know how to play chess?"

"Sort of." Kay and Sir Ector played often, but neither had ever let him touch the expensive chessboard. Still, Arthur was pretty sure he had the basic idea down just from watching.

"Well, then, I'm in luck," Lucas's mom teased, a twinkle in her crinkled blue eyes. "Maybe I'll win for once. Lucas and his father are always trampling me."

She led Arthur into the house's living chambers and pulled the chess box from a nearby shelf. Together, they set it up and began to play. When Arthur checkmated her king after only a few dozen moves, she laughed at her defeat. (Unlike Sir Kay, who would tip over the board in fury and storm away if he lost.)

"Sort of?" she teased him. "You meant *sort of* amazing, didn't you?"

Arthur beamed at her compliment, his insides warming. "Another round?" he suggested. Distracted by the game, he could keep thoughts of his future reality at bay.

"What's going on down here?" interrupted a sleepy voice. They looked up to see Lucas, decked out in plaid nightclothes, peeking down the stairs.

"We couldn't sleep," his mother explained. "So Art here has decided to graciously kick my butt at chess instead."

"I think our cat could beat you at chess, Mom," Lucas said as he padded down the stairs.

His mother rolled her eyes. "Yeah, yeah," she replied. "Well, since you're both up, how about a game of Risk? I'll conquer all your continents and achieve world domination before you can even crawl across Europe!"

"Oh, you think so, do you?" Lucas crowed. "Well, then it's on, Mom. It's totally on." He turned to Arthur. "What about you?"

Arthur agreed happily, though he had never heard of the game. And as Lucas returned with the board, he marveled to himself how a night that had started out so horribly had turned out to be so great. He guessed it made sense; everything in the twenty-first century was great.

Forget going home. He would stay here, in the twenty-first century, forever—and try to forget all about his best friend, Guinevere.

CHAPTER 27

"Who ARE you?"

Stu's eyes flew open, jerked out of sleep by the voice. He tried to sit up in bed, only to realize there was a knife at his throat.

Held there by none other than Princess Guinevere herself.

"Who are you?" the girl demanded again. Her eyes burned with self-righteous anger.

"Hey—hey! Watch it with the knife!" he protested.

"Not until you answer my question."

He blinked, still groggy from sleep. "What are you talking about? I'm Arthur, obviously." Guinevere's father had practically forced his daughter on Stu earlier that day, as if she was some kind of prize cow. At the time, he'd felt bad for her—what must it be like to be forced to marry a guy just because he was king? No wonder she ended up falling in love with Sir Lancelot instead.

"You're a liar," she growled, pressing the blade harder against his throat, nicking his skin in the process. Stu could feel a tiny drop of blood drip down his chest, and his heart began to beat faster.

"What—why do you say that?" he gurgled. Did she suspect something was up?

"Arthur is my best friend in the world," the princess replied. "You may look like him, yes, but only through some kind of sorcery. I would swear on my mother's grave that you are not my friend."

Stu let out a breath, realizing he was totally busted. Sure, he could pretend to be Arthur in front of strangers, but if Arthur and Guin had been good friends, the jig was definitely up.

"Take the knife away and I'll explain," he said, trying to keep up his courage so as not to get his throat slit.

The princess narrowed her eyes, then reluctantly withdrew the blade, still keeping it close to her side and pointed in his direction.

He struggled to sit up in bed, looking around. "How'd you even get in here?" he grumbled. "I thought I had guards at the door." First Lot, now Guinevere. Medieval security was not all it was cracked up to be.

"I flew in through the window. The *real* Arthur gave me some of his shape-shifting powder," she explained. "Which you would have known, if you were him." She frowned. "Now talk."

He let out a resigned breath. *Here goes nothing*, he thought. "Fine. You're right," he said. "I'm not really Arthur. I'm Stuart Mallory and I come from the twenty-first century. The future. Merlin turned me into an Arthur look-alike until the real Arthur came back from his...um...quest. Which has been quite an experience, let me tell you. I don't know if you saw that fight with King Lot but—"

"Quest?" Guinevere interrupted. "What quest?"

"You wouldn't believe me if I told you," he said. "Maybe if we go find Merlin—"

But she wasn't having any of that. "Try me," she said, hand still on the knife.

And so Stu—against his better judgment—did. And Guinevere listened to the whole tale without interrupting. When he had finished, she sat quiet for a moment.

"This is all my fault," she said at last. "If I hadn't dropped the scabbard down into the Well of Dreams, none of this would have happened."

"Merlin sent Sophie to bring Arthur home," Stu assured her. "And believe me, the second he gets here, I'll be giving him the throne. I mean, it's been interesting and all, but I miss my computer." *And Sophie*, he thought. He wondered for the thousandth time how she was doing. Was she still mad at him? Was that why she hadn't returned with Arthur? Had she decided to abandon him here forever?

He shuddered. No. She wouldn't do that. Would she?

He looked up, realizing that the princess had climbed off the bed and was back on her feet, a determined expression on her face.

"What?" he asked, a little worried.

"Your Sophie is taking too long," she told him. "If she's unable to complete her quest, then I will go retrieve Arthur myself."

"Oh, I don't really think you should . . ." Stu began, trailing off as Guinevere raised her knife again. He exhaled. Seriously, did everyone in this freaking place have to have the undying urge to kill him? "Fine. Maybe that's a good idea, actually." He wasn't in the position to turn down any offers of help.

Guinevere walked to the window, a fistful of sparkling powder in hand. Then she turned back to Stu. "I'll be back as soon as I can," she said. "Try not to mess anything up while I'm gone."

Stu nodded, though in truth he wondered if it was already too late.

CHAPTER 28

"Get out of the way!"

Guinevere's eyes opened groggily, her head pounding as she looked around, not knowing where she was or how she'd gotten there. It appeared she'd awakened in some kind of large field, almost like a jousting field, but with strange white lines and numbers painted on the grass. She rubbed her eyes, trying to remember. Suddenly it all came screaming back at her.

Arthur. The Well of Dreams. The future.

"You're going to get trampled!"

Still dazed, Guinevere tried to focus. Her eyes fell on a group of helmeted men, charging toward her at top speed. *Oh dear.*

She struggled to her feet, but tripped over her long gown, splashing into the mud instead. The men didn't slow down. She tried to stand again—desperately looking from left to right—wondering which way she should run—

SLAM! One of the men who had been running backward, not looking where he was going, crashed into her. She hit the ground with a thud, and a moment later the man fell on top of her, crushing her with his weight.

"Ow!" she cried, struggling to get out from under him.

He rolled off her and leaped to his feet. "Are you all right?" he asked solicitously. But then Guinevere looked up at him and he stiffened, staring down at her from beneath his helmet. "Guinevere?" he asked in a voice no louder than a whisper. Her eyes widened. How did he...?

A whistle blew, but he ignored it. Instead, he pulled off his helmet. Guinevere's mouth dropped open as she realized the boy who had tackled her was none other than Arthur himself.

Relieved, she scrambled to her feet and threw her arms around him, not caring, for the first time in her life, if anyone saw her do it. After all, in a sense the two of them were practically betrothed, even if Arthur didn't know it yet.

"Oh, Arthur!" she cried, burying her face in his shoulder. He smelled the same—warm, woodsy—though he was dressed unlike anyone she'd ever seen. "I'm so glad I found you."

She waited for him to hug her back, but his hands remained at his sides and his body felt rigid. Unyielding. Surprised, she drew back. Her eyes searched his scowling face. "What's wrong?"

"What are you doing here?" he demanded angrily. "Did Merlin send you?"

She shook her head, confused. "I came on my own," she said. "I had to find you and tell you what's happened back home. Something big! You'll never guess."

"They want to crown me King of England? After I pull a sword from a stone?"

"Yes!" she cried, surprised. "How did you know?"

He huffed. "The Google told me. In fact, it told me everything that happens to me for the rest of my life."

Google? Was that some sort of oracle? "Then you know why I'm here," she said. "We need to get you home so you can take the throne and we can get started. We have so much to do—there's no time to waste!"

His eyes narrowed. "We?"

"We're to be married, Arthur," she informed him happily. "Isn't that wonderful? It'll be just as we always talked about." She smiled at him. He didn't smile in return.

"Hey, Arthur! You coming, man?" called one of the men on the field. Arthur nodded and held up one finger, then turned back to Guinevere, looking distracted.

"You shouldn't have come," he said in a cold voice. "You

should go home and tell Merlin I'm not coming back. He'll have to find someone else to be king."

Before Guin could respond, he stalked back to the others. She watched him go, her stomach twisting in knots. Then, not knowing what else to do, she walked off the field, sank down onto a nearby metal bench, and dropped her head in her hands. What was going on here? Why was Arthur acting like this? This should have been a dream come true for them. Instead, he was acting like he didn't want to be king.

That he didn't want her.

"Oh, Arthur," she whispered. "What happened to you?"

"Are you okay?"

She looked up, her vision blurred by her tears. Standing above her was a boy—tall, wavy black hair—very handsome. He plopped down beside her on the bench, his intense green eyes searching her own in concern.

"I'm Lucas," he said. "Wide receiver. Out with a busted knee. I know it's probably none of my business, but I saw you crying and I just figured I'd come over to see if you needed any help."

She sighed. She needed more help than she could possibly even ask for. But what could she say? That she was stuck in the future with no idea how to get back? That the boy she loved was acting insane?

Suddenly Stu's words came barreling back to her.

"Sophie," she managed to squeak. "Do you know a girl named

Sophie?" From what Stu said, Sophie was the only person here in this millennium who would believe her wild tale.

"Sophie Sawyer?" Lucas asked. "Sure. I know her."

"Can you ... find her for me?"

Lucas nodded. "I think I have her number in my cell." Pulling out a strange rectangular device, he started pressing on the surface with his finger. "Yup. Here she is. You want me to call her?"

Guinevere nodded thankfully.

"No problem," Lucas said with a teasing grin. "Always happy to help a damsel in distress." He winked. "Not that you don't look like a girl who's capable of saving herself, of course ..."

"Obviously," she declared, not able to help a small smile. It was about time someone recognized that. Maybe boys in the twenty-first century weren't as pigheaded as the ones in her own time. That would certainly be a welcome change. Especially after the reaction she'd just gotten from Arthur.

Lucas grinned back at her with white, perfectly straight teeth. "All right, I'll call Sophie," he said. "Who should I say is looking for her?"

"My name is Guinevere," she said. "Tell her Stu sent me."

CHAPTER 29

Morgana paced the wooded path between the school and the "parking lot," waiting for her minion to return with information about Arthur. She'd spent most of the morning in the "library" studying up on the twenty-first century and its mysteries, but was still having difficulty formulating a plan to dispose of Arthur and retrieve the scabbard. Back home—where her magic was strong—it might have been an easier task. But here, weakened and far from the source of her power, she could only conjure up minor spells. And with the scabbard having made Arthur invincible, none of them were going to do the trick.

From a distance her eyes locked on Mortimer, running up from a nearby field, an eager expression on his face. It'd been almost too easy to pull him over to her side. No magic necessary. Just a sympathetic ear and a willingness to listen when no one else would, and he was putty in her hands.

"Hi, Morgana," Mortimer said shyly as he slowed on approach, his eyes darting nervously from side to side. "I wasn't sure you'd be here." He gave her a bashful grin and Morgana resisted the urge to roll her eyes. No wonder the world fell apart when men began to run it.

"So," she said, taking him by the hand and leading him over to a nearby wooden bench. His palm was disgustingly sweaty and he smelled a little like onions. "Tell Morgana what you learned today," she instructed, urging him to sit down beside her. "Did you discover our enemy's weakness?"

To Morgana's delight, Mortimer gave a firm nod. "There's this girl," he informed her. "Down by the football field. She and Arthur had some kind of argument. He looked really upset afterward and kept making mistakes in practice." He beamed, evidently very proud of himself.

Morgana considered this. "This girl," she said. "What does she look like?"

Mortimer's brow wrinkled. "Well, she was wearing a weird dress."

"Define 'weird.'"

"Like something you'd see at a medieval fair."

Morgana stared at him, surprised. Had yet another time

traveler come to town? Someone Arthur knew, perhaps? Someone he would be upset to see?

"Anything else you can remember about this girl?" she asked hopefully.

But Mortimer shrugged. "Not really." Then his eyes brightened, locking on to something behind her. "Wait—there she is! Walking to the parking lot with Sophie Sawyer!"

Morgana whirled around, her mouth dropping open as she saw who Mortimer was pointing to. Could it really be? Princess Guinevere herself, in the twenty-first century, completely unprotected? Yes, it had to be. She'd know the princess anywhere. Her lips curled into a satisfied smirk. This was almost too good to be true!

She rose from her seat. "You did well," she told Mortimer hastily. "I may call upon you again in the future."

Mortimer grinned from ear to ear. "And maybe we can sit together at lunch sometime?" he called after her.

But Morgana didn't bother to answer. She was rushing down the path, following Guinevere and her friend. The princess was absolutely the perfect weapon to bring her brother down. She wasn't about to let her out of her sight.

CHAPTER 30

"This is insane. I don't even know a Lancelot."

From her spot on the bed, Sophie gave Guinevere a pitying smile. The princess leaned back in her chair, staring at the computer.

"The Google lies!" she added, glancing over at Sophie with a distraught look on her face. "It has to. I would never do something like this!"

"Unfortunately, history says you do," Sophie replied carefully. "And it sounds like Arthur knows it."

Guinevere rose from her chair, pacing the room. "And here I thought everything was going to turn out so well once I found out he was to be king. He's my best friend, you know," she added. "And I'm sure he'd make the most excellent husband." She ran a hand through her long blond hair. "But now he believes I will be a terrible wife. That I will betray him for another man. A man I don't even know." She glanced glumly at the computer. "All because some magic box tells him so."

Sophie sighed. And here she thought she'd been so clever with her little "show Arthur the video game" plan. She'd wanted him to see visions of glory and honor—of him becoming the most legendary king in the world. She'd conveniently forgotten the rest of the story. His betrayal by his only love. His not-so-happily ever after. No wonder Merlin hadn't wanted him to know his future. It was a destiny no one would want to live.

She couldn't blame Arthur for not wanting to go back. But, at the same time, he couldn't stay. The timeline was already going wonky. Who knew how bad it would get if Arthur stayed here longer?

And then there was Stu. Poor Stu, who was stuck in medieval times, trying to fill in for a king. It had been two days since she'd left him standing there without even saying good-bye. Did he think she'd abandoned him forever?

"This is all my fault," Guinevere said. "If I hadn't dropped the scabbard down the well, he never would have come here."

"Believe me, I feel guilty, too," Sophie said. "But blaming ourselves isn't going to get the boys back where they belong. We have to come up with a plan. Even if it means dragging Arthur back to the past by his ear."

Guinevere laughed at this. "Do not think I wouldn't," she said. Then she sighed. "Arthur has a good heart, Sophie. He is smart and kind and he cares about other people, too. He just doesn't understand the impact of what he's doing. If we can just explain to him what's happening, I'm sure he'll change his mind." She pursed her lips. "Well, at least about going back. Mayhap not about me."

She looked so sad. Sophie opened her mouth, wanting to assure her everything would be okay. But at that moment her bedroom door burst open. Dad, forgetting to knock as usual, poked his head inside.

"You girls ready to head out to the search?" he asked. "We can grab pizza on the way."

Sophie cocked her head. "Search? What search?"

"Haven't you heard?" Dad gave her a surprised look. "It's been all over the news. That kid from your class is still missing. Practically the whole town is out looking for him."

Oh. Right. Stu.

"Well, they're wasting their time," she muttered under her breath.

Her father gave her a sharp look. "Do you know something, Sophie?" he demanded, his eyes drilling into her. "If so, you need to tell the police immediately. A boy's life is at stake here."

It took everything inside Sophie to swallow back her retort.

Don't you think I know that? she wanted to scream. But that would only bring up more questions.

"No. I don't know anything," she said at last, staring down at her lap. "I don't even know the kid."

In a way it wasn't a lie. After all, in this new world she was living in, she and Stu had probably never even met—except maybe in passing. She thought about the countless afternoons they'd spent together, hanging out, playing video games, watching movies. Countless memories that no longer mattered. Because in this world, they didn't exist.

A horrible thought struck her. If she got Stu home now, would everything go back to the way it was? Or would he become the new Stu? The one who didn't know her from a hole in the wall?

And here she'd been worried about him playing soccer . . .

Her father's face softened. He gave Sophie a pitying look. "I'm sorry," he said. "I know this must strike close to home for you. It does for me, too."

Sophie stared at him, realizing he was mistaking her upset for her own mother's disappearance. Sometimes she forgot how hard that had been for him, too. She'd been so young when it happened. Had her dad blamed himself for Sophie's mother like Sophie was now blaming herself for Stu? Was he trying to help find Stu now to make up for the past?

She found herself nodding. "Give us a few minutes to get ready."

Dad looked relieved. "Excellent. I'll call in the pizza." He turned to Guinevere. "What do you like on yours?"

The princess gave him a baffled look and Sophie fought the urge to laugh. She couldn't believe her father had just asked the legendary Princess Guinevere her Domino's preferences.

Sophie jumped in to save her new friend. "We'll have pepperoni."

To her surprise, her father frowned. "What's a pepper-oni?"

Sophie stared at him in shock. Had the ripples in time actually eliminated her favorite pizza topping as well as everything else?

This needed to stop. Now.

CHAPTER 31

"All right, knights, gather round. Here's what we're going to do," Arthur announced, gesturing for his team to meet in a huddle. The players formed a semi-circle, waiting for his command. However, this time Arthur wasn't offering up some masterful offensive play; he had something far nobler in mind.

When he'd first learned that Stuart Mallory was still missing, he realized he needed to step in. Whether he was Lucas's brother or not (a fact that still confused Arthur to no end), Stuart was in need of aid and Arthur was convinced he was the knight for the job. Back home he would have remained helpless in this quest—a mere servant boy with no power to do anything useful. But here he had an army at his disposal. After all, that was what knights had been created for—to right wrongs, help people in need. And he was positive that when they returned victorious, having rescued Stu from a dragon or an evil witch or whatever it was that kept him away, Sophie would finally understand why he should stay in the twenty-first century.

If only his army would be a bit more enthusiastic.

"This better not take long," Garrett grumbled. "The game starts at seven and I forgot to DVR it."

"And I'm supposed to play *Call of Duty*," Connor declared. "I promised my cousin. Not to mention it's freaking freezing out here." He pulled his jacket tighter around his body for emphasis.

"Yeah, and I'm starving," added Tristan. "How long do you think we have to be out here, anyway?"

Arthur frowned. "All night, if necessary!"

"Not all night," their coach interjected. "The police have instituted a curfew. Everyone needs to be back here before dark." He glanced at his watch. "That gives us about an hour. Then we'll go get pizza."

Everyone cheered at this. Arthur sighed.

"Go ahead," Lucas encouraged him, pointing to the map Arthur had borrowed from the police. "Let's make a plan."

Arthur nodded, laying out the map and grabbing the tokens he'd borrowed from Lucas's game of Risk from his pocket, spreading them out onto the forest floor. "Lucas and Tristan, you take the west flank," he instructed, placing a green token on the map. "Garrett and Connor, you take the north. Percy and Graham can scour the east. Be careful though," he added. "Watch out for the swamp, here." He placed a red token to mark the rough terrain. "And I will cover the southern area with Mortimer." He looked up. "If you find yourself in trouble, make a sound like this." He chirped a swallow's call. "And the rest of us will come to your aid."

"Or, you know, send a group text," Garrett pointed out. The others laughed.

"Um, right." Arthur shrugged, having no idea what he was talking about. "We'll meet back here in an hour. Good luck and be careful. Remember you are on a noble quest and you will—"

"Get pizza when we're done!" interrupted Connor, raising his hand in a fist. The others cheered.

"Let's doooo eeeet!" crowed Percy.

As they broke from the huddle, Arthur watched a metal carriage pull up to the search site. His eyes widened as the vehicle stopped and none other than Guinevere herself stepped outside, along with Sophie and another man.

His heart panged in his chest. It was all he could do not to run to her, throw his arms around her, and squeeze her tight. Thank her for coming, for caring enough to want to help. To apologize for how he'd treated her on the football field earlier that day. Blaming her for something she hadn't done yet. Something she might never do.

He squared his shoulders. He needed to apologize. Now. She'd come all this way to find him. She deserved that at the very least.

"I'll be back," he told the knights.

His heart pounded as he forced himself to approach her, feeling as if he was stuck in the swamp he'd warned Percy about. *It is only Guinevere*, he tried to remind himself. *Your best friend. How can you be afraid of her now?*

But he *was* afraid. Afraid he'd lost her forever.

As he drew closer, he realized she looked different. Like him, she now wore twenty-first-century clothing. A long-sleeved white tunic and baggy blue trousers. The kind of outfit that might be better fit for a boy. Yet on her it looked stunning.

"Guin—" he started.

"Well, look who's here."

He whirled around. With his eyes on Guinevere, he hadn't seen Sophie step up beside her. He cringed. Was she going to yell at him again?

"The knights and I are on a noble quest," he declared. "To find a missing boy."

Sophie's face filled with anger. "Are you freaking kidding me?" she demanded. "You're here searching for Stu? Do you even have any idea—?"

"Sophie, do you mind if I talk to Guinevere alone for a

moment?" he interrupted, a little annoyed. Clearly the girl was determined to be angry with him, no matter what he did.

"Sure. Whatever. He's all yours," she muttered to Guinevere, heading over to the main police tent and leaving the two of them alone.

Guinevere gave him a wary look. "So *now* you want to talk to me?"

He hung his head. "I'm sorry about before," he said. "You just . . . took me by surprise."

"So did you when you took off to another world without even telling me first."

"I didn't mean to. I was only trying to get the scabbard."

"Right." She kicked the ground with her foot. "Thanks for that, by the way."

"I would do anything for you, Guin. I hope you know that."

He looked up and saw that her eyes were misting with tears. "And I for you," she said, giving him a beseeching look. "Arthur, Sophie showed me what you read online. And I know it makes me sound terrible. But I swear to you, it will not come true. I could never betray you. You have to believe me!"

And suddenly Arthur realized he did. After all, this was Guinevere. His best friend. His true love. The girl he'd known and trusted since he was a boy. How could he doubt her word now? Or her loyalty to him? What he had read didn't make any sense.

He took a deep breath. "I believe you," he said quietly. "Maybe that makes me a fool. But I do. I know you, Guin. And I trust you with all my heart. I always have." Feeling daring, he reached out and slipped his hand into hers. It felt so soft. So right. He had to trust in that. Trust in her.

"Thank you," she whispered, squeezing his fingers. "You don't know how much this means to me. To have you by my side—it's all I ever wanted." Her eyes shone with excitement. "Just think of it, Arthur. You and I, ruling the kingdom, side by side. Righting all the wrongs in the land, just as we always dreamed about. No longer will families live in fear. No longer will knights run wild. We can create a land of equality and liberty and justice—"

"Or we could stay here instead!" Arthur blurted out.

She dropped his hand abruptly, staring at him with a confused expression. As if the idea had never occurred to her. And maybe it hadn't. She hadn't been in the twenty-first century for more than a few hours. She had no idea of the wonders of this world. But she would love it here, he suddenly decided. And together they could find a true happily ever after.

"Don't you see? It's perfect!" he told her. "This way we can avoid all the bad stuff that's destined to happen to us back home. I mean, you'll never even meet a Lancelot, never mind fall in love with him. You'll never betray me. And the kingdom won't be destroyed. No one will die. I won't die . . ." He trailed off, catching the dismayed expression on her face. "What?"

"Arthur, think about what you're saying!" she cried. "You think you can just live here—abandoning your people back home? They've been praying for years for a great king to pull the sword from the stone and rescue them from oppression. And now you have the chance to become that king. To help children like Thom and mothers like Sara. To give them a better life and bring peace to the land. How could you possibly turn your back on them now?"

Her words pierced like a thousand bee stings. Mostly because he knew she was right. But at the same time . . .

"Guin, I've read my own story," he pleaded. "If I go home, I die. I'm murdered in cold blood by a man who wants my throne. What kind of good can I do if I'm dead? I can accomplish so much more here, in this world. Like right now!" he added excitedly. "I'm here to save a lost boy! He needs my help and—"

Guinevere laughed bitterly. He stopped, confused. "What?"

"Don't you get it?" she asked. "You won't find Stu lost in the woods if you searched a thousand years. You won't find him anywhere in this world."

"What are you talking about?" he demanded. "He's not . . . dead, is he?"

Guinevere shook her head. "He's back home, filling in for you. Merlin made him look just like you so he could pull the sword from the stone, since you weren't around to do it. And now he's ruling your kingdom, trying to keep things together while you're off playing football." She spit out the word "football," as if expelling poison.

Arthur stared at her, shocked. "But why would he do that?"

"Because someone had to. And evidently you're too much of a coward." She glared at him, her eyes full of fire. "You know, I thought more of you, Arthur. But really, in the end, you're no better than Agravaine himself."

And with that, she stormed off. Arthur watched her go, too stunned even to follow. Was she telling the truth? Could Stu really be back in time, fulfilling Arthur's destiny, saving Arthur's people, and risking his own life to do so—all because Arthur was too afraid? He felt shame wash over him at the thought.

Well, maybe it was all for the best, he told himself miserably. Someone like him—someone so cowardly—didn't deserve to be a knight. A king. And they certainly didn't deserve a girl like Guinevere. Who knew? Maybe Stu would do a better job than him in the end.

"Hey, Art? You coming?" Lucas called out to him. "Let's get this search started, bro!" The other knights shouted as well, gesturing for him to hurry up. But what was the point? Obviously this was a stupid idea from the start. Just like all his other ideas.

"You go on," he muttered. "I'm going to wait for the pizza."

CHAPTER 32

Well, that didn't go well, Guinevere thought, watching Arthur walk away.

Still, what else could she have said? That she'd stay here with him? Abandon everyone back home to war and death so the two of them could live a comfortable existence in the future? Sure, they might manage to escape their own destiny, but what harm would it cause everyone else? People like Sara and her children. They needed a ruler like Arthur. He couldn't turn his back on them now.

Arthur might be content to be selfish, but Guin wasn't.

Frustrated, she slammed her fist against a tree, regretting the move the moment her hand connected with the trunk. She pulled it away, wincing at the scrapes on her knuckles. She knew she should go find Sophie, but what was the point? They'd just be wandering around the woods for no reason, searching for a boy who would never be found.

"Whoa, you look like you're ready to kill someone."

Guin looked up. Lost in her thoughts, she hadn't heard Lucas come up beside her. He studied her face with worried eyes.

"Are you okay?"

"I wish not to talk about it." Pain shot up her hand and she rubbed it ruefully.

"Did you just punch someone out?" Lucas asked, eyes widening at the tears in her knuckles.

"Unfortunately no. Though he well deserved it."

Lucas laughed. "Remind me to stay on your good side," he said. Then his eyes brightened. "Don't worry, I've got the perfect cure."

"What's that?" Guin asked warily.

"An extra-extra-extra-large cherry Slurpee from 7-Eleven. Guaranteed to ease any pain."

"A what?"

Lucas's face lit up in excitement. "Dude! You don't know what a Slurpee is?" he asked. "It's, like, the best drink on earth."

"I see. And where might one find such a gift from the gods?"

"Well…" Lucas lowered his voice to a near whisper. "It would involve a highly dangerous quest. I don't know if you're up for that…."

Guin squared her shoulders. "I can handle myself."

"Very well. But we have to be quiet. We don't want to get caught."

Guin nodded, following Lucas past the search tent and toward the field of cars. "I should tell Sophie where I'm going," she hedged.

"We'll only be a minute," Lucas assured her. "She won't even know you're gone." He glanced back, as if to be sure they weren't being followed, then pulled Guin behind a wooden fence and gestured for her to peek through a knothole.

"7-Eleven is just beyond the parking lot," he explained. "But the lot is being patrolled by a policeman. And if he catches us, he'll report us to my coach and then we'll be in for it."

"Are you sure you want to take the risk?" Guinevere asked, sudden excitement thrumming through her veins. Her sense of adventure had been piqued.

Lucas grinned. "Trust me, it's worth it for your first-ever Slurpee." He peered through the knothole again. "We'll have a better chance if we split up. That way if one of us gets caught, the other can escape." He pulled away so she could look through the hole. "See that big sign? Meet me there."

Guin took a peek at the sign. It seemed so far away. But she didn't want Lucas to think she was scared. "Very well," she declared, pushing down her fear. "I'm ready."

He gave her a mock salute. "Good luck!"

And with that, they were off, each bounding in separate directions. Guin reached the parking lot first, ducking behind a brown car, then poking her head up to look through its windows. She spotted the guard a few rows down, looking back up at the search area. Sucking in a breath, she made her move, running to the next car and diving behind it. From across the parking lot, she saw Lucas do the same and smiled to herself. This was fun!

She continued, moving slowly, not rushing, not taking risks. It wasn't a race, she told herself. Safety was more important than speed. Soon she reached the end of the parking lot and was ready to make her final run for the sign.

But just as she was about to go, she realized the police officer was on the move, heading in the same direction she'd last seen Lucas. Her heart pounded. She had to save him! She glanced around the parking lot, searching for some distraction. Her eyes alighted on a medium-size stone, just under the car. She grabbed it and threw it as hard as she could. The stone collided with a window, and a moment later, a high-pitched sound started wailing through the air. Guinevere stifled a screech of surprise.

"Hey!" The guard ran toward the blaring car. Guin turned back to Lucas. He flashed her a huge grin, then did a show-off flip, landing just behind the sign. She had to hold her hand over her mouth to keep from laughing, realizing she needed to make her own move before the officer came back.

A moment later, she was at the sign. Back with Lucas.

"That was amazing," she cried. "I was positive we would get caught!"

"I would have if you hadn't thrown that rock," Lucas declared, hands on his knees, trying to catch his breath. "I owe you my life."

She smiled. "I would exchange that life debt for one Slurpee."

He grabbed her hand and shook it hard. "Deal. Now let's go before anyone realizes we're gone."

They crossed the street and into the 7-Eleven, which turned out to be a wonderland of food and other fascinating delights. Guin picked up a rainbow-colored package from one of the shelves, turning it over in her hands, wondering what on earth a "Skittles" could be.

But Lucas grabbed it and placed it back on the shelf. "No distractions." He led her over to the Slurpee machine, placed a giant cup under the swirling bowl, and pushed a lever. A moment later, the cup was filled to the brim with bright-red liquid.

"Cherry Slurpee for my brave adventurer," he declared, handing the cup to her.

"Thank you, kind sir," she quipped, putting the cup to her lips and taking a large sip. The icy liquid filled her mouth, taking over her senses, and—

Slamming into her head!

"Ow!" she cried, dropping the cup in shock. Red liquid splattered everywhere as she clutched her head with both hands. Pain shot through her entire body, forcing tears to her eyes. "Winds and rain!" she cried in agony. "What was in that drink?"

She looked up, realizing Lucas was laughing hysterically.

"What?" she demanded, a little insulted. That had really hurt!

"Welcome to your very first brain freeze," he teased. He reached down and picked up her fallen cup, throwing it into a hole on the counter.

She did a double take. "The Slurpee freezes your brain? Why would anyone want such a horrible thing?"

Lucas snorted. "You just need to learn to drink it slower," he told her. "And preferably through a straw." He filled another cup, grabbing a small white tube and sticking it in, instructing her to sip.

"I don't know," she hedged.

But Lucas pressed the drink into her hands, catching her eyes with his own. "Trust me," he said.

Guinevere took the cup and held her breath as she took a tentative sip, praying she wasn't making a mistake. The liquid hit her mouth, surprising her again with its intense flavor and sweetness. She dared a small swallow and her lips involuntarily quirked into a smile. "Mmm," she said, and sipped again. "This is exquisite!"

"It is indeed," Lucas replied, making his own drink. "The Slurpee is the cure for any distress."

She chuckled. "I think you may be right."

They paid for their drinks, then left the store, retracing their steps toward the parking lot. When they reached the sign, Lucas turned to her, raising his Slurpee in a mock toast. "To our brave adventure!" he crowed. "And to the lovely damsel who clearly has no problem saving herself."

Guin's cheeks flushed at his words, but she managed to touch her cup to his. "Thank you. The Slurpee was indeed a magical cure."

"Told ya!" Lucas cried, his smiling eyes catching her own. "I'm always right in matters of sweet, delicious, oversize beverages."

"I never doubted it for a moment," she teased back. Then, on impulse, she leaned forward and kissed him quickly on the cheek. "Thank you," she whispered in his ear.

"No, thank *you*," Lucas replied, kissing her back.

This time squarely on the mouth.

CHAPTER 33

Guinevere broke from the kiss, backing up in horror. "Sir! You forget yourself!" she protested, covering her mouth with her hand.

Lucas stared down at her, confused. "What do you mean?" he asked. "I thought—"

"You kissed me," she cried. "You can't kiss me. I belong to Arthur."

"You're with Arthur?" Lucas's eyes widened. "Why didn't you tell me that?"

"You never asked."

"Oh, man." He groaned, pacing the parking lot. "Man, oh, man. I'm sorry. I had no idea. Arthur's my friend. I never would have kissed you if I'd known."

He looked so distressed that Guinevere's heart softened. "I know," she assured him. "It was my fault for kissing you first. I only meant it as a friendly gesture. I never meant..." She moaned. "Oh, winds and rain! I'm as wicked as the Google says I am!"

Lucas shot her a confused look. "What?"

"Never mind," she said quickly. "It matters not. But know that I love Arthur with all my heart." She gave Lucas a sorry smile. "You're very nice. And you make me laugh. But my heart belongs to him."

"I totally get it." Lucas nodded slowly. "Arthur's a lucky guy. I hope we can still be friends."

"Of course," she cried, relief washing over her. "We will be friends. But now I must go find Sophie. I've been gone too long and she must be worried."

"Do you want me to come with you?"

"No!" She shook her head, more violently than she'd meant to. But still—she needed to get away from Lucas, and fast. "I mean, I'll be fine. Thank you."

Lucas looked like he wanted to argue, but thought better of it. "Okay," he said. "I'll see you later. And Guin?"

"Yes?"

"I'm really sorry."

She smiled at him, her heart aching a little. "Me too."

Guinevere turned and headed through the parking lot, back

to the rescue area. She didn't see Sophie; maybe she'd started searching without her. She walked into the woods, calling Stu's name, even though she knew he wouldn't answer.

As she walked, her mind raced, thinking about what had just happened. Thankfully no one had seen them—that would have been a disaster. Arthur already doubted her. The last thing she wanted to do was prove him right.

As Guinevere walked, darkness started to fall, and she paused, realizing that while lost in thought, she'd ended up lost in the woods as well. She scanned the trees around her, searching for some sign of life. Some other rescue group, perhaps. But the forest seemed as silent as the grave and just as dark.

She turned and attempted to head back in the direction from which she came. "Hello?" she called out, but there was no answer. How far had she wandered and for how long? And how big was this forest, anyway? Sophie had called it a nature preserve, saying it had miles of trails. But Guin had no idea how long a mile was.

Suddenly her ears caught a low rumbling sound, causing her heart to leap in her chest. What was that? And where was it coming from? She had no idea what sorts of beasts lurked in the darkness of this strange new world, and she had no desire to find out.

"Hello?" she cried out again. This time her voice cracked on the word. She hugged her arms around her chest. The temperature had dropped dramatically and the thin coat Sophie had let her borrow was doing little to keep out the chill. Why oh why had she been so stupid—to wander off without looking where she was going? It was really dark now, and she had no light to guide her way.

Just as Guinevere was about to despair, she caught a spark to her right. Just a small glow, but a glimmer of hope all the same. Excited, she changed directions.

"Hello?" she cried. "Is someone there? Please help me! I'm lost!"

"Over here!" a high-pitched female voice answered.

Guinevere pushed her way through a thick copse of trees and entered a clearing, where she found a small fire. A girl, some years older than herself, sat in front of it, warming her hands. With long black hair and purple eyes that seemed to glow in the firelight, she was perhaps the most beautiful girl Guinevere had ever seen and, at the same time, appeared strangely familiar. Then Guin noticed she was wearing the same uniform as the other girls who attended Sophie's school. Perhaps she'd seen her by the football field earlier that day.

She approached eagerly. "Thank the goddess I found you!" she exclaimed, dropping to her knees to warm herself by the fire. The heat felt good against her frigid skin.

The girl remained silent, watching her with intense, catlike eyes. A little unnerved, Guinevere rambled on. "I was lost in the woods and have been trying desperately to find my way back to the place with the 7-Eleven," she added. "Do you by chance know the way?"

Silence. A chill tripped up Guinevere's spine, though she wasn't sure why. Only that suddenly the fire didn't seem so warm.

"Um, do you know Sophie?" she tried again. "I came here with her and we got separated. She's probably worried about—"

"You're very beautiful," the girl interrupted, still watching her intensely. "No wonder he likes you."

Guinevere tensed, wondering if she'd made a mistake approaching this stranger. "What?" she asked, her voice trembling. "What are you talking about?" Something was wrong here. Really wrong. "You know what?" she added, rising to her feet. "Never mind. I'm sure I can find my own way back."

She turned to leave . . . only to have a bolt of lightning crash down in front of her, inches from where she stood.

Guinevere leaped back, startled. She whirled to find the girl still watching her, calmly, her lips now curled into a sinister smile. Did she just . . . ? But that was impossible.

Wasn't it?

"So sorry," the girl purred. "But you're not going anywhere, Princess Guinevere." And at that very moment, Guinevere realized exactly where she'd seen her before.

And when.

"Mother, protect me!" she whispered, her heart in her throat. "You're Morgana!"

"So then I said to him, 'It's about time we have a hot *guy* at this school.' And he said..."

Sophie stifled a yawn as Ashley—aka her new-world bestie—continued to prattle on as they walked through the woods, shining their flashlights in all directions, calling Stu's name. If only the girl knew she was supposed to hate Sophie's guts. It would make things a lot easier. And quieter.

She wondered where Guin had taken off to. She'd turned around for one second so the princess could talk to Arthur, and when she'd turned back she was nowhere to be found. Though neither was Arthur. Was it too much to hope that Guin had succeeded in her mission and they were already back home?

"And then he took my hand and kissed it. Like something out of a movie!"

Evidently not, since her world was still doomed.

She turned to Ashley. "Look," she said brightly. "There's two paths! Why don't you take that one and I'll take this one! Then we'll cover double the ground."

Ashley glanced down the path hesitantly. "We're supposed to stay with our partners...."

THE ONCE AND FUTURE GEEK

"We are! We're just . . . separating for a second. And then we'll meet back here."

Please go, please go, please go, she begged mentally.

Suddenly a wind whipped through the forest. A blankness seemed to wash over Ashley's face.

"How about I take this path?" she suggested in a flat voice. "And you take that one?"

Sophie stared at her. So shocked she was dumbstruck. Then somehow, she found a way to nod. "Great idea."

And with that, Ashley was skipping happily down the path, leaving Sophie behind. Sophie watched her go, newfound wonder washing over her. Had her weird powers actually worked here—in the twenty-first century? How cool would that be? Maybe she needed to try them on Arthur . . .

A terrified cry broke through the darkness. Sophie froze. Was that Ashley? Had Sophie sent the poor girl into harm's way? But no. It sounded more like . . .

Guin burst from the bushes, eyes wide and terrified.

"Run!" she cried. "It's Morgana!"

Sophie's heart skipped a beat. Morgana? The sorceress? The ultimate villain that had slaughtered her and her friends in *Camelot's Honor* just a few days ago?

She was here? In real life?

Sophie dug in her heels, switched directions, and tore off after

Guinevere as fast as she could. The cold wind whipped through her hair, stinging her ears, but she pressed forward, knowing both of their lives could depend on it. After all, she'd seen what Morgana could do in a video game. And in real life, as Merlin said, there were no do-overs.

They crashed through the underbrush, dodging trees. Running so fast that for a moment Sophie actually thought they might have a chance to get away. But then she felt an odd tingling at the base of her skull. As if she could actually feel the sorceress gaining ground behind them. Which was so not good. Guin and Sophie were both tiring. They wouldn't be able to run much farther....

"In here!" Guin cried, grabbing Sophie's arm. She almost lost her footing as the princess dragged her to a small ranger station, nestled in the woods. Thank goodness Guin had seen it. Sophie would have probably run right past.

The two girls dived through the door, which was thankfully unlocked. For a moment, Sophie held out hope a forest ranger would be there to help them, but the shack was empty. The ranger was probably out on the search.

Sophie turned off her flashlight and sank to her knees, gesturing for the princess to do the same—so they couldn't be seen through the windows. She closed her eyes, trying to listen. To hear if Morgana was near.

"I can't believe it," she whispered, half to herself. "Morgana. What is she doing here?"

But even as she asked the question, she already knew the answer—straight from *Camelot's Honor*. Morgana was always trying to kill Arthur. Which was why, in the game, they had set off to try to kill her instead.

A quest, Sophie realized with a grimace, they still hadn't managed to complete.

"But why is she after you?" she whispered to the princess. "I mean, she just wants Arthur, right?"

"But Arthur has the scabbard," Guinevere reminded her. "The scabbard protects him from harm. As long as he has it, she can't touch him."

"So she's going after you instead," Sophie concluded. "She thinks if she kidnaps you, Arthur will trade the scabbard for your life."

"And then there will be nothing to stop her from killing us all," Guinevere added miserably. "And taking over the kingdom for herself." The princess shuddered. "We can't let that happen, Sophie. We can't let her destroy my world."

Or my future, Sophie realized. With Morgana taking over, these tiny time ripples they'd been experiencing—like the absence of pepperoni pizza—would grow to tidal-wave proportions, perhaps even leading to the end of the world as they knew it.

"We need to get back to my house," she told Guinevere.

"Maybe I can contact Merlin through the video game. If anyone would know what to do, it'd be him."

Guinevere opened her mouth to reply, then clamped it shut as they heard a crashing noise outside.

"Did you think you could hide from me?" Morgana called out a moment later. "Did you think my magic wouldn't track you down?" She cackled, a harsh, bitter sound cutting through the night. "Now come out or I will *make* you come out. And I cannot promise it will be in one piece."

Sophie glanced around the cottage, searching for another exit, but saw none. They were trapped. She bit her lower lip, trying to think, her heart racing in her chest. There had to be a way to get past the sorceress. But how? They certainly weren't equipped to fight her head-on. She knew from the legends, not to mention *Camelot's Honor*, that Morgana was a powerful sorceress, and they didn't even have any weapons. Even Stu had his homemade gun when taking on King Lot.

Then again...She thought back to Ashley skipping down the path. About Stu pulling the sword from the stone. Him fighting off King Lot.

The tingling in Sophie's skull returned with a vengeance. Maybe she wasn't entirely helpless after all.

She turned to Guin. "We're getting out of here. On the count of three, get up and run as fast as you can. I'll take care of Morgana."

"But how?" Guinevere asked, scrunching up her face.

Sophie bit her lower lip. "Just trust me, okay?" she said, though in truth she wasn't sure she trusted herself.

But she had to try. Closing her eyes, she concentrated as hard as she could, just as she had when Stu pulled the sword from the stone and then again at the fight. She fixed Morgana in her mind, then pushed at the thought as hard as she could.

Stay back. Stay back. STAY BACK.

A cry of rage ripped through the night. Sophie's eyes flew open. Guinevere was at the window, watching. Guinevere turned, her eyes wide. "She's tripped over some roots. Now's our chance!"

The two girls sprang from the cabin, sprinting with all their might. From behind, they could hear Morgana screaming. Sophie dared a peek back, just in time to see the sorceress rise to her feet, her purple eyes glowing in the darkness. She raised her arms, her fingers crackling with electricity.

"You won't get away!" she cried.

Sophie grabbed Guin, pulling her to the ground. They collapsed into a pile of leaves, just in time to duck the bolt of lightning shot in their direction. Morgana screeched in rage at having missed, and for a moment, Sophie waited breathlessly for another round. But it seemed the sorceress needed some recovery time between spells. Like in the game, she had to restore her mana.

Stay back, Sophie commanded. *Get tangled in some more roots.* It couldn't hurt to be specific.

She turned to Guin. "Go. Now!"

The two girls scrambled to their feet, running as fast as they could down a winding path. Sophie prayed it would lead somewhere safe, and fast. She was exhausted and not sure how much longer she could run. Or for how long Morgana would be stuck in the roots.

Her prayers were answered as they burst onto a small road just in time to meet an oncoming car, head-on. The car swerved to avoid them, screeching to a halt.

To Sophie's surprise, her father poked his head out of the driver's-side window.

"There you are!" he cried. "What are you doing way out here? I thought I told you to come back before dark. The search party was about to start searching for *you*! Do you know how dangerous these woods are at night?"

Sophie knew. All too well. She gestured to Guin and the two of them hopped into the backseat, slamming and locking the doors behind them.

"We need to go home! Now!" Sophie cried. She peered out the window and caught movement in the bushes. Morgana must have escaped the tree roots. Their only hope was to make a quick getaway.

But Dad wasn't in such a hurry. "Home? I thought we'd go get ice cream!" he said with a smile, glancing at the girls in the rearview mirror, not making any movement to get away. Sophie wondered what her dad would do if she dove into the front seat and hit the gas pedal herself.

"Yeah, but…" Sophie glanced at Guin, then back out the window. Morgana stumbled from the forest a few yards down the road, her hair sticking out in every direction and leaves plastered to her school uniform. Not exactly the best look for an all-powerful sorceress of Arthurian legend. Sophie would have laughed if she wasn't so scared.

Morgana's eyes locked on to the car. She took a step forward.

"I have a test!" Sophie blurted out. "I have to study. Please! Let's go! Now!"

Morgana broke into a run, her steps eating up the road. Sophie winced. She was almost upon them. The sorceress stopped, raising her hands in the air, her fingertips crackling with electricity again. From beside her, Guinevere let out a frightened *eep*. Sophie couldn't breathe. Was this it? Was it game over forever?

"GO!" she screamed, one last time.

"Okay, okay," Dad muttered, stepping on the gas. "It was just a suggestion."

As they pulled away, a bolt of lightning crashed down from the sky, striking the very spot where they'd been parked only seconds before.

"Did you hear something?" Dad asked, glancing backward.

"No!" Sophie and Guin shouted in unison. Then Sophie added, "Just drive!"

Dad shook his head, mumbling something that sounded a lot like "Kids!" under his breath. Sophie collapsed in her seat, allowing herself a breath of relief as they pulled onto the main road and headed back home. That was way too close.

"How did you do that?" Guinevere hissed after Dad turned on the radio and the sounds of music blocked out their conversation from the front seat. "How did you manage to stop her?"

Sophie shivered. "I have no idea."

CHAPTER 34

Stu brandished his sword, his eyes not leaving his opponent. Circling slowly, watching, waiting for his opening. He knew from years of gaming that every villain had at least one fatal flaw. Though sadly, in real life you couldn't look it up on the internet.

And then—there it was! As his enemy raised his sword, his shield shifted ever so slightly to the right, exposing a small vulnerable spot under his chin. Just for a second, but if Stu could time it right . . .

The knight readied for another blow. *Now!* Stu sprang forward, stabbing with his blade, striking just above his enemy's throat.

"Oh yeah, baby. You're so dead!" he cried triumphantly.

Sir Gawain grabbed the sword with a gloved hand and playfully shoved it away. "Not bad, not bad," he said, pulling off his helmet. He threw Stu a grin. "Keep this up and we'll make a knight of you yet."

Stu lowered Excalibur, his face flushing with pride. He rubbed his shoulder; the lessons made him sore all over. But having a true master knight teach him how to fight made every ache and pain worth it.

"That's enough for today," Gawain pronounced, sheathing his sword. "After all, you've got your big meeting this afternoon. I'm sure you'll want to spend some time preparing for it."

Stu nodded, trying not to look nervous. Today was the day all the tribal lords from around Britain would come and swear their fealty to him. In exchange, he was supposed to offer them a battle plan that would protect their shores against the Saxon invaders that had been spotted just off the coast.

If only these seasoned warriors knew they were putting their people's lives in the hands of a guy whose sole war experience came from playing *Call of Duty* on the Xbox...

"I need to get out of here for a bit," he told Gawain. "Get some fresh air outside the castle walls."

"Very well, I'll have one of the lads saddle a couple of horses for us," Gawain replied, starting toward the stables. Stu stopped him.

"Actually I feel more like walking. And, no offense, but I'd like to go alone." Since becoming king, he'd been constantly surrounded by servants, guards, hangers-on. It was getting a little old, to tell the truth.

Gawain frowned. "I don't like you leaving the castle by yourself, sire. It could be dangerous."

"I won't go far. To the river and back. And I'll bring my sword, just in case." He gave the warrior a pleading look. "Just a few minutes to clear my head."

Gawain didn't look happy, but finally assented. And so Stu headed out from the castle walls, following the narrow dirt road that wound through some grassy hills and wildflower-strewn fields. The warm sun beat down on his back as he sucked in a breath of probably the freshest air he'd ever breathed in his life (even if it did smell a bit like horse manure).

It was funny; once upon a time this would have been a dream come true. To leave real life and all its pressures behind. To enter a world where he was literally king. It was as if he'd stepped into a real-life video game, just as he'd always wanted. But now that he was here? He was kind of bored. He missed his old life, complicated as it might be. He missed video games, Sophie. Even soccer, for goodness' sake.

Would Sophie ever come back? Would he ever be able to go home? Or was this it? Was this his life from now on?

He shook his head. He could dwell on all of this later. First he had to save the land from war. Once he'd finished uniting Britain, he could worry about finding a way out of this whole mess. In the meantime he should—

"Oh, alas!" interrupted a screeching female voice. "I am doomed! The raging waters threaten to consume my very soul!"

What was that? Stu frowned. He looked around, trying to determine the source of the sudden melodramatic cry. Yet there didn't appear to be anyone in sight. Then his eyes fell upon a small wooden bridge, spanning the river, just a few yards away.

The voice came again. "Is there no brave and gallant knight who will come save me in my time of need? No one to come to my aid?"

Stu ran to the bridge, leaning over and peering down. The so-called raging waters lapped lazily along the shores as the sun cast sparkles on the river's otherwise placid surface. As he watched, a rather ornate wooden rowboat drifted into view. In its belly, atop a pile of embroidered blankets, lay a girl around his age with long brown hair and a fancy-looking white gown, sobbing uncontrollably as she floated downstream.

"Alas, I am lost! Lost and dead if no one shall save me!" she called out.

Stu squinted down at her. Truth be told, she didn't appear to be in any immediate danger. The boat wasn't leaking, as far as he could tell, and the water didn't look more than a few feet deep.

"Uh, are you okay?" he called as she floated by. But her boat disappeared under the bridge before she could answer. Stu ran across to the other side to wait for her to reappear.

"If only a brave knight were to come by and see my desperate plight!" the girl's voice echoed from under the bridge.

Stu squared his shoulders, making up his mind. After all, he was supposed to be King Arthur here. And King Arthur rescued ten damsels in distress before breakfast, according to the legends. He climbed over the wooden railing and pinched his nose as he dropped down into the water.

Unfortunately for them both, his timing was a bit off and he managed to clip the side of the boat as he hit the water, causing it to capsize and throwing its passenger into the muddy river. Stu grimaced, scrambling to his feet (the water turned out to be only waist-high) and pulling a slimy reed from his hair just as a young knight astride a white horse crossed the bridge. He looked down at them, gave a small, amused-sounding snort, then urged his mare on toward the castle.

One of the men arriving for his big meeting today, Stu realized. What a great way to make a first impression.

The sound of splashing beside Stu caught his attention. He had almost forgotten about his damsel in distress. The girl had managed to right herself and was currently attempting to wade through the water in the direction the knight had gone.

"NO!" she cried. "Wait! Come back!" She thrashed toward the shore, her progress slowed as her dress caught on a fallen branch. She tugged furiously on the fabric and Stu heard a loud rip. She shrieked in fury and pounded her fists against the water's surface.

"Are you okay?" Stu asked, wondering if perhaps he'd just tried to rescue a crazy person.

She turned to him, her brown eyes blazing fire. "How could you?"

"How could I what? Save your life?"

She managed to pull herself and her soaking skirts up onto the embankment, collapsing onto the muddy shore. "I didn't need saving, you doltish dunce!"

Stu felt his hackles rise. "You could have fooled me with all that 'save me, save me' stuff you were shouting a few minutes ago."

The girl rolled her eyes. "What I mean is, I didn't need to be saved by *you*." She pulled a few sopping leaves from her hair and sighed deeply. "I had it all planned out so perfectly. I would fall helplessly into the river, just as he galloped by. I'd cry out and he'd hear me. And he'd stop and save my life—like any good knight would. And then, when his eyes fell upon me, he'd realize who I was. His true love and destiny. The girl he never meant to leave behind." She scowled at Stu. "But then you had to come along and muck it all up."

Stu would seriously never understand girls. "*Who* did you want to save you again?" he asked, bewildered. "That knight on the bridge?"

"He's not just any knight, you know. He's Sir Lancelot. The bravest knight in all the world."

Stu gulped. *That* was the legendary Sir Lancelot? King Arthur's soon-to-be number one knight and best friend? Now Stu really hoped the guy hadn't seen his botched rescue.

"And now I've missed my one chance to get him to notice me," she moaned. "You might as well have left me floating down the river to die of my own despair."

Stu squinted at her. Something about her tale suddenly struck him as strangely familiar. "What did you say your name was?"

She looked up, her big brown eyes brimming with unshed tears. "I am Elaine, Lady of Astolat."

Uh-oh. Stu stifled a grimace. According to what he'd learned in his English-lit class last year, this Elaine chick *was* supposed to float down the river and die of despair, thus inspiring a bunch of stories and paintings by famous writers and artists throughout history—from Lord Tennyson to Meg Cabot.

So much for not changing history while he was here. He half wondered if he should push her back into the water. But no, he couldn't do that to her. History was just going to have to deal with one extra nondead maiden. No big deal, right?

"Don't worry," he tried to assure her. "Someday your prince

will come. And let's face it, no guy—not even Lancelot—is worth dying for, right?"

"You're right. I'm sorry. I've been ghastly since I met you." Elaine sniffled, looking over at him with sorrowful eyes. "And here you were trying to save my life. Rescuing me from my watery grave." She stole a glance back at the castle. "Unlike *some* knights I know!" she shouted loudly.

Stu shrugged. "Well, anyone would do the same in my place."

"But they didn't! You did!" she cried, a sudden worrisome gleam sparking in her eyes. She scooted closer to him. "You're a true hero! *My* hero!"

"I don't know about—"

Elaine grabbed Stu by both ears, yanking him forward and planting a big smacking kiss on his surprised mouth. Her lips were slimy from the muddy water and her breath smelled vaguely like fish.

"Whoa! Hang on a second!" Stu cried, struggling to back away. But her fingers pinched his ears and wouldn't let go.

"O brave and noble hero who rescued me from the darkest pits of despair!" she crowed, pulling him into a headlock and rocking him against her chest. "From this day forward I shall declare you my knight and true champion!"

"Gurk!" It was about all he could say—given that his larynx was being crushed. And suddenly Stu had a pretty good idea of why Lancelot had taken off running.

Thankfully, she loosened her hold. "Did you say something, my love?"

"Um, that's very nice of you," he stammered. "But I can't be your champion. I...I..." His brain raced, trying to think of an acceptable excuse. "I...I belong to someone else!" he blurted out triumphantly. *Argue that, medieval maiden!*

Elaine dropped him like a hot potato, causing his head to slam against the riverbank. "What?" she cried angrily. "Who could this be? What vile harlot would dare to rip away my true love—my very heart?"

"Her name is Princess Guinevere," he announced, trying to sit back up. "We're supposed to get married."

Elaine cocked her head in question. "I thought she was betrothed to King Arthur."

"Right. And I *am* King Arthur."

Elaine burst out laughing.

Stu stared at her. "What's so funny?"

"Oh, my lord, you are as amusing as you are handsome."

"I'm telling you. I am. I am King Arthur," Stu repeated, not knowing why he was even bothering.

"And I'm the Lady of the Lake," she replied. "Look. I've seen King Arthur. You, my lord, are no King Arthur."

"But I..." Stu trailed off, his eyes suddenly catching his reflection in the river.

Oh no.

He did a double take. Gone were the insta-muscles. The handsome face, the big feet. The glamour that had made him king had completely vanished—it must have washed off in the river somehow. And now only Stu Mallory's face stared back up at him.

And here he thought Merlin had been kidding when he said the glamour spell was "dry-clean only."

Stu cringed. This was not good. The lords of the realm would soon be gathering in the war room, all of them depending on him to lead them to battle. If he didn't show up looking like the same King Arthur who pulled the sword from the stone . . . well, they were going to start asking questions. In fact, he'd probably be lucky to avoid being burned at the stake for trying to trick them.

He had to find Merlin. Get a new glamour before the meeting started. If he was lucky, maybe he could find him back at the Crystal Cave. He still had the directions that Sophie had given him before she left.

"I'm sorry," he said to Elaine as he scrambled to his feet. "It's been real. But I've got to go now. I've got something super important to take care of and I don't have much time."

She rose to meet him, her gown and hair still dripping wet. "I'll go with you."

"That's *really* not necessary."

"You saved my life. I'm in your debt."

Stu raked a frustrated hand through his hair. "Do what you want. But don't slow me down. I'm under a major time crunch here."

And with that, he turned and started back up to the bridge, Elaine racing after him eagerly. "Thank you, m'lord. You won't regret it!"

But Stu was pretty sure he already did.

CHAPTER 35

After a bleary night of little sleep, Sophie dragged herself into school the next day, still haunted by the nightmares that had chased her until dawn. Horrible visions of Morgana tracking Stu down and unleashing her fury upon him—with Sophie powerless to stop her. She'd woken up screaming her mother's name. As if Mom could somehow hear her and come to her aid.

But her mother was long gone. Sophie was on her own.

She somehow made her way to history class, plopping down at the nearest desk. To make her morning even better, the teacher announced a pop quiz, walking up and down the aisles, handing out the papers.

"You with us this morning, Miss Sawyer?" the teacher asked,

stopping in front of Sophie's desk. "Or are you planning to spend A-period napping?"

Sophie's cheeks burned as her classmates giggled. "I'm fine," she replied, taking the test from the teacher. At least it would probably be easy. This was her best class, after all. She was sure whatever was on the quiz would be a cakewalk.

1) In what year did the Saxons conquer England?

...Or not.

Sophie looked up from the quiz, scanning the room. Sure enough, everyone else was busy circling and writing in answers, as if nothing were amiss. Even though Sophie knew for a fact that the Saxons never conquered England. Namely, because King Arthur had defeated them during his reign.

Uh-oh.

2) Name the Saxon emperor who married High Queen Morgana.

Saxon emperor? Queen Morgana? *Oh no.* This was not good.

3) What was the real name of the impostor king who disappeared three days after his crowning and ended up being burned at the stake for treason?

a) Lancelot

b) Gawain

c) Stuart

Sophie almost fell out of her chair. *Oh no! No, no, no!* She peered over at the test-taker next to her, praying she was somehow mistaken. But no, he was circling C.

Her stomach lurched. She had to get out of here and figure out what had gone wrong. Raising a hand, she asked, "Can I go to the nurse? I think I'm going to puke."

It wasn't far from the truth.

The teacher sighed, but gestured to the hall pass sitting on his desk. "You'll have to make up the quiz tomorrow."

Tomorrow. There might not be a tomorrow the way things were shaping up.

History could spiral onto an alternative track. One where your future may no longer exist. Meaning you may no longer exist.

And here she'd thought the pepperoni-pizza thing was bad.

After exiting the classroom, she broke into a run, racing to the school library. After signing up with the librarian, she plopped down at a terminal and pulled up Google. Hands shaking, she typed "King Arthur" into the search box and held her breath.

KING ARTHUR: The name given by impostor Stuart Mallory, who attempted to steal the throne from Queen Morgana after pulling

the sword from the stone. Three days after his coronation, the day
before he was supposed to lead Britain to victory over the Saxons,
he disappeared. The battle was a massacre and eventually led to the
Saxons taking over England. The impostor king was soon found and
burned at the stake.

Sophie leaned back in her chair, hardly able to breathe. Something had gone wrong. Really, really wrong. And it had led to a disaster of epic proportions. Not to mention the end of her friend's life.

Her mind treated her to a vision of poor Stu, all alone, strapped to a stake, the flames licking at his feet as Morgana watched, cackling in victory.

She couldn't let this happen!

Though, in a way, hadn't it happened already?

She scanned the website again, heart pounding, trying to figure out a plan. Though this event had technically already happened in her time, there might still be a chance to stop it from happening in Stu's. The battle against the Saxons happened three days after Stu's coronation. Which would be tomorrow! Her pulse quickened. Maybe there was still time to set things straight.

"Sophie, are you all right?"

She whirled around at the sound of the voice, surprised to see Arthur standing behind her.

"You!" she cried, anger surging through her. She sprang from her seat and grabbed him by his collar, shaking him with all her might. "This is all your fault!"

"Quiet!" the librarian scolded from behind her desk. But Sophie was through being quiet. She was going to knock some sense into this little once and future twerp's head if it was the last thing she did. She had one more chance to save Stu and she wasn't about to blow it.

Arthur looked at her guiltily. "What?" he asked.

"Do you have any idea what you've done?" Sophie demanded. "What your little field trip here has cost the world?" She grabbed him by the ear and dragged him over to the computer. "Read this!"

Arthur scanned the web page and paled. "But that isn't right."

"No, it's not right. It's not right at all. But it's happening all the same. All because you decided you wanted to play football."

Arthur stared at the computer, a dismayed look on his face. "'The Saxons slaughtered everyone,'" he read. "'Women, children. The few who survived were forced into slavery or left to starve.'" He swallowed hard. "I wonder if Sara and her children escaped."

"Guess you'll never know," Sophie replied, her voice laced with sarcasm. "But hey—at least you guys will be a shoo-in for the championship. If there's any world left to play in, that is, after this all shakes out."

"But I didn't mean . . . I mean, I thought . . . what about Stu?" Arthur blurted out. "He was supposed to take my place. I figured he'd do a better job than me," he added, looking crestfallen. "Seeing how terribly I've handled everything so far. To be honest, I'm not sure I'm even cut out to be king. I think Merlin might have made a mistake."

She stared at him in surprise, the truth hitting her with the force of a ten-ton truck. Suddenly she understood, for the first time, exactly why Arthur had refused to go home. Not because he was having fun here. Not because he was afraid for his life. (Though both those things might be true.) But deep down, she realized, he was simply afraid of failing. Of letting everyone down.

She thought of the Arthur she'd met back in medieval times. Abused by his foster brother, the butt of every knight's jokes. All his life he'd been told he was nothing. Of course he'd be riddled with doubt.

"You underestimate yourself," she stated, realizing it was time for a good old-fashioned pep talk. "All your life people treated you as a nobody. But look at what you've done here—in only a few days. You proved yourself a born leader—rallying the football team to search for Stu. And you showed your skill in battle, leading your team to victory on the football field." She wagged her finger at him. "In just a few days you got everyone to love you, honor you, respect you. Trust me, that's not easy in junior high."

"But—"

She waved him off. She wasn't finished yet. "So why not take all that you've accomplished here and use it back home? When you put your mind to something, Arthur, you're unstoppable."

"But you forget, I *do* fail at home," he said miserably. "The Google says I die, killed on the battlefield after my knights turn against me."

"We all die," Sophie reminded him. "What matters is how we live. Do you want to be remembered as Britain's most legendary king? Or would you rather die in obscurity, reminiscing about your glory days of school sports?"

She paused for breath, wondering suddenly if she should try her powers on him. Magically convince him to do the right thing. But no. She couldn't do that to him. He had to want this himself, or it would never work. At least not long-term.

For a moment, Arthur was silent and she held her breath, praying she hadn't gone too far. Then he squared his jaw and straightened his shoulders, his face taking on a determined expression that made Sophie's heart soar with excitement. Now *this* was the King Arthur of legends!

"You're right," he declared, so loudly he earned another shush from the librarian. "I've spent far too long running away. It's time

I go home and make things right." He glanced at the computer screen. "I'm not too late, am I?"

"I'm not sure," Sophie admitted. "Merlin told me that our two time periods run on parallel tracks. Meaning the big battle against the Saxons—the one that will change history—will be fought tomorrow morning. *If* we get back there now and you lead your troops to victory—well, there may still be time to set things right."

CHAPTER 36

Arthur dove through the halls, a man on a mission. Now that he'd made up his mind to go home, he knew there was no time to waste. According to Sophie, the tribal lords were assembling, waiting for his guidance. The entire history of the world depended on his making this meeting on time.

But he couldn't go without Guinevere.

He stopped short at the cafeteria, scanning the early lunch crowd. He found the princess, sitting alone at a far table, staring down at her hands. His heart leaped. There she was. The most wonderful girl in any century. He'd never love anyone like he loved her. He just prayed she'd forgive him for being such a fool.

"Guinevere!" he cried over the din of the cafeteria, pushing through throngs of students, ignoring their protests as he made his way to his princess. She looked up at his voice, her blue eyes brightening.

"Arthur!" she cried. "I've been looking everywhere for you!"

"And I for you," he admitted, his heart practically bursting from his chest at her words. She'd been looking for him! That meant he wasn't too late. He still had a chance to say he was sorry. To tell her he wanted her to be his wife and that he was ready to go home once and for all. "Look, Guin," he said, sitting down beside her and grabbing her hand in his. "We have to talk."

"Yes . . . ?" she asked, her trembling voice threaded with hope.

"Please forgive me," he said. "I've been selfish and cowardly, running away from my destiny. But you were right. And I'm done running."

Her hand tensed. "What are you saying?"

"I'm saying it's time to go home," he replied, flashing her a grin. "It's time for me to take the throne and become King of England."

She stared at him for a moment, searching his face, as if looking for some kind of trick. But then she allowed herself a smile—a huge smile that lit up the entire cafeteria. "Oh, Arthur!" she cried.

"I'm so sorry for ever doubting you, Guin. I trust you with my life. I know you would never betray me. No matter what the

Google says." He leaned forward, until their lips were inches away. "I love you, Guinevere. I love you more than—"

Beep, beep!

Startled, they broke apart, interrupted by an entire cafeteria full of beeping. Arthur scanned the room, confused, as all the students around them reached for their cell phones.

"What's going on?" Guinevere asked, looking startled.

Arthur shrugged. He knew only a little about cell phones. They were designed to deliver messages and photos and sometimes videos to others. He watched as the students stared down at their phones, laughing and jeering in delight. Whatever message they had been sent was evidently highly entertaining.

Then, one by one, their eyes lifted from their phones...

...turning straight to him and Guinevere.

Arthur's heart started pounding. Was the cell-phone message directed at him somehow? Were they laughing at his expense? It seemed impossible, but he couldn't think of another explanation.

"Arthur?" Guinevere cried, looking a little frightened. "What's going on here?"

Arthur rose to his feet and grabbed a phone from a nearby student, ignoring his protests. He pressed a button, and a moment later the video started playing on the small screen. Guinevere peered over his shoulder, then gasped loudly, falling away.

Arthur dropped the phone and it hit the ground with a loud

clatter. But the video kept playing, as if mocking him from the floor. A video of his beloved Guinevere . . .

. . . kissing Lucas.

He staggered backward, his world spinning out of control.

Lucas and Guinevere?

Guinevere and Lucas?

It couldn't be!

Somehow he managed to turn to the princess, his whole body shaking so hard he was amazed he was still standing upright.

"After all you said," he managed to squeak out. "After all you promised." His voice cracked and he couldn't continue.

"Arthur—" Guinevere tried, tears rolling down her cheeks. "It's not what you think!"

"Did you kiss my best friend?" he demanded. "Did you betray me like the Google said you would?"

"It wasn't like that! Yes, Lucas kissed me but I—"

"Get out of my sight!" he cried. "I never want to see you again."

He pushed past her, fleeing the cafeteria, the laughter and jeers burning his ears—the dreadful video replaying in his brain, over and over.

Lucas kissing Guinevere. Guinevere kissing Lucas.

Sophie was right. You couldn't run from your destiny.

CHAPTER 37

Guinevere had no idea how she managed to keep her dignity as she walked slowly toward the cafeteria exit, feeling the stares of the other students burning into her back. It was all she could do not to break into a run—tears streaming down her cheeks. But she was a princess. She had to find a way to rise above.

But though she kept her head held high, inside she was crumbling, her heart breaking into a thousand pieces. They'd been so close—Arthur had wanted to go home and make things right at last. He'd wanted to marry her and work to save the kingdom. Everything they'd ever talked about—every dream they'd ever had—was *this* close to coming true. And then the video had come and ruined it all.

If only the video had played a few seconds longer—showing her breaking from the kiss and telling Lucas it was a mistake. That she loved Arthur and would never betray him. But no. Whoever had shot the video shortened it so Arthur would believe she was every bit as wicked as history said she was. And now everything was ruined.

She wondered what Arthur would do. Would he still return home? She hoped so—the kingdom did not deserve to be punished for her mistakes. She thought of Sara and her new baby and her other children. If her moment of weakness had hurt them, Guin would never be able to forgive herself.

As she wandered down the hall, she came across a small chapel, doors wide open but completely empty. She found herself drawn inside, sinking down into one of the pews, head bowed. When reading her story online, she'd discovered that after the whole thing with Lancelot had been made public, she'd ended up joining a convent, swearing off men for the rest of her life. Maybe that wasn't such a bad idea.

But oh, Arthur.

Her heart ached as she tried to imagine life without him at her side. He'd been her best friend for so long—and they'd almost had a chance to become more. But now—

"Um, Guinevere?" A male voice cut into the room. She whirled around, surprised; she hadn't heard anyone enter. A skinny black-haired boy with a pockmarked face hovered in the doorway, looking awkward and uncomfortable.

"Yes?" she asked, rising to her feet.

"I was sent to find you," he told her. "Arthur wants to talk to you."

Guinevere's heart thudded. "He does?" she asked, her voice barely a whisper. She told herself she shouldn't get her hopes up—that he probably just wanted to yell at her some more. But at least it would give her a chance to urge him to go home. To not let others suffer because of her mistake.

The boy nodded. "He's in the auditorium," he explained. "I can take you to him."

"Thank you," she said, gushing, exiting the pew and following him out the door. "I really appreciate you coming and telling me." She paused. "What's your name?"

"Mortimer," the boy replied, his face coloring to a pink blush. He shifted from foot to foot. "Um, so yeah, let's go."

Guinevere practically skipped down the hall as she followed Mortimer to the auditorium. Her mind raced with the words she should say to Arthur. Should she beg forgiveness? Try to explain what had really happened? Or just urge him to keep with the plan of going home? Who knew? Maybe he'd already talked to Lucas, who'd cleared things up. Maybe he had already forgiven her.

Oh, she hoped so! She really hoped so.

Mortimer stopped in front of a set of double doors, a sign proclaiming AUDITORIUM above them. He gestured with his hand. "After you," he said.

Guinevere thanked him and pulled open the door, her heart beating wildly in her chest. "Arthur?" she called out as she stepped into the darkened room. "You wanted to talk to me?"

Suddenly the door slammed shut behind her and a spotlight clicked on, illuminating a lone figure on the stage. Her heart froze as she realized it wasn't Arthur at all.

It was Morgana.

CHAPTER 38

W here was he? Sophie glanced at the library clock for the tenth time, then at the door. Didn't he realize how short on time they were? If Arthur missed his big meeting with the tribal lords, that was it. It would be too late. The Saxons would win the war, history would be altered forever, and Stu would never have a chance to come home. She paced the library floor, wringing her hands. *Come on, Arthur!*

Maybe she should have gone with him to find Guinevere—refused to let him out of her sight. But he'd seemed so passionate—so determined to make good on his promise to fulfill his destiny, she'd figured she'd give him the benefit of the doubt.

Had it been a mistake?

"No. Think positively," she whispered to herself.

At least she could prepare for the moment when they did return, she decided, settling back down at the computer. She typed: *www.camelotcode.com.*

Clicking enter, she leaned back in her chair, waiting for the page to load. But instead of the familiar blank page with the web counter she'd seen before, she got an unexpected message.

Web Page Not Found

Wait, what? That wasn't right. Maybe she'd typed the URL in wrong. She tried again, this time being careful to type in every letter correctly. But no luck.

She leaned back in her chair again, her mind spinning as she stared at the message. This couldn't be. It was impossible and yet . . . She pulled out her phone, scrolling through old texts to find the one Merlin had sent her with the web address. But in her heart, she knew, even as she searched, that she hadn't gotten the website wrong.

The website no longer existed.

Time had changed. History had changed. And in this new world, the website Merlin had created no longer existed. Meaning, no matter how much Arthur wanted to go back, he couldn't.

And everything would end up like *Wikipedia* said it would.

She moaned, sweat breaking out on her forehead as she tried

the web page one more time. Maybe something was wrong. Maybe the Wi-Fi was down. But no, the other pages loaded up perfectly. This one just wasn't there.

"No!" she cried. "This can't be happening." She banged her head on the keyboard in frustration. How could she have gotten this close—only to have yet another door slam in her face?

Stu, I'm sorry, she thought. *I don't know what else I can do.*

She squeezed her eyes shut. She needed to think—to come up with a plan. But they were running out of time. She'd been so busy, she realized, concentrating on getting Arthur to go home that she'd taken for granted that actually getting him back would be simple.

She loaded up her browser again, this time typing in the *Camelot's Honor* web page. Maybe if she downloaded the game onto the school computer, somehow she could reach Merlin and he could tell her what to do.

But that web page was gone as well. There was no record of a game called *Camelot's Honor* ever existing. Which made sense, she supposed. After all, if there was no King Arthur in this new world, then there would be no game created around his life. Meaning her only connection to medieval times had been shredded forever.

As she stared at the computer screen miserably, a tall shadow crossed behind her. The librarian, she guessed, coming to complain about her outburst. She sighed deeply, rubbing her eyes.

"I'm sorry," she muttered, before the librarian could reprimand her. "I'll be quiet. I'm just having a tough time here."

"That's what I heard," replied the figure behind her, in a strangely familiar voice. One Sophie hadn't heard in the last five years.

"Mom?" she cried, spinning around in her chair.

CHAPTER 39

Arthur plopped down onto the locker room bench, his heart heavy and his mind tormented. He knew he had to get to Sophie—that time was of the essence—but at the same time, he couldn't just leave things here in such a mess.

How could Guinevere do this to him? How could she betray him for another—no, not just another! His best friend! It hurt more than he could bear.

It was hard to believe how excited he'd been just a few minutes ago—imagining a whole future with her by his side. He could have faced it all—even death—if he'd known that she loved him and would be there for him till the end.

But now, what was left? He'd fulfill his destiny, sure. Too many people were counting on him for him to just walk away. But how could he find the strength to do it, without Guin by his side?

"I thought I might find you here."

He whirled around to see Lucas enter the locker room. Arthur felt his hands involuntarily clench into fists. Half of him wanted to punch the boy who was supposed to be his friend. But at the same time, how could he blame him? History was playing out exactly as it was supposed to. And if Guinevere really loved Lucas more than Arthur? Well, who was he to stand in their way? More than anything in the world, he wanted her to be happy. And if she was happy with Lucas, then he needed to face that reality along with the rest.

"Hey," he said with a heavy sigh.

"Look, man, I wanted to tell you. I mean, right after it happened." Lucas ran a hand through his hair. "Seriously, I didn't know you guys were together. I never would have made a move if I did. You're my friend and friends don't do that."

"I don't blame you," Arthur replied, staring down at his hands.

"Well, don't blame her, either," Lucas urged. "'Cause trust me—she was having none of my moves. Totally flipped out on me for kissing her."

Arthur looked up. "What?" he whispered, a strange hope welling inside of him against his better judgment.

"See for yourself," Lucas said, handing him a cell phone. The video began to play again and Arthur winced as he watched the kiss. He started to turn away.

"Keep watching," Lucas scolded. "This is the uncut version, off Mortimer's phone. Little sneak. I caught him laughing about it in the hall. He thought he was so cool, sending that to everyone. But don't worry, we'll have the last laugh. Once I see what other videos he's got on his phone."

Arthur nodded, forcing his eyes back to the screen. Just in time to watch Guin break away from the kiss, her face awash in horror, just as Lucas had said.

I love Arthur with all my heart.

The words were simple, but they made his heart soar. How could he have ever thought of leaving her behind—that she would be better off without him? She loved him! She hadn't betrayed him at all! The Google was wrong. Everyone was wrong. He should have trusted his heart from the beginning. Trusted her.

"I have to find her!" he cried. "Before it's too late!"

"You're already too late."

The boys whirled around to see Mortimer standing in the doorway. The boy gave them a smug smile.

"What did you say?" Arthur asked in a whisper.

"Your Guinevere is gone," Mortimer declared. "Morgana has taken her back to her castle. And if you don't bring her the scabbard? You'll never see your precious princess again."

CHAPTER 40

"**M**om?"

It was a dumb question; though Sophie hadn't seen her mother in five years, there was no mistaking the woman standing in the library. She was exactly the same—same beautiful, long blond hair, same serene blue eyes. Even her face had remained ageless, without any of the crinkles Sophie's friends' mothers had at the corners of their eyes.

Sophie flew from her chair and into her mother's arms, holding on to her as tightly as she could as tears streamed down her cheeks.

"Oh, Mom!" she cried. "I've missed you so much."

She pulled away then, feeling sheepish. After all, if her mother's return was only a by-product of the time shift, her mother would have always been there in this new timeline—she would never have left in the first place. And, if so, she'd probably be pretty confused as to why her twelve-year-old daughter was suddenly hugging her like crazy.

"Um, sorry," Sophie stammered, forcing herself to regain her composure. "I know you're probably going to say I just saw you this morning and—"

"You didn't see me this morning, sweetie," her mother corrected gently. "I've only just arrived."

"You have?" Sophie asked, furrowing her brow. Her mother's appearance wasn't due to a change in history? Then why was she here?

It was then that she noticed her mother's outfit for the first time. A simple white tunic dress that fell to her feet, tied with a silver belt.

The kind of outfit you'd find in medieval times.

"Oh, Sophie," her mother said, smiling down at her, tears welling up in her own eyes. "I've missed you so much." She squeezed her back into a hug. But Sophie couldn't relax in her mother's arms. Not with her brain burning with questions.

She reluctantly pulled away. "Not that I'm not thrilled to see you, Mom," she managed to say. "But why are you here?"

Her mother's face took on a serious look. She led Sophie over to a table and sat her down. "I think you know," she told her. "It involves a certain time-traveling monarch?"

Sophie almost fell off her chair. "How did you . . . ?"

"I don't know the whole story," her mother admitted. "Only parts. And I just found out or I would have been here sooner. Merlin chose to hide what was going on, hoping to fix things himself. However, the last time shift was so momentous and changed so much history . . . well, it wasn't hard to see that something had gone wrong." She looked lovingly at Sophie. "You called for me last night. Do you remember?"

Sophie nodded dumbly, remembering her dream. Had it been something more?

"It was lucky you did," her mother told her. "It got me worried about you and I decided to make a trip to the Well of Dreams. It was then that I glimpsed Arthur and put two and two together."

"Well of Dreams? You know about the Well of Dreams?" Sophie's head was spinning at this point.

Her mother nodded. "There's so much I want to tell you," she said. "But first we need to—"

Suddenly the library door burst open. Arthur and Lucas stumbled into the room, white-faced and out of breath. "What's wrong?" Sophie asked, rising to her feet. She looked behind them. "Where's Guinevere?"

Arthur closed his eyes, looking miserable. "She's been—" He stopped short, opening his eyes and staring at her mother. To

Sophie's surprise, he immediately fell to his knees, bowing his head before her.

"My lady," he whispered. "You have come!"

His lady?

Strangely, Sophie's mother did not seem at all surprised by Arthur's sudden weird behavior. Instead, she rose from her chair and walked over to him, taking his hands in her own and pulling him to his feet.

"I am disappointed in you, my child," her mother scolded him gently. "What you have done, how you have acted—it is most unbecoming of knight or king."

"Knight? King?" Lucas hissed at Sophie. "Who is that lady and what is she talking about? And what does this have to do with Guinevere?"

Sophie put a finger to her lips. There would be time to bring poor Lucas up to speed later. In the meantime, she watched with, admittedly, some satisfaction as Arthur's face turned bright red at her mother's reprimand. *Go, Mom!*

"I've been a fool," Arthur admitted. "I've destroyed my country and my true love is now in the hands of my worst enemy."

"Wait, what?" Sophie asked, alarmed. "Where's Guinevere? Is she okay?"

Arthur hung his head. "Morgana has her."

Sophie's mother frowned. "This is more serious than I thought," she declared. "We must get you back immediately."

Arthur looked up at her, his eyes filled with hope. "Then it's not too late?" he breathed. "I can still set things right?"

"It is never too late for one with a brave soul and a pure heart," she assured him. "Are you truly ready to meet your destiny head-on, no matter what the cost to your personal happiness?"

Arthur nodded furiously. "I'll do anything. Just give me a chance. Please!"

Her mom released his hands. "Then, Arthur of Pendragon, it is time for you to go home."

"But how?" Sophie blurted out. "The website is down!"

Arthur turned to her. "Sophie . . . she is one of the Companions," he informed her. "She doesn't need a website."

Sophie looked at her mother in confusion. "A what?"

Her mother gave her a rueful smile. "I'm sorry, sweetie," she said. "I know I have a lot to explain. Our time is short, but let me tell you what I can." She turned to Arthur. "This is something you need to hear as well."

Sophie wondered at first if Arthur was going to protest—say they didn't have time to waste. But instead, he just nodded. Evidently one did not argue with a "Companion"—whatever that was. Her mom gestured for all three of them to sit around the table.

"You may have heard of Arthur being called the once and future king," she began. "And this is true. The Arthur you see here is not the first. Nor will he be the last. His great spirit has been reborn many times, throughout the ages—whenever the world is in need of a true hero with a good heart." She smiled lovingly at Arthur, who stared back at her in adoration.

"But," she continued, "there are many others out there, filled with greed and lust for power, who wish to destroy this precious spirit in order to bring about a lawless world they can rule for their own purposes."

"People like Morgana," Sophie surmised.

"Yes," her mother agreed. "And so Viviane, the Lady of the Lake, in her divine wisdom, commissioned a sacred sect of druid warriors to travel the strands of time and watch over this spirit during each and every rebirth. They call us the Camelot Companions."

Sophie felt a thrill trickle up her spine. She thought back to that night, five years ago, when her mother had left. When she told Sophie she had to go and save the world. Though she liked to imagine it, Sophie had no idea she'd meant it literally!

"I was never supposed to meet your father," her mother confessed. "I was here on assignment, but I was never supposed to fall in love, never meant to have a child. It is frowned upon for Companions to have ties to the mortal world. It creates complications when we're called away." She sighed deeply. "You can't imagine how hard it was for me to leave you. But my mission was too important. Morgana had stolen the scabbard from Uther

Pendragon and sent him to his grave. If we hadn't worked to get it back from her, she would have used it to bring England to its knees. Arthur would have been slain and the world thrown into a thousand years of chaos." She shrugged. "Not that it made it any easier to leave my baby girl behind."

"You did what had to be done," Sophie said assuredly, pride washing over her at her mom's story.

Her mother smiled. "Trust me, not a day went by in which I didn't think of you, wishing I had never left you, wondering if someday we would be reunited." She reached out and stroked her daughter's hand. "And now we are, though I wish it were under better circumstances."

Sophie took a breath. "Do you think..." she started. "Do you think I could have inherited some of your powers?"

"Why do you ask?" her mother said.

Sophie recounted her adventure with Morgana the night before, and told her about Stu's battle with King Lot, and about her somehow helping him pull the sword from the stone.

When she had finished, she realized her mother was frowning. "What's wrong?"

"It seems clear that you have indeed been given the gifts of a Companion," her mother said. "And we are very lucky, in a sense, that you were here to watch over Arthur when we could not. But, Sophie...being a Companion is not an easy life."

Sophie didn't care. She'd been given a gift. And it had saved her friends' lives. And maybe even the entire world itself. At the end of the day, that was pretty awesome.

"I think I can handle it," she declared.

Her mother laughed. "Of that I have no doubt." She reached into her pocket and pulled out a small, clothbound book, handing it to Sophie. "It's a primer," she explained. "It will give you some background on the Companions and also some beginner spells to try. Once you've mastered those, I'll send you a new volume."

"Whoa!" Sophie flipped through the book, amazed, and paused on a familiar page. "Wait, this is that bird spell! The same one I used to do in *Camelot's Honor* when I was trying to fight Morgana." She looked up. "I don't know what to say."

"Say you'll help me rescue Guinevere!" Arthur broke in. "If you really have powers . . . well, I'll need all the help I can get!"

Sudden excitement stirred in Sophie's heart. She looked to her mother. "Can I?"

Her mother's brow furrowed, but she nodded. "As much as I'd like to save you from hardship, this was clearly your quest from the start. It is only right to allow you to see it through to the end." She paused, then added, "Unfortunately, I won't be able to come with you."

Sophie's heart sank. "What? Why not?"

"My sisters and I must start to pull together the strings of time that have become unraveled by all of this. Every ripple of change could become a tidal wave in another era. Time must be set right."

"I understand," Sophie said. As much as she didn't want to leave her mother again—so soon after she'd found her—she knew she had her own destiny to fulfill. "Will I see you again?" she asked, her voice a little shaky, afraid of what her mother might answer.

"Of course," her mother said, leaning over to kiss the top of Sophie's head. "I promise, no matter what, I will find you. And then we will talk. For real."

Sophie grinned widely. "I can't wait." She turned to Arthur. "You're ready for this?"

"I was born ready."

"Wait! What about me?" Lucas butted in. Everyone turned in surprise, having forgotten he was even in the room. "I want to help Guinevere, too," he declared. Then muttered under his breath, "And maybe someone could explain what the heck is going on?"

CHAPTER 41

"Stu!"

Stu whirled around, his mouth dropping open in shock as his eyes fell upon the best sight he'd seen since first arriving in medieval times. Sophie herself, running toward Merlin's Crystal Cave.

As soon as she reached him, she threw her arms around him, almost knocking him over with her enthusiastic hug. "You're here! You're actually here!" she cried.

"I've *been* here!" he reminded her, trying not to laugh. "You're the one who's been MIA."

"Oh. Right. Sorry about that," she said as she released him. "We ran into some...complications. But we're here. Me, Arthur—even Lucas." She turned and gestured to the two boys who were stepping out of the woods. "Don't worry, we've caught Lucas up on everything that's happened so far."

"Wow. I can't tell you how happy I am to see you," Stu admitted. "I came here looking for Merlin but he's nowhere to be found. I was beginning to lose hope."

"So this is the guy who's been pretending to be me?" Arthur asked, giving Stu a critical once-over. "He doesn't look anything like me."

"Yeah, Stu, what happened to your disguise?" Sophie asked.

Stu blushed. "It's a long story. But it doesn't matter now. You guys got here just in time." He turned to Arthur. "You have to get to the castle. The tribal lords are all gathering. They're waiting to hear your battle plan against the invading Saxons."

To Stu's surprise, Arthur shook his head. "The tribal lords will have to wait," he declared. "Morgana has kidnapped Guinevere and taken her to her castle. We have to rescue her before we even think of doing anything else."

Stu raised an eyebrow. "Uh, I don't know, dude. The Saxons are on their way. And if you don't lead the men to battle, you're going to get completely slaughtered."

"He's right," Sophie said. "Remember what we read on *Wikipedia*. If the Saxons win the battle, everything will be ruined. People will die. The kingdom will be taken over. You'll be burned at the stake."

Arthur slammed his fist against a nearby tree. "But

Guinevere," he moaned. "It's my fault she was kidnapped. And I'm the only one who can save her."

Everyone fell silent for a moment. Then Stu stole a glance over at Sophie, an idea forming in his mind. "Are you sure about that?" he asked. Sophie shot him a surprised look. He shrugged. "I mean, *we* could do it, right?"

"You?" Arthur sputtered, in an insulted voice. "But you have no training."

"Actually, that's not true," Stu replied slowly, his mind now racing with a plan. "In fact, I think Merlin's been training us for this fight for years." He turned to Sophie, his eyes shining. "Right, Soph? I mean, who knows better than us how to take down Morgana?"

Sophie gnawed on her lower lip. "Well, at least the video-game version."

"But we can use the same strategy in real life," Stu said, excitement rising. "I've been practicing my swordsmanship with Gawain since I got here. I'm really good now!"

"Well, I do have my mom's spell book," Sophie mused. "It even has that bird spell from the game."

Stu raised an eyebrow. "Wait. Your mother?"

"Oh yeah. Long story but she's back," Sophie replied. "One of the better things that happened since you were gone."

"I'll say," Stu marveled.

"In any case," Sophie continued, "without Merlin, we don't

have a healer. There's no way we can survive the fight without him."

Arthur frowned. "Where is Lord Merlin, anyway?"

"I haven't seen him since the sword-and-the-stone thing," Stu admitted. "It's like he totally disappeared."

"That's very odd," Arthur said. "Merlin's too old to travel much. He's always here at the Crystal Cave. Using his magic box...um, computer," he corrected.

The four of them fell silent. Then Lucas looked up. "His computer," he said. "Is it connected to the internet?"

Arthur looked at him blankly. But Stu knew the answer to this one. "It must be," he said. "Otherwise he wouldn't be able to play *Camelot's Honor*."

"Maybe we can find a clue there," Lucas suggested. "Does he have a Facebook? Twitter? Or maybe we can hack his e-mail."

Stu looked at his stepbrother admiringly. "Now you're thinking like a geek!"

The four of them ran into the Crystal Cave and followed Stu and Arthur to the back room. Once there, Lucas cleared away the clutter and sat down in front of the computer, typing furiously.

"Since when do you know anything about computers?" Stu couldn't help but ask, peering over his shoulder. "I thought your world revolved around sports."

"Um, actually a lot has changed since you were in the

twenty-first century," Sophie informed him. "In fact, the two of you aren't even stepbrothers anymore."

"Really? Does that mean I get my own room?"

"Here it is!" Lucas exclaimed. He glanced over at Arthur. "By the way, you might suggest the guy get a more hack-proof password. It only took me three tries to guess it."

"So what does his e-mail say?" Sophie interrupted. "Do you know where he is?"

"Hmm. Let's see . . . there was an e-mail exchange between him and some chick named Viviane," Lucas said. "Evidently she's pretty mad at him for not telling her about the whole Arthur switcheroo."

Stu tapped his foot impatiently. "And?"

"And it looks like she demanded he come see her in Avalon," he added. "In his last e-mail, he says he's on his way."

"Awesome. Maybe he's still there now!" Stu cried excitedly. "We can go find him and tell him about Morgana and get his help with the battle. With him on our side, I'm sure we'll win!"

"Of course!" Sophie exclaimed. "Merlin was always so insistent about needing all three of us to bring down Morgana. I bet he wasn't just talking about the video game."

"So how do we get to Avalon?" Stu asked, turning to Arthur.

Arthur looked at him blankly. "I have no idea."

"Oh," Stu said. He should have known it wouldn't be that easy. "I don't suppose you can Google Map it?" he asked Lucas.

"Unfortunately, Google Maps doesn't really cover mystical islands from a thousand years ago," Lucas replied.

"Right." They fell silent. It had all seemed so perfect! But if they couldn't find Merlin...

"Oh, Lord Stuart? Where art thou?"

Ugh. Stu groaned as Elaine burst into the cave, skipped over to the group, and threw her arms around his waist, looking up at him with big, pathetic, puppy-dog eyes. Just the thing to make the bitter moment complete.

"Uh, who's this?" Sophie asked.

"Who are *you*?" Elaine demanded, giving Sophie a sour look. "And why are you bothering my lord and protector?"

Stu sighed, working to pry her hands from his body. "Chill, Elaine," he commanded. "This is Sophie. The friend I was telling you about."

Elaine narrowed her eyes. "Oh. You," she said disdainfully. "I remember you from the joust."

Sophie matched her gaze. "You mean the time you were rooting for Stu to die?"

"Um, hello?" Arthur interrupted. "We're wasting valuable time here. Guinevere needs to be rescued. And if you can't do it without Merlin, then I'm coming with you. At least this way we'll have extra muscle and maybe—"

"Ooh, Merlin! I love Merlin!" Elaine interrupted. "He used to always show up at Avalon with these things he called Twinkies, which, if you haven't tried them, are the best food in the entire world!"

"Elaine, we know what Twinkies are," Stu interjected impatiently. "And we don't need—"

"Wait, did you say Avalon?" Sophie asked, looking at the girl with new eyes. "Do you know where Avalon is?"

Elaine gave her a sneer. "Of course I do," she replied haughtily. "I spent three years there, training. I told you that at the joust, remember?"

Stu whooped in excitement. Maybe saving the girl's life hadn't been such a big mistake after all. "Is it far?" he asked. "Can you take us there?"

"I would take you to the ends of the earth, if it pleased your lordship," Elaine swore, batting her eyelashes in Stu's direction.

Sophie snorted. Stu sighed.

"Okay, then here's what we're going to do," he said. "Elaine, Sophie, and I are going to head to Avalon to find Merlin and get him to help with Morgana. In the meantime, Arthur, you head back to the castle to meet with the tribal lords."

"But..." Arthur's face twisted with anguish again. "Are you sure I can't come with you? I mean, I'm the one that Morgana wants."

"Which is exactly why you can't go," Sophie reminded him gently. "Look, I know you want to be all knight in shining armor for Guin. But remember what you promised my mother. What do you think Guinevere would want you to do?"

Arthur frowned and scuffed his boot against the dirt. "Guinevere would want me to save the kingdom," he said, not sounding too happy about it.

"Don't worry," Stu chimed in. "We won't let anything happen to your princess. We'll retrieve Merlin, head to the castle, obliterate Morgana, and rescue Guinevere. She'll be back in your arms before you know it." He gave Sophie a small smirk. "And this time, not even Dad aggro will be able to stop us!"

"I'll go back to the castle with you," Lucas told Arthur. "I can help you strategize. I don't know if you know this, but I play a mean *Great Battles: Medieval* video game. And you've seen my epic skills at Risk." He turned to Stu and Sophie. "Don't worry, I've totally got King Arthur's back."

Stu shook his head in Sophie's direction. "Your mom being back, Lucas playing video games. You've been living one crazy alternate future without me."

Sophie patted him on the back. "You don't know the half of it," she said. "What are we waiting for? Let's go make history."

CHAPTER 42

The isle of Avalon was no ordinary island. Shrouded in mist, it was the magical retreat of the druid priestesses who worshiped the Great Mother. Legend had it that it was originally created by the fae folk, and that some of them still made their home there, in another dimension, between the curtains of mist. Some legends even spoke of the Holy Grail itself being hidden deep underground, beneath the mighty hill, known as the Tor.

In Sophie's time, it was a bustling tourist attraction and no longer even an island—the lake surrounding it had grown marshy over the years, becoming one with the land. But back in medieval times it still seemed mysterious, magical, and more than a little spooky.

Though Elaine was, perhaps, the most annoying person Sophie had ever met, she had to admit that they would never have found the island without her. Elaine had chartered a boat from a small lakefront village and rowed them into the mist. Sophie couldn't see her hand in front of her face when they were in the middle of the lake—never mind any island—and would have been pretty much lost forever, but somehow Elaine knew exactly the path to take, and soon they found their way to the other shore.

Sophie jumped off the boat, grateful to be back on dry land. She peered up and down the shoreline. "How big is this island?" she asked worriedly. The mist was still thick, and it was starting to grow dark. "And where would Merlin have gone to meet the Lady of the Lake?"

Elaine pulled the boat up onto the beach. "You ask a lot of questions," she noted sourly. "Follow me. I shall lead you to the village. Surely Merlin will be there to greet us. And if not, Viviane, our Lady, will know exactly where to look for him."

She grabbed Stu's hand and started dragging him up the hill. He glanced back at Sophie, giving her a *Save me!* look. Sophie stifled a laugh. It was so good to be with her best friend again. Just like old times.

As they walked up the steep hill, slowly so as not to lose their footing, Sophie wondered how long Morgana would keep Guinevere hostage before she decided to kill her. If they got there too late—if Guin were already dead—well, she didn't know how she'd be able to return to Arthur with the news.

No. She couldn't think like that. She had to keep the faith.

"Hello? Can I get some dinner down here?"

The three of them stopped short, looking at one another. *Was that—?*

"Perhaps some pea soup? I'm very fond of pea soup!"

"Merlin?" Sophie cried. "Is that you?"

"Yes, yes, it's me, and I'm starving! Don't you druids ever eat? And don't bring me those horrid mushrooms this time. They're terrible for my digestion."

"Come on!" Sophie urged the others, diving through the mist, no longer caring that she didn't know the way. She could follow Merlin's voice as he continued to complain about the mystical island's menu.

A few moments later the mist fell away, revealing a small clearing surrounded by large trees. In the center stood a particularly huge, gnarly oak tree. Sophie's eyes widened as she realized Merlin himself seemed to be caught in its branches.

"Sophie! Stu!" Merlin cried, looking both embarrassed and relieved. "Thank the winds and rain you're here!"

"What happened?" Sophie asked, rushing toward him. She tried to pull away a branch that had wrapped itself around his forearm. But to her surprise, the tree shifted, a thin branch reaching down from above, slapping her hand.

"Hands off the prisoner!" the tree scolded in a low-pitched female voice. Sophie let out a surprised shriek and stumbled backward in shock. Did the tree really just speak to her?

"Now, that's just rude," Merlin said to the tree. "I'm allowed to have visitors, you know."

"We need your help," Stu informed the magician, approaching with caution. "Morgana has kidnapped Guinevere!"

"By Excalibur's blade!" the magician cried. "I told him that girl would bring nothing but trouble." He peered at the three of them. "And where is Arthur? Tell me you got him back."

"We did," Sophie assured him. "And we sent him to the castle to plan tomorrow's battle. But only after we promised we'd rescue Guinevere for him."

"That boy has a one-track mind," Merlin grumbled. "But I guess you're right. He needs Guinevere to rule by his side. I suppose a rescue isn't too much to ask."

"This is what you've been training us for, right?" Stu interjected. "Why we've been playing *Camelot's Honor* all this time."

"Yes, yes. Except..." Merlin gave them a rueful look. "I'm not sure I'll be much help to you. You see, Viviane was angry at me for not telling her about the missing scabbard and Arthur being gone. To punish me, she's trapped me in this tree for the next thousand years. So I'm afraid you may have to do without me. Maybe find a pickup group in the next town?"

"No way," Stu exclaimed. "We're a team. We're sticking

THE ONCE AND FUTURE GEEK

together." He unsheathed Excalibur, the blade shining brilliantly in the fading light, and raised it to the tree.

"No, no!" Merlin cried quickly. "You can't just cut it! It's magical!"

Stu lowered his sword reluctantly.

"Well, maybe I have a spell?" Sophie suggested, pulling out the little book from her pocket and skimming through its pages.

"No one can free him but a daughter of Avalon," the tree informed them haughtily. "And obviously there are none of *those* around." It sniffed. How could a tree sniff?

"Are you sure about that?"

Sophie whirled around, surprised to see Elaine stepping into the clearing. She stomped up to the tree.

"And who might you be?" the tree asked with a yawn.

"I am Elaine," she declared, squaring her shoulders. "The Lady of Astolat."

Merlin shot Stu a suspicious look. "No offense," he said to the girl. "But aren't you supposed to be dead?"

"I would have been!" Elaine chirped happily. "But Lord Stuart rescued me just in time!" She glanced over at her hero with adoration. Stu shuffled from foot to foot, refusing to meet Merlin's eyes.

"Never mind that now!" Sophie interrupted. "Can you free Merlin or not?"

"Perhaps…" She shrugged. "If someone *important* were to ask me to."

Sophie squeezed her hands into fists. "Seriously, I have had about enough of—"

"It's okay!" Stu interrupted, jumping in between the girls. He shot Sophie a pleading look, then turned to Elaine. "Would you mind freeing Merlin for me?" he asked. "I'd be…forever grateful."

Elaine smiled smugly at Sophie. Then she waved her arms, muttering something under her breath. A moment later, the tree's branches loosened, sending the magician crashing to the ground. He climbed to his feet, rubbing his back, then gave the trunk a little kick.

"Bloody irritating thing," he muttered. "Though I suppose it is better than the rack." He turned to Sophie and Stu. "Now, where were we?"

"We were rescuing Guinevere," Sophie reminded him. "Morgana took her to her castle. Wherever that is." Hopefully Merlin would know and they'd no longer be dependent on Elaine.

"Tintagel." Merlin nodded. "What an interesting choice."

"Because?"

"It was there that I went to claim Arthur as my own," he explained. "When he was a baby. I wanted to hide him away until he was old enough to take the throne." He frowned. "Morgana certainly wasn't happy with me that day."

"So she wanted to get her brother back to the castle? Where it all began?" Sophie asked.

"Perhaps. The castle has been abandoned for many years and lies in ruin on the shores of Cornwall."

"Cornwall," Stu repeated. "Isn't that really far from here?"

Merlin tugged on his beard, calculating. "If we traveled by foot, it would take weeks—maybe a month."

Sophie's enthusiasm faltered. Weeks? A month? That was too long.

Then she remembered her mother's spell book. She'd only skimmed through it, but she was pretty sure there was something about...

"Teleportation!" she cried. Of course! After all, hadn't her mother just used it to get them back here in the first place?

Everyone looked at her, puzzled. She held up the book. "The Companions can teleport people. And I have the spell to do it!"

Stu's eyes lit up. "Sweet! Then what are we waiting for? Let's take down Morgana once and for all."

CHAPTER 43

"So if we moved Sir Ector's men here and then had King Leodegrance's men gather here, we could send Gawain and his brothers through this pass right along here—to put on the pressure," Lucas suggested, setting up the small stones representing each army on their dust-drawn map of England's eastern shore. "This way we could surprise the Saxons and cut off any escape route they might have."

Arthur stared down at the map, nodding thoughtfully. "I'd want to leave Sir Bors's men here," he suggested, grabbing a rock and placing it due east. "Just in case they tried to sneak in by the sea."

"And then you can keep King Percival's men back here, for reinforcements," Lucas agreed.

"Perfect," Arthur cried. "Will it actually work?"

Lucas gave him an impish grin. "It's your basic zone defense with a little blitz thrown in for good measure. Definitely effective on the football field. I do it all the time in Madden. Even works against the Patriots."

"I can't wait to see the Saxons running home with their tails between their legs," Arthur finished, rubbing his hands together in excitement.

"Me too," Lucas said, looking Arthur up and down. "Man, who would have thought when I found you, shivering on the front steps of the school, you'd turn out to be so legendary!"

"Well, I had a little help from my friends," Arthur reminded him. "In fact, I owe you pretty much everything."

"Meh." Lucas brushed off the compliment. "Just do me one favor."

"What's that?"

"Throw a really big party when you get back from defeating the Saxons. I'm in the mood to celebrate! After all, it's not every day you get to time-travel to the Middle Ages. I want to see some action! Maybe even score a dance with a real medieval chick."

"Just as long as it's not Guinevere," Arthur warned.

"No way, man, she's all yours. I prefer brunettes, anyway."

Arthur smiled. "You're a good friend, Lucas Lake. I am lucky to have you."

At that moment Gawain poked his head through the door. "They're ready for you, m'lord."

Arthur turned to Lucas. "Wish me luck."

Lucas clapped him on the shoulder. "You don't need it, man. You're going to be awesome."

And with that, Lucas watched his friend turn and walk out of the room, head held high, just like a real king. A chill tripped down his spine.

"Go get 'em, Arthur," he whispered.

He rubbed out their map and scattered the rocks they'd used to represent the knights. After all, every good football player knew not to leave a strategy lying around in plain sight. Then he rose to his feet and headed out of Arthur's chamber and toward the kitchen. He was starving—not a good day to have missed lunch to make up a test.

"You!" A girl's voice startled him. "You were with Lord Stuart!"

He whirled around, surprised to be recognized. His eyes fell upon Elaine, standing in the hallway, wringing her hands together.

"What are you doing here?" he asked, approaching her cautiously. "I thought you went with Stu and Sophie to find Merlin."

She nodded, casting her eyes to the floor. "I was," she said. "I freed Merlin from a tree. Just as Lord Stuart asked of me."

"Well, that's good..."

"But then they left me! Merlin said I could not join them in their fight. And that terrible girl teleported me back here while they went on to Tintagel. Even though I could have totally done it myself." She looked up at Lucas with big brown dejected eyes. "First Lancelot, then Stuart," she whimpered. "I swear I am destined to be rejected by every knight in the land." She leaned against the wall, then sank to the ground, wrapping her arms around her knees. "He should have just let me die in despair."

"Aww, come on, you don't mean that!" Lucas cajoled. He dropped down to his knees in front of her. "You've got a whole life ahead of you. You're pretty, you're sweet, you're obviously talented—some lucky knight is totally going to scoop you up." He poked her in the shoulder. "And if they don't? No big deal. Back in my world, girls don't just sit around, waiting for a guy to come rescue them. They go and do their own thing."

"Do their own thing?"

"They have careers. Hobbies. They travel," Lucas explained. "I mean, what do you like to do? What makes you happy?"

"I like to ride horses," Elaine sniffed through her tears.

"Really? Me too." Lucas offered her his arm the way he'd seen knights do in movies. "What do you say we hit the stables? See if they'll let us saddle up a couple ponies and take a ride."

"Really?" she asked. "You'd really go riding with me?"

Lucas smiled. "I'd be honored to."

CHAPTER 44

The stench of death hung heavy in the air as the group made their way into the forbidden fortress. Dark shadows danced menacingly across battle-scarred walls while the windows rattled in warning. A nightmare scene fit to frighten even the bravest of heroes, and Lord Vanquish knew he and his companions were far from that.

Yet still they pressed on, through cobweb-draped halls, down crumbling stone steps. Ducking low-hanging archways, crossing rotted-out floors. They couldn't stop now. Not when they were so close—their final enemy lying in wait just beyond the ancient iron-barred doors rising up before them.

* * *

"Do you mind cutting out the play-by-play?" Sophie hissed, interrupting Stu's overly dramatic monologue. "I'm nervous enough without having you go all medieval ESPN on me."

"Aww, come on," her friend protested. "I'm just trying to psych everyone up for battle!"

"Stu…"

"I mean, aren't you even the least bit excited?" he asked, his eyes dancing. "We're finally going to take down Morgana!"

Sophie's face softened. "Yeah," she admitted. "It *is* pretty cool."

"Pretty cool indeed," Merlin agreed. "But I'm with Sophie on the running commentary. A medieval fighter should be seen and not heard. Or not even seen, actually. Be like a ninja!"

Stu's eyes lit up. "Now that I can do!"

Sophie watched as her friend started an elaborate, sneaky ninja walk down the cobwebbed corridor, turning at the appropriate intersections. At the end of the hall, a shred of light shone through a crack under a heavy wooden door. Stu turned to Sophie and Merlin. "This is it, isn't it?" he whispered. "I remember this door from *Camelot's Honor*. It leads to Morgana's lair. I'm sure of it!"

Merlin nodded. "I think you're right," he agreed, after consulting the map he'd conjured up on arrival. Magical GPS. Pretty handy.

Sophie's heart slammed against her rib cage. After all, while things had seemed fine and good in theory from the safety and comfort of Merlin's cave, being outside a real sorceress's door was an uncomfortable reality check.

Because this was no video game. The dungeon wouldn't reset and there'd be no do-overs if they failed.

Because they'd be dead.

She thought suddenly of her dad back home. Had he noticed, yet, that she was gone? What would he do if she didn't come back—if she disappeared just as her mom had? Her dad could be a pain sometimes, but she knew he loved her. And it would devastate him if she didn't return.

She squared her shoulders. All the more reason to get this done with. Once and for all. So she could return to her father, and make her mother proud.

Save Guinevere. Save the world. And bring back pepperoni pizza to boot.

She turned to Stu, her heart suddenly feeling very full. "May the Merlin be with you," she mouthed.

Stu grinned. "And also with you."

Merlin rolled his eyes. "Obviously I'm right here, guys. Now come on. Let's do this thing!"

And with that, they pushed the doors open, stepping into the sorceress's inner sanctum. Just like in the game, it was a windowless chamber with black walls and high ceilings disappearing into the darkness.

Sophie glanced at her friends. This was it. This was really it.

Her heart skipped a beat as Morgana stepped into the light. Unlike in the game, there was no sound track. No haunting music to accompany her approach. But that didn't make it any less scary.

Morgana regarded them. Her mouth twisted. "Where is Arthur?" she demanded.

"He's a bit busy right now," Sophie shot back, hoping Morgana didn't hear the tremble in her voice. "So you're going to have to deal with us instead."

Morgana snorted. "Foolish children," she said. "Do you really think you can defeat me?"

Sophie glanced at Stu. That was their cue.

Stu rushed toward the sorceress, Excalibur raised and ready. Merlin followed at a distance, keeping him in healing range while Sophie bided her time, hovering near the door. She watched as Stu slashed at Morgana with his blade. As expected, instead of knocking her down, the sword bounced harmlessly off her skin. Just like in the game, a magical bubblelike shield protected her from any harm.

Morgana laughed maniacally, raising her hands above her head. A swirling cloud of dark smoke began to envelop her figure as she drew energy from the elements to strengthen her black spell. A moment later a firebolt flew from her fingers. But Stu was ready, effectively blocking the blow with his shield.

"Nice," Sophie whispered, feeling a trill of pride. Stu wasn't kidding when he said he'd been practicing.

Morgana fell back, attempting to refresh her magic supply. But Stu wouldn't give her a break, launching immediately into his next attack. His sword, once again, bounced harmlessly off her force field, but Sophie got what he was trying to do. While he couldn't hurt Morgana in her current invincible state, he could keep her attention focused on him so Sophie could make her move. It was called "tanking" in the video game, and Stu was proving to be as good a tank in real life as he was in *Camelot's Honor.*

She watched as the sorceress's shield cycled from red to green to blue. According to Merlin, when it turned purple it was time to go. She reached into her pocket, fingering her mother's book, going over the spell in her head.

As Stu charged again, Morgana managed to unleash another firebolt. It was weaker than the first one, but aimed true, and Stu, midswing, wasn't able to block it in time. Sophie stifled a scream as he fell backward, flames engulfing his body.

Luckily, Merlin was ready, waving his arms, his wrinkled face scrunched up in concentration. He screamed out a word Sophie couldn't understand and the fire extinguished immediately. Stu scrambled to his feet, shaking himself off and giving Merlin a thumbs-up as he launched back into combat position.

Sophie exhaled, thankful they hadn't tried to do this without their magical teammate. It would have been a short battle for sure.

Suddenly Morgana's shield shifted to a brilliant purple.

Sophie drew in a breath as her mother's voice echoed through her head. *You know what to do, darling.*

Here went nothing. She uttered the magic words under her breath. Tossed the magical powder over her head.

Bam! Pow! The transformation was nearly instantaneous—her body sprouting wings and feathers—folding in on itself until she emerged as a giant hawk.

Go, go, go!

As Sophie shook out her feathers, Morgana made another strike at Stu, this time slashing at him with a bolt of lightning. Sophie gasped as the electric voltage crackled through her friend's body, causing him to convulse uncontrollably.

"Merlin!" she squawked, realizing too late that, as a bird, she was no longer able to speak.

Luckily, Merlin needed no instruction, muttering something under his breath and waving his arms again. At first nothing happened, and the wizard scowled as he repeated the words and gestures. Thankfully, this time the crackles faded and Stu's body fell to the ground. Merlin cast a second spell and Stu rose to his feet, panting hard, but looking ready to fight again.

Sophie swallowed. That was a close one. She had to get moving.

Taking a deep breath, she flapped her wings as hard as she could, forcing herself to take flight. The wind rushed through her feathers as she soared up into the darkened ceiling of the room, using the techniques she'd learned from Arthur when escaping from the tower.

Don't struggle, he'd said. *Let the wind take you.*

Once she was feeling confident, she dared a peek at the action below. Just in time to see Morgana turn on Merlin, her face twisting in satisfaction as she shot a torrent of water at the wizard. The water froze, encasing the healer in a block of ice. Sophie watched in horror as Merlin's surprised face froze solid, his arms and legs pinned into place. Stu rushed over, trying to chip away at the ice to free him, but the process was too slow.

It was all up to Sophie now.

She pointed her beak down and dove at the sorceress, landing on the top of her force field. Her talons dug into the now-milky-white sphere as she tried to find the weak spot she knew from the video game. But the sphere was like rubber, unyielding to her claws, and Sophie found herself bouncing off and flailing into the sky, just as Morgana turned to attack Stu again.

As Sophie tumbled helplessly through the air, Morgana sent a firebolt at her friend, engulfing him in another sea of flames. He collapsed to the ground, writhing in agony.

And this time there was no one to heal him.

"No!" Sophie cried, swallowing back her fear and forcing

herself to find her balance. She dove at the sorceress, no longer worrying about skill or style or fear of flying. She locked on to her enemy's force field and closed her eyes, imagining with all her might popping the shield and leaving the sorceress vulnerable to attack.

Mom, she thought as hard as she could. *Help me now!*

The shield burst and flew away. Morgana looked up in surprise. She pointed a gnarled finger in her direction. A blast of heat hit Sophie square in the chest, sending her flailing to the ground, human-shaped again. As she hit the ground, her ankle crunched hard on the stone floor.

Screaming in pain, she forced herself to rise to her feet anyway. There had to be something she could do. She could not let Stu die in vain. If only she could reach Excalibur.

But the sword was lying with Stu, on the opposite side of the room. Limping, Sophie backed up, away from the sorceress, until her back met the stone wall behind her. Desperately, she tried to summon up another round of magic, but the last attack had drained her and she was unable to pull up anything from within.

"No one can protect you now!" Morgana shrieked, lifting her arms, readying her next spell. Helpless, Sophie closed her eyes, trying to come to terms with the fact that they'd failed to take down the sorceress once again.

And this was their last try.

But instead of fire or lightning or icy pain, there was a sudden scream. Morgana's scream.

Sophie's eyes flew open, just in time to see the sorceress's body fall at her feet. Morgana looked up at her with pain-filled eyes.

"It can't be!" Morgana cried, before slumping down onto the cold stone floor. It was only then that Sophie noticed there was a sword wedged between the sorceress's shoulder blades.

The sword Excalibur, to be exact.

She looked up in confusion, her eyes falling upon Stu, who stepped over the sorceress's body and pulled Sophie into a strong embrace. She collapsed against him, scarcely able to believe he was all right. He wasn't dead.

A sudden wail interrupted their celebration, echoing through the chamber and sending chills down Sophie's spine. She watched as a shimmering purple cloud spiraled up from Morgana's lifeless body and began to rise into the ether.

"What the...?" Sophie began.

"You may have won this battle," Morgana's disembodied voice called out, followed by an evil-sounding cackle. "But the war is far from over. By the goddess, I will come back, stronger than ever. Nothing will stop me from destroying this once and future king—once and for all!"

And with that, the cloud poofed away, the voice faded, and Sophie, Stu, and Merlin were left alone in the chamber.

Trembling, Sophie turned to Stu. He shrugged impishly. "The best games always do leave room for a sequel," he quipped. "Or at least an expansion pack."

"What happened?" she demanded. "I thought you were dead."

"Me? Dead? No way. I'm a level-eighty warrior! I'm not going to be taken by some noob mage." He grinned. "Besides, Arthur gave me his magical scabbard, which is like the best game hack ever."

Sophie didn't know whether to laugh or cry, so she did some kind of awkward combo of both, hobbling over to Stu and throwing her arms around him once again, squeezing him tight.

"Whoa! I still need to breathe!" he joked.

"You were amazing," she declared. "A real hero."

"You were pretty heroic yourself!"

"See what happens when we work as a team?" Merlin interrupted, joining them, soaking wet. Thankfully, it seemed, Morgana's ice spell had melted with her death.

Sophie squealed and hugged the magician. "That was so epic!" she cried, and Merlin laughed, nodding his agreement.

"It was indeed epic," he declared. "But we're not quite done. We still need to collect Princess Guinevere, you know. I think Arthur would be rather disappointed if you came home without her."

Sophie and Stu looked at each other. In the excitement of battle, they'd almost forgotten the real reason they were here.

"Don't worry," Merlin said, catching the looks on their faces. "I think I can manage that part alone. You two wait here and I'll retrieve the princess."

Once he was gone, Sophie turned back to Stu. "I'm so sorry," she babbled. "I never should have asked you to go and become King Arthur. If something had happened to you—"

"Are you kidding me?" Stu cried. "This was the most amazing experience ever. I wouldn't trade it for all the world."

CHAPTER 45

The hall had been cleaned within an inch of its life and the dogs kicked out to the kennels. A bountiful feast had been laid out on the tables, and two brand-new thrones sat up on a dais, gleaming with gold and jewels. The court musicians played a rowdy tune, and everyone from the highest lord to the lowest serf found themselves a corner to dance in.

But Arthur had eyes for none of it. Only her.

"M'lady, may I have this dance?" he murmured, approaching and bowing low.

"Why, I would be honored, m'lord," Guinevere replied demurely, lowering her eyes as she returned the bow, her thick lashes sweeping daintily against her pale cheeks. Arthur's heart stirred all over again. Gone were the T-shirt and jeans, and in their place was a silver gown threaded with intricate embroidery that sparkled in the candlelight. He had to admit, as much as he liked twenty-first-century attire, this was better. So much better.

He pulled her into his arms and onto the dance floor. The musicians, catching his eye, launched into a romantic ballad, the bard singing soulfully of their recent victory against the Saxons. The plan Arthur had worked out with Lucas had gone off without a hitch, and the army had sent the Saxons fleeing the island in record time.

History was restored, Morgana had been defeated, and Guinevere was back in his arms.

"I'm so sorry," he found himself saying for the thousandth time. "I never meant to—"

"Quiet, King," she commanded, her blue eyes sparkling. "It was all a big misunderstanding and it's time we moved on. After all," she added, "we have a lot of work to do."

His heart soared at her words. "Does that mean you'll stay? You'll stay and be my queen?"

"You are my true love," she assured him. "No matter what that stupid Google says."

Arthur's heart swelled at her words. "Well, you know what they say," he replied. "You can't believe everything you read."

* * *

On the other side of the room, Stu led Sophie around the dance floor. Who would have thought her geeky best friend would be such a good dancer? Thank goodness Merlin gave her a magical cast for her broken ankle to help her heal quickly. At this point, she wasn't even limping.

"Well, I don't know about ruling the kingdom, but Arthur sure knows how to throw a party," Stu said, twirling her around.

"Totally," she agreed. "But as fun as this is, I'm anxious to get home."

"Me too. After all, we still have to beat *Camelot's Honor*," he said with a laugh. "It's gonna seem weird doing it now, though. After already doing it in real life."

Sophie smiled. "Sorry you had to miss the pizza party," she said. And to her surprise, she really meant it.

He waved her off. "There will be tons more pizza parties," he replied. "This is kind of a once-in-a-lifetime thing."

"I know, but also...I'm sorry I gave you a hard time about the whole soccer thing. I was just...jealous, I guess. I thought you were leaving me behind."

"Are you kidding? You're my best friend. I'm not leaving you anywhere," he proclaimed, giving her a scolding look.

She laughed. "I'll hold you to that."

His expression turned serious. "Just so you know? I only joined the team 'cause of my dad. I was sick of him always cheering on

Lucas and forgetting about me." He hung his head. "I guess I just wanted to be the hero of the family for once."

Sophie stared at him, surprised. "Why didn't you tell me?"

"I was just . . . embarrassed. I thought you'd think I was lame."

"Stuart Mallory, I will never, ever think you are lame."

"Good to know." He grinned. "'Cause I think I might stay on the team. I know it's weird, but I kind of like it."

"I don't think it's weird at all. Just make sure you save SOME time to play video games," she teased.

"Duh. After all, the *Camelot's Honor* expansion pack is coming out soon."

"Which we are clearly going to rock," Sophie declared. Then she spotted something over his shoulder and turned him to see. "Ooh, don't look now, but I think you might finally be free of your stage-five clinger." Across the dance floor Lucas and Elaine were waltzing cheek to cheek.

"No way!" Stu cried. "Lucas and Elaine? Who would have thought?"

"Your stepbrother always was one to help a damsel in distress."

"True enough," Stu replied. "It's just too bad they'll have to part ways soon. Once we head back to the twenty-first century."

"Let's just hope she doesn't try to come back with us."

"Aw, she's not that bad," Stu said.

"You're just saying that 'cause she thinks you're awesome."

"Well, is she really that wrong?"

Sophie groaned. "This being king thing has really gone to your head, hasn't it?"

Stu opened his mouth to respond, but before he could, a figure stepped into their path. Merlin had cleaned up for the occasion, his white beard gleaming.

He turned to Sophie. "My dear," he said, "would you come with me? There's someone who wishes to speak with you."

"Uh, yeah, sure," she replied. She gave Stu a wave. "Don't eat all the desserts without me."

"I promise nothing," he replied with a mischievous grin.

Sophie followed Merlin out of the grand hall and into the empty castle courtyard. The night air had a distinct chill and she found herself wrapping her arms around her body for warmth. She looked around, wondering who on earth would want to talk to her. After all, she admittedly didn't have a lot of besties in ye olde medieval England.

It was then that she saw her. Dressed in a snow-white gown that fell to her feet, the soft moonlight illuminating her long golden hair. Sophie gasped. She'd always thought of her mother as beautiful. But tonight she looked like a goddess.

"Mom!" she cried. "You made it!"

Sophie threw her arms around her mother, burying her head in her chest. Her mother's arms wrapped around her, stroking her hair with loving fingers. She leaned down to press a kiss against Sophie's head.

"I'm so proud of you, my dear," she said, pulling away and looking down at Sophie with admiring eyes. "You acted bravely. Selflessly. You managed to save the world."

"I'm sure anyone would have done the same," Sophie reasoned. But inside she was bursting with happiness at making her mother proud.

"Anyone would not," her mother corrected in a firm voice. "Only a precious few hold the needs of others above their own. And fewer still act bravely and risk their own lives to save those in need. Today you have proven yourself a true Companion. One of us."

Sophie looked up, surprised. "Really? I'm a real Companion now?"

Her mother nodded serenely, leading her over to a nearby stone bench and gesturing for Sophie to sit down beside her.

"You are a Companion by birthright," Sophie's mother told her. "But that doesn't mean you don't have a choice. Tomorrow morning you can jump into the Well of Dreams and never look back. You can live a long and happy life, get married, have children of your own. And nothing will take you from them or cause you pain..." She trailed off.

"Or?" Sophie prompted, her breath in her throat.

"Or you could choose the life of a Companion," her mother continued. "Join the eternal struggle of right versus wrong. Good versus evil. You can travel through time to serve and protect generations of potential chosen ones. I won't lie to you, daughter. It's a dangerous life. I cannot see the future for you if you choose to live it. You may die. You may be hurt. You may lose the ones you love. But you may also make a difference." She smiled serenely. "You may also save the world."

Sophie beamed. "Just like you."

Her mother chuckled. "I suppose so," she said. Then she gathered Sophie's hands in hers and looked her in the eye. "I cannot tell you what to do. But you must choose now. And you will be held to this choice forever."

Sophie squared her jaw. "I want to be a Companion," she declared. There really was no other choice.

Her mother leaned forward and kissed her lightly on the cheek. "Very well, daughter," she said. "From this day forth, a Camelot Companion you shall be!"

And with her words, a spark flashed from the heavens, slicing through the sky and bathing Sophie with white light. She shivered as electricity ran up and down her body, causing the hairs on her arms to stand up on end. It was the most intense, powerful feeling she'd ever experienced, and she didn't want it to end.

But all too soon the light faded. The darkness returned. And her mother was handing her a scrap of parchment paper.

"What's this?" Sophie asked eagerly. "My first assignment?"

Her mother laughed, shaking her head. "No. It's my Skype ID," she replied. "From now on, if you want to chat, you can hit me up on this."

Sophie looked down at the paper, then up at her mom. "No way!" she cried. "I can Skype you?"

"Just don't go all crazy now," her mother added. "Those inter-time dimensional Wi-Fi charges aren't cheap."

"And what about... my missions? When do they start?"

Her mother held up her hands. "Perhaps next week. Perhaps next year. Perhaps you will never be called upon at all. But when you are needed, probably at a time when you least expect it, you will be called." She patted Sophie's knee. "In the meantime, I suggest you study hard. I'll be checking in on your report cards, you know. Remember you've still got to make up that history test you skipped out on earlier this week."

Sophie groaned. "At least maybe I'll have a chance at passing it now that history's been restored."

Her mother rose to her feet, pulling Sophie up with her. "Thank you, my dear. The Companions owe you a great debt. Everyone will be thrilled to know you have joined us."

And with that, she kissed her again, then snapped her fingers and disappeared. Sophie stared at the empty space where her mother had stood a moment before, tears rolling down her cheeks. Then she looked down at the parchment paper and felt a little better. This wasn't a real good-bye. Just a see-you-later.

And besides, she had to go find Stu and tell him all the crazy news. He was going to die when he found out!

And so, Sophie headed into the party, rejoining the boys and Guinevere, who dragged her into a circle for a group dance. As she kicked up her heels and got down with her friends on the dance floor, she marveled at how something that seemed like such a happily ever after could actually be just the beginning.

EPILOGUE

One Month Later

"Woo-hoo! Go, Stu!"

Sophie yelled and cheered—on the edge of her seat as Stu ran down the field, dodging the players from the rival team. Once in position, he lined up, ready to make his shot. Sophie held her breath, her heart beating a mile a minute as his foot connected with the ball and sent it flying through the air toward the goal. The goalie raised his hands to catch it but fell short. The ball slammed into the net for a goal—just seconds before the timer clicked to zero.

The Knights had won the game. The crowd went wild.

Sophie glanced over at Lucas and grinned, clapping so hard

her hands were starting to hurt. Lucas let out a whooping cheer, rising to his feet. "That's my brother!" he cried. "Go, Stu!"

A moment later Stu appeared in front of them, flushed and sweaty, but with a big smile on his face. Sophie jumped up from her seat and threw her arms around him. "That was amazing!" she cried. "I had no idea you were so good!"

"Told you," Lucas declared, fist-bumping his stepbrother. "You sure you don't want to join the football team? We can use strong runners like you."

Stu laughed, shaking his head. "No way. One sport is enough for me." He turned to Sophie. "Now let's go get some pizza."

"As long as it's pepperoni," Sophie teased, and everyone laughed.

Yes, pepperoni pizza was back on the menu and Stu and Lucas were once again stepbrothers. Sophie's mother, along with the Companions, had managed to weave the threads of time back together and set them straight. Sophie was no longer friends with a cheerleader, and *Camelot's Honor* was once again a best-selling video game. And no matter how busy they got with real life, Sophie and Stu always made sure they set aside time to play. Even though, admittedly, after beating Morgana in real life, it sometimes seemed a bit anticlimactic.

In fact, everything had turned out better than Sophie could ever have hoped for. And she didn't even mind having Stu on the soccer team. In fact, she found she actually enjoyed going to the games and had met a ton of cool new people in the stands. Two of whom were field-hockey players who had convinced her to try out herself in the spring.

She was even getting along better with her dad, now that she wasn't on the computer 24/7, and tried to make an effort to keep up with the dishes, as per her mother's Skype requests. And now that she knew her mother was not coming back? She was okay with Dad dating Cammy, too. (She just hoped it didn't get too serious and she ended up with Ashley as her stepsister.)

In all, life had turned out to be a pretty happily ever after.

As she and Stu walked away from the soccer field, heading to Pizza Cave to join the team for a post-victory bite, Sophie felt her phone vibrate in her pocket. She pulled it out, squinting down at the text on the screen.

    Rex quondam, Rexque Futurus

Her eyes widened. The Camelot Code. Did this mean she was receiving an assignment from the Companions at last?

"Uh, Stu?" she said. "Take a look at this."

All month long she'd been on edge, jumping at every beep, wondering if or when she'd get the call. And now here it was. But what did they want? A few details might be nice.

Stu peered over her shoulder. "Do you really think it's them?" he asked.

"Well, there's only one way to find out."

Suddenly Sophie's heart was pounding in her chest. Once she said the words, she realized, she'd be on her way. Leaving her pretty awesome real life behind again, to head out on another quest to save the world. Whatever it might be—however much danger it might entail—there would be no turning back.

"I—I guess this is it," she stammered, her voice quavering. She didn't relish feeling like such a wimp. After all, her mom didn't shy away from her assignments. But still... "I'll just say the words and—"

"Actually," Stu interrupted, "I think we should both say them."

She stared at him in surprise. "W-what? But you're not...?"

"Not a Companion? So what?" He patted his chest proudly. "I still know a thing or two about saving the world!"

Sophie bit her lower lip. "Are you sure about this?" she asked him. "After all, we have no idea where this assignment will take us."

"All the more reason we should stick together," declared Stu. He grabbed her hand, squeezing it tight. A happy feeling rose within her and she realized she was no longer afraid. She and

Stu were a team now. And no matter where they ended up or what they'd be asked to do, they would do it together.

"On the count of three, then," she announced, her mouth curving into a smile. "One...two..."

ACKNOWLEDGMENTS

This book went through an incredible twelve-year journey to finally find its happily ever after, and so many people supported me along the way. I love and appreciate all of you more than you can know!

First off, I want to thank the team at Disney Hyperion. I've felt a little like Cinderella at the ball becoming one of your authors. To my editor, Kieran Viola—thank you for believing in me and this book! From your very first acquisitions letter I knew I had found the Holy Grail of editors, and I am continually inspired by your enthusiasm and editorial insights. Let's work on a billion books together, okay?

To Stephanie Lurie, who is a legit fairy godmother, for

pulling the manuscript from the pile and sending it to the ball. And to Tyler Nevins and Pétur Antonsson for an amazing cover that looks straight out of a Pixar film. Thank you, Mary Mudd, for all your help and answers to my pesky questions. And Dina Sherman for introducing my book to librarians and teachers— my favorite gatekeepers! And to Amy Goppert, as well as the rest of the sales, marketing, and publicity team who work hard to get these books into the hands of readers—you are my heroes.

To my agent, Mandy Hubbard, whose enthusiasm and energy make it so much fun to be a writer. Thank you for taking a chance on me and this book! And to Kristin Nelson for all the work you put into this book over so many years. It would not be what it is today without you.

To Diana Peterfreund—you are the Louise to my Thelma. May we have many more years of cosplay, sushi, and friendship. And to my fellow Texas SCBWI authors and Lodge of Death ladies—thank you! I'm so privileged to be a Texas author and have so many talented peers. And to my intrepid assistant, Sarah Simpson Weiss. I don't know how you do it—but I'm glad you do!

To Jacob—the most supportive husband on the planet. It's been an amazing ten years together and I can't wait for many, many more. And to my daughter, Avalon. You are as magical as the Arthurian island for which you are named. I am so lucky to be your mom! And to the rest of my family—both the Mancusi and the Beach side. Your unflagging support over the years has made all of this possible. And to my local friends and fellow neighborhood moms, who lure me out of my writing cave with promises of game nights, pool parties, and big baskets of chips and queso. I'm so fortunate to have such awesome friends!

Lastly, thank you to all the librarians, teachers, and booksellers out there (especially those from Texas!) who work tirelessly every day to connect kids with books they will love. You are truly my rock stars and it wouldn't be half as fun to be an author without you!